I0660811

Edwin Abbott Abbott

Philomythus

An Antidote Against Credulity - a discussion of Cardinal Newman's Essay on

ecclesiastical miracles

Edwin Abbott Abbott

Philomythus
An Antidote Against Credulity - a discussion of Cardinal Newman's Essay on ecclesiastical miracles

ISBN/EAN: 9783337178758

Printed in Europe, USA, Canada, Australia, Japan

Cover: Foto ©Andreas Hilbeck / pixelio.de

More available books at **www.hansebooks.com**

PHILOMYTHUS

An Antidote against Credulity

A Discussion of Cardinal Newman's Essay on Ecclesiastical Miracles

BY

EDWIN A. ABBOTT

" How long will ye love vanity and seek after falsehood? . . . Stand in awe and sin not "
PSALM iv. 2

London
MACMILLAN AND CO.
AND NEW YORK
1891

The Right of Translation and Reproduction is Reserved

PREFACE

THE great need of the coming age appears to be a faith that shall be at once deep, honest, morally helpful, not tremulous, and not foolish. Faith in an indisputable God must be detached from faith about disputable incidents. We must learn to distinguish between knowledge of material facts, and confidence in spiritual realities ; and to combine a resolute trust in Righteousness with a resolute distrust in all history (whether of things animate or inanimate) that is not commended to us by appropriate evidence.

No timorous soul can draw this distinction or effect this combination. He who is always quoting to us, "Stand in awe and sin not," against the "sin" of rejecting what "may possibly" be true, and never quotes it against the "sin" of accepting what is in all probability untrue, is not a safe guide for himself ; still less, for others. Caesar's craven lieutenant, who mistook some bushes for the Helvetian enemy and spoilt the great general's well-laid plans by "reporting, for seen, what he had not seen", is but a type of many a superstitious "Philomythus" who, in

his pusillanimous eagerness to believe what is "safe," has
"reported for seen, what he has not seen", and has led
astray whole battalions in the army of God.

Abstract denunciation of this theological timidity appeared
to the author likely to be less effective than a concrete ex-
hibition of the results to which a keen-witted, pure-hearted,
and sincerely pious man may commit himself, by giving way
to this safety-seeking spirit in what ought to be dispassionate
historical investigation.   The better the man, the more
conspicuous the warning to be derived from his errors.
For this reason, Cardinal Newman's *Essay on Ecclesiastical
Miracles* has been selected as the subject for a discussion,
intended to suggest an antidote against that kind of unconsciously dishonest and conveniently credulous Assent
which springs from a misplaced application of Faith to
historical facts.

BRAESIDE, WILLOW ROAD
          HAMPSTEAD, N.W.
March 25, 1891

CONTENTS

INTRODUCTION

CHAPTER I

IS PROBABILITY "THE GUIDE OF LIFE"?

CHAPTER II

NEWMAN'S DOCTRINE OF PROBABILITY AND FAITH

CHAPTER III

"LEGAL PROOFS"

CHAPTER IV

THE DOCTRINE OF PROBABILITY APPLIED TO MIRACLES

CHAPTER V

"WHAT IS THE HARM OF THIS?"

CHAPTER VI

CHAPTER VII

NEWMAN'S INQUIRY INTO PARTICULAR MIRACLES

CHAPTER VIII

A GRAMMAR OF ECCLESIASTICAL ASSENT

CHAPTER IX

AN ART OF ECCLESIASTICAL RHETORIC

CHAPTER X

TWO SPECIMENS OF ECCLESIASTICAL COMPOSITION

APPENDIX

PHILOMYTHUS

INTRODUCTION

§ 1. *The Nature of the Proposed Discussion*

It is an invidious thing, in ordinary circumstances, to attack the opinions of an eminent man recently dead, and justly and widely admired. But as the late Cardinal Newman was himself no ordinary man, so the circumstances now tending to the diffusion of his opinions are of no ordinary kind. The Master of Balliol tells us that on the last occasion when he saw Mr. Ward (one of Newman's foremost allies in the Tractarian movement, who joined the Church of Rome in 1845), he asked him "whether he thought there was any hope of a great Catholic revival, and in what way it was to be effected. The answer was curious. He said 'Yes!' and he thought that the change would be brought about (1) by a great outpouring of miraculous power in many parts of the world ; (2) by the rise of a new Catholic philosophy, for which portions of Cardinal Newman's *Grammar of Assent* would form a fitting basis."[1]

This prophecy, made apparently about thirteen years ago might remain on record as merely "curious ;" and an isolated

[1] *Life of Ward*, by Mr. Wilfrid Ward, p. 439.

B

incident of this kind would not have much weight against
what, I believe, has been the prevailing opinion in England—that the principal value of the *Grammar of Assent*
consists in its psychological interest and its bearing upon
the complex character of its author. But a Romanist
prelate, not many months ago, held up to admiration the
Grammar of Assent as a work whose logical character
would henceforth prevent any one from even entertaining
the supposition that conversion from Anglicanism to
Romanism implied weakness of understanding in the converted ; and Mr. Wilfrid Ward has recently expressed his
opinion that " the theory of faith which slowly shaped
itself in the Tracts and Parochial Sermons, which was
more exclusively (? extensively) developed in the Oxford
University Sermons, and which was yet further amplified
and elaborated in the *Grammar of Assent* (published in
1870) lives and will ever live as a permanent contribution
to the philosophy of religious belief." Lastly, all English-
speaking people have been invited to contribute to a testi-
monial to Cardinal Newman ; and, among the objects of
this effort, one, recently announced (though, I believe,
more recently dropped) was to be the encouragement of the
study of his works, and, these, it is to be presumed,
principally, if not entirely, his religious works, or those
bearing on religious questions.

Since, then, certain people are speaking their minds in this
very plain way, and saying "Cardinal Newman's religious
works *ought to be* generally read," it seems only fair, and
nothing more than a kind of self-defence, that those who
think some, at all events, of his works to be hurtful in their
bearing upon religion, should say with equal plainness,
" Some, at least, of Cardinal Newman's works ought *not* to
be generally read," and should give their reasons for thinking

so. One can say this, and give one's reasons for it, without in any way impugning the sincerity, or denying the fascinating gracefulness, of the Cardinal's character.

§ 2. *Newman's Treatment of Facts*

I do not intend, in the following pages, to deal much with abstract questions; but rather to show that Newman's methods of reasoning, whatever they may be in theory, do not work in practice. Taking the *Essay on Ecclesiastical Miracles* as a practical exemplification of the results which follow from the adoption of some of Newman's most characteristic *dicta*, such as (177)[1], "A fact is not disproved because it is not proved," and (171) "A fact is not disproved because the testimony is confused and insufficient," and (179) "How does insufficiency in the evidence create a positive prejudice against an alleged fact? How can things depend on our knowledge of them?" and (231) "As if evidence were the test of truth!"—statements which appear to Mr. R. H. Hutton[2] so very true as to be truisms, and to Professor Huxley so very false as to be almost insolent—I shall try to show that they are indeed true, so very true that they would be scarcely deserving of deliberate examination, if they were not almost always used by Newman in such a context *as to suggest, a little later on, some other and quite different statement which, besides being not a truism, is also not true.*

In dealing with practical applications of Newman's theory, we are, comparatively at all events, on safe and solid ground. And one need be on very solid ground in criticizing New-

---

[1] Bracketed numbers refer to the pages in the *Essay on Miracles*, ed. 1890.

[2] *Cardinal Newman*, by Mr. R. H. Hutton, p. 60.

man's statements. Transparently clear in appearance, his
general propositions abound in reservations, qualifications,
peculiar usages of words—pitfalls, masked batteries, line
after line of concealed entrenchments on which he can fall
back in case of a retreat; and, if you attack a general
statement of his, you can never feel sure, at the last, that he
will not explode both his assailant and himself, by blowing
his own proposition to pieces and proving that it never had
any meaning at all. What ordinary Englishman, for instance,
could say (259) that "we *have no doubt* about" a narrative
—the narrative being a story that a Bishop changed water
into oil by his prayers—and yet that "we cannot bring ourselves to say positively that we *believe* it"? There is a
meaning in this. It is not nonsense. But what care and
toil are needed to extract from this and similar apparently
lucid nonsense the obscure and latent sense![1]

It is only, therefore, in dealing with *facts* that we can
catch our Proteus in a net from which he cannot extricate
himself. If, for example, you can show that, while he
bitterly accuses Kingsley[2] of ignoring the words "it is
said," "it is *reported*," (in one of the lives of the Saints) as
indicating the legendary character of the story containing
these expressions, Newman himself *repeatedly ignores the
same words in quoting Eusebius*[3]—this is an undeniable

---

[1] "We have *no doubt* about it, yet we cannot bring ourselves to say
positively that we *believe* it, because belief implies an habitual presence
and abidance of the matter believed in our thoughts, and a familiar
acquaintance with the ideas it involves." I cannot understand this,
as applied to "belief" in the truth of *facts*.

[2] *Apologia*, 1st ed. p. 38, "Now will it be believed that this writer
suppresses the fact that the miracles of St. Walburga are treated by the
author of her life as mythical?" and see *ib.* p. 40 as to the omission of
the words "*was told* and believed," "*says* her history," &c.

[3] For example (242), "another sight still more strange happened,"

instance of culpable neglect ; and it is rather less excusable in Newman, not writing in controversial haste. Again, in one of the passages above quoted from Eusebius, that historian himself *quotes two other authors*, but adds, at the end of the narrative of some disputed legend, this distinct warning, " But on this. matter *let each of my readers form his own conclusion.*" Now Newman *first* (242) *omits these words of warning*, and then goes on to make Eusebius (251) "*attest,*" where he has distinctly *declined* to "*attest*" anything at all. Surely, in the face of such derelictions as these, you are safe in saying at once, " This is too bad, even in a man with a strong bias, and would be inexcusable in a thorough scholar, however biassed." If further, you find him devoting a score of pages (348-368) to a particular " Inquiry " into an alleged miraculous cure of blindness, and not giving a single reference to any of the authorities for the miracle—what scholar can blame you for saying, " This betokens a gross contempt for facts, and an absence of all expectation that his readers will seriously inquire for themselves with his 'inquiry' to help them "? If, again, you find him trying to prove the miraculous .

ought to have been, "*it is reported that,* or, *the story goes that* (λόγος ἔχει) another sight . . . happened" ; and *on the very same page,* translating, in inverted commas, Tertullian's testimony to the existence of a letter of Marcus Aurelius, he *omits words* (see below, p. 153) *which show that Tertullian really knew of no such letter, and that* it was a mere guess, or, as Bishop Lightfoot calls it, a " *hazard* of Tertullian." Again (255-6) Newman relates *two* stories from a single section of Eusebius, the former essentially miraculous, the latter not. The *former,* Eusebius introduces with " *they say that* " (φάσι), which is maintained throughout ; the latter he relates, in the indicative, on his own responsibility, as a *fact.* But Newman, though he adds afterwards (258) that " Eusebius notices rather pointedly that it was the tradition of the Church," ignores *the marked distinction made by the historian between the miraculous and the non-miraculous parts of the tradition.*

efficacy of a certain oil that flows from the bones of St. Walburga by "a chain of evidence," and neglecting to obtain evidence (which he might have procured in a week by a letter to the bishop of the diocese in which St Walburga's monastery is situated) as to the efficacy of the oil during the last two hundred and fifty years, who again can blame you for declaring that this would be most culpable laziness, if it did not proceed from a contempt for that very evidence which he professes to be fabricating into a "chain"?   Lastly, if he introduces you to a grand miracle entitled "The *Change* of the Course of the Lycus"; then introduces you to a new description of it as the "*Restraint* of the Course of the Lycus," that is to say, in plain English, "The *Keeping* of the Lycus in its *Original Course*"—an act that might have been effected by natural means ;—then lays stress upon this miracle as being (267) "verified" by a "monument set up at the time," and by an "observance"; and then informs you that the "monument set up at the time" was a "tree," and that this tree had once been the Saint's staff, but had *miraculously* been changed to a tree, and that the "observance" was the conversion of the people in consequence; then— what are you not justified in saying?   Indeed, you hardly know what to say, consistent with the desire to say nothing unkind against one who in the supposed interests of religion can honestly make so great a sacrifice of the faculties with which God has endowed him for the attainment of truth.

As I proceed, I feel more and more the great difficulty of my task.   My object is to prove that Newman's logical principles tend to make ordinary people superstitious, credulous, and lazy ; superstitious, because, instead of looking God's facts in the face, and seeking to know

them through the faculties which He has given them,
men under these fettering principles are constantly tempted
to crouch before Him and say, " We will believe anything
to have happened or not to have happened. Only do Thou
tell us by some special sign, some conspicuous authority, what
Thou wouldst have us believe ; " credulous, because in
such a frame of mind as this, to believe any lying legend
that " may possibly be telling of Him " seems safer than to
reject it ; lazy, because this miracle-mongering mood dis-
poses men to expect that the truth about facts should be
itself conveyed to them by means little short of miraculous,
without any painful effort on their part to use their minds
and understanding. But in proving this I am beset with
difficulties. An ordinary Englishman enjoys Newman's
easy-flowing style ; has not time to penetrate its fallacies,
still less to verify his references or examine the context of
his quotations ; and cannot bring himself easily to believe
that a theologian of such established reputation is not only
radically inaccurate about facts, but also supremely and
contemptuously indifferent to facts, as a basis for belief in
an alleged miracle. This therefore I must endeavour to
show.

But, before going further, a short extract may be of use
in preparing the reader for the *kind* of miracles which
Newman once (1826) rejected, but, under the influence of
his later theory, is prepared to defend. In his earlier *Essay
on Miracles* (1826), he enumerated, as being " unworthy of an
All-wise Author " the following portents (29) : " that of the
consecrated bread changing into a live coal in the hands of
a woman who came to the Lord's Supper after offering in-
cense to an idol ; of the dove issuing from the body of
Polycarp at his martyrdom ; of the petrifaction of a fowl
dressed by a person under a vow of abstinence ; of the

exorcism of a demoniac camel; of the stones shedding tears
at the barbarity of the persecutions; of inundations rising up
to the roofs of churches without entering the open doors; and
of pieces of gold, as fresh from the mint, dropt from heaven
into the laps of the Italian monks."

But in the present edition of that Essay, the following foot-
note is added at the end of the extract, "[*Vide*, however
Essay ii., *infra*, n. 48—50, 54, 58, &c.]" Turning to these
passages in the second *Essay*, we find it argued that there
is in Nature a principle of (150) *deformity* and of *the ludicrous*;
that (151) "there is far greater difference between the
appearance of a horse or an eagle and a monkey, or a lion
and a mouse, as they meet our eye, than between even the
most august of the Divine manifestations in Scripture and
the meanest and most fanciful of those legends which we are
accustomed without further examination to cast aside;" and
thus, we are invited to infer that (152) "it may be as shallow
a philosophy to reject them," *e.g.* the petrifaction of a fowl by
a special suspension of the Laws of Nature by the Almighty,
" as to judge of universal nature by the standard of our own
home." To such results is Newman led by his assumption
that Miracles are (97) the "characteristic of sacred History"
and that to treat the history of the post-apostolic Church
without taking Miracles into account would be (981) "to
profess to write *the annals of a reign, yet to be silent about the
monarch.*"

3. The Argument from the Three Classes of Ecclesiastical Miracles

Now let us consider Newman's method of inquiring, and
of preparing us for the inquiry, into Ecclesiastical Miracles.
Early in his Essay he draws a very marked distinction be-

tween Scriptural and (99) "Ecclesiastical Miracles, that is, Miracles posterior to the Apostolic age," which are "on the whole, different [1] *in object, character, and evidence,* from those of Scripture on the whole, so that *the one series, or family, ought never to be confounded with the other.*" The Scriptural Miracles (115-6) are generally public ; they are evidences of a Divine revelation, and (220) not tentative ; they are (116) wrought for a definite object by persons conscious of a Divine guidance ; they are grave, simple, and majestic, (117) compactly and authentically narrated. Ecclesiastical Miracles, on the other hand, are often (116) of a romantic character, wild and unequal, (220) frequently tentative and private, spiritual accomplishments, so to speak, (221) of individuals ; often (116) scarcely more than extraordinary accidents or coincidences ; supported by (116) exaggerated evidence (117) or by mere floating rumours, popular traditions, vague, various, inconsistent in detail ; (116) "they have sometimes *no discoverable or direct object,* or but a slight object ; they happen for the sake of individuals, and of those who are already Christians, or for *purposes already effected,* as far as we can judge, by the miracles of Scripture."

Startled by these candid admissions, we ask what ground there is for thinking that these inadequately proved and often purposeless portents actually occurred ; and we find an argument alleged as a "first principle." It is this (*Apol.* 1st ed. Append. 49): "What God did once, He is likely to do again." In other words, "Because God is supposed to have suspended the Laws of Nature once for a definite purpose, and in certain ways, ('grave,' 'simple,'

---

[1] The edition of 1843 has "*very* different." Here, and elsewhere (unless specially excepted), italicized words in quotations are italicized by the present writer, *not* by Newman.

' majestic '), therefore it is a likely supposition that He has repeatedly suspended, is suspending, and will suspend, the Laws of Nature, in *quite different* ways (*not* "grave," *not* ' simple,' and *not* ' majestic ') for *quite different* purposes, and often, so far as we can judge, *for no purpose at all.*"

Wildly absurd though this may appear, it is really Newman's *main argument.* In comparison with this "first principle" of the Antecedent Probability of Ecclesiastical Miracles, he tells us plainly that mere facts and evidence are of very little account (190) : "in drawing out the argument on behalf of ecclesiastical miracles, *the main point to which attention must be paid is the proof of their antecedent probability. If that is established, the task is nearly accomplished.*"

With Antecedent Probability, however, we shall deal more fully hereafter. What claims our present attention, is another, though subordinate, argument, viz., that we ought to look favourably on a great number of these doubtful or moderately probable Ecclesiastical Miracles, because some at least can be proved to be certainly true. Accordingly he tells us (134) that in his review of the miracles belonging to the early Church, " It will be right to include certain isolated ones which have *an historical character*, and are accordingly more celebrated than the rest " ; and he proceeds to enumerate seven, beginning with the well-known story of the Thundering Legion, and ending with that of the African Confessors who spoke after their tongues had been cut out. He then adds (135) : " *These, and other such*, shall be considered separately before I conclude ; " and he concludes his Essay by an inquiry (241-387) into the evidence and character of these seven miracles (adding two others that can hardly be described as having " a historical character," viz., the Change of the Course of the Lycus, by Gregory

Thaumaturgus, and the Change of Water to Oil, by Narcissus). The Inquiry is preceded by a brief Introduction (228-240) on the "Evidence for Particular Miracles." In this, he admits (229) that some ecclesiastical miracles are certainly false ; but then he urges that some are certainly true ; and he says that, as regards a great number of ecclesiastical miracles that are neither certainly true nor certainly false, the reader, while prejudiced *against* them by the false miracles, ought to be prejudiced *for* them by the true ones.

This is fair enough, so far—if true. But the reader must carefully observe that there is no question here of Scriptural Miracles. The whole argument turns upon this, that the miracles under discussion are (229) "of the *same family*," *i.e., Ecclesiastical.* His thesis is, that the multitude of "neither certainly true nor certainly false " Ecclesiastical miracles ought to be regarded favourably because (besides other reasons) some " of the *same family* " are certainly true ; and that they ought not to be at once rejected because others " of the *same family* " are certainly false. Here is the whole passage.

After stating in the previous section that he intends to examine particular miracles, Newman begins the next section thus (229) :—

"An inquirer, then, should not enter upon the subject of the miracles reported or alleged in ecclesiastical history, without being prepared for fiction and exaggeration in the narrative to an indefinite extent. This cannot be insisted on too often ; nothing but the gift of inspiration could have hindered it. Nay, he must not expect that more than a *few* [*Ecclesiastical miracles*] can be exhibited with evidence of so cogent and complete a character as to demand his acceptance ; while a great number of *them* [*i.e. Ecclesiastical miracles*], as far as the evidence goes [*i.e. apart from Antecedent Probability*, which, *to Newman, seems* (190, *quoted above, p.* 10) "*the main point*"] are neither certainly true nor certainly false, but have very various degrees of probability viewed one with another ; all of *them* [*i.e. the middle class of Ecclesiastical miracles*] recommended to his devout attention by the circumstance that *others of the same family* [*i.e.* (99) *miracles not of the Scriptural "family" but of the Ecclesiastical "family"*] have been proved to be true, and *all* [*i.e. the middle class of Ecclesiastical miracles*] prejudiced by his knowledge that so many *others* [*i.e. "so many other Ecclesiastical miracles"*] on the contrary are certainly not true."

Does not this passage clearly show that, in the selection of his few "particular" miracles, Newman was bound—if he had the slightest respect for evidence—to take the greatest care to select those for which he can produce the fullest and strongest evidence ? Upon the proof of this select " few " depends his power to "recommend " a great number of others to his reader's "devout attention "—so he has himself told us.   He has also warned his readers that "not more than a few can be exhibited with evidence of so cogent and complete a character as to demand his acceptance."   Then surely we are justified in inferring that, of these precious "few," none will be omitted.   Or, if the "few" are too many for his pages and for the special inquiry which he proposes to devote to them, then at least we may expect that the evidence for those very few which he is forced by his excess of material to select from the "few," shall be not only "cogent " but "most cogent," not only "complete " but "absolutely complete."

Again, suppose for a moment that one of his very few "historical " miracles should fail him, or at least so far fail

him as not to be available for controversial purposes, and
that he himself should be obliged to admit this; suppose
the discovery of some natural phenomena coming to light,
say in 1860, should show that the very miracle for which
the most "cogent and complete" evidence had apparently
been produced in his essay of 1843, must henceforth be
regarded as disabled from "recommending" the vast multitude of doubtful ecclesiastical miracles to the "devout
attention" of his readers; and suppose that Newman
himself should candidly make this admission and publish
it, say, in 1865—should we not infer that, before publishing
a new edition of the *Essay on Miracles* in 1870, he would
substitute for the disabled miracle—upon which so very
much depended for his "devout" readers—one of the other
few or very few miracles for which he had space to produce
his "cogent and complete" evidence ? If he should not do
so, there would be the less excuse for such neglect, because
we happen to know that he had at hand in 1864 another
"historical" miracle, not included in the Nine—a miracle
that is notorious among Protestants and Romanists alike,
for which Newman tells us the evidence appeared to him
irresistible. "I think it," he says (*Apologia*, 1st ed., p. 57),
"*impossible to withstand the evidence* which is brought for the
liquefaction of the blood of St. Januarius at Naples." [1] I
shall presently show that the above-mentioned suppositions
are verified, but that our inference as to what would be the
consequence is not verified. One of the Nine great Miracles
—and by far the most important in the estimation of any

---

[1] "Putting out of the question the hypothesis of unknown laws of
nature (which is an evasion from the force of any proof), I think it impossible to withstand the evidence which is brought for the liquefaction
of the blood of St. Januarius at Naples, and for the motion of the eyes
of the pictures of the Madonna in the Roman States."

good judge ; one, at least, on which Newman himself justly
lays the greatest stress, because of (381) its "completeness," (382) "the opportunity of testimony," (384) "its
entireness," (385) its "permanence," (380) the "variety,
consistency, and unity" of the testimony, and that too
"from eye-witnesses of the miracle"—will be found to be
given up ; but neither in the edition of 1870 nor in that of
1890 is any substitute provided.

Were we dealing with ordinary men, we should be almost
compelled to attribute such conduct as this to tergiversation.
But against Newman it is impossible not only to substantiate
such a charge, but even to imagine that it could be brought
by any rational being acquainted with his character. It is
simply a contempt for facts—a contempt so great that he
might, without much exaggeration, be said almost to prefer
to believe in a miracle that is unsupported, rather than in
one that is supported, by a basis of facts ; and he hardly
conceals his contempt for the Protestant reader who cannot
help asking for evidence.

§ 4. *The Argument from Potentiality*

Hence arises the great danger of Newman's position.
It is this, that, though he is dealing with facts, and is
tempted to alter and suppress inconvenient facts, he can
yet place himself beyond the appeal to facts—so far as
concerns their miraculousness. As to some of the faults
mentioned above, grave though they are, there might be
nevertheless some hope. A man who has been guilty
merely of omissions, neglects, or misconceptions, you might
possibly hope to convince of his errors. But the fatal
characteristic of Newman's position is that, even when he
has made all these admissions, he can still fall back upon a

reserve which is absolutely impregnable to the attacks of common sense. Newman was in no sense a student; but still he had the literary faculty, and you could certainly have induced him to confess that he was wrong in mis-quoting Eusebius, in misdescribing the so-called *Change* of the Course of the Lycus, and in not giving his authorities for the miraculous cure of blindness at Milan; possibly you might even have shown him that from a constant repetition of his theoretical assertion (180), "The direct effect of evidence is to create a presumption in favour of the alleged fact," he has been led in practice to neglect the word "direct," and occasionally to attach worth to what is worthless, through neglecting the context and circumstances and "*indirect* effect" of evidence; but all these triumphs, supposing you could attain them, would be but a scratching of the surface; they would not penetrate below, or touch the rooted and superstitious credulity which is the real cause of the evil.

Not that, of course, the superstition which is at the bottom of this credulity, is often openly avowed. It generally disguises itself and has various masks to be assumed according to various circumstances, such as, "It *may* be so," "It is at least a *pious belief*," "We do not say it *is* so, but, *if* it is so, then is it wise to reject what possibly *may* be from the Lord?" and the like. Against these what argument can avail? You may perhaps hope to move this advocate of "pious belief" in probable facts, by urging that it is not right to accept what is probably an error, and possibly a lie, about any subject, least of all about God. He smiles and tells you that Queen Victoria has many romances told about her, and (*Apol.* 1st ed. p. 54) : "Do you think *she* is displeased at them?" Note, just in passing, the clever "parallel"—we will devote a section hereafter (p. 227)

to Newman's "parallels"—between Almighty God, reported as a Petrifier of unlawfully dressed fowls, and an
Exorcizer of demoniac camels, and Queen Victoria reported
as (*ib.*) "mistaken for the housekeeper by some blind old
woman," or "meeting beggars in her rides at Windsor," or
"running up the hill as if she were a child"!!

But to return to our "pious believer." You may de-
monstrate to him that natural causes are fully sufficient
to explain a certain result hitherto supposed to be
miraculous.   He will listen with equanimity, he will
admit with candour.   But do you seriously suppose
that he will on that account give up to profane history
what had once been consecrated to God by the name
of a miracle?   In theory, he may.   In theory, he will
(*Apol.* 303) "frankly confess that the present advance of
science tends to make it probable that various facts take
place and have taken place, in the order of nature, which
hitherto have been considered by Catholics as simply supernatural."   But, in practice, he would resort to almost any
device sooner than abandon a miracle to Liberalism ; and
one of these devices is *Potentiality*.

Just as a jury—so, at least, Newman says—would not (303)
"think it safe to find a man guilty of arson if a dangerous
thunderstorm was raging at the very time when the fire
broke out," so we ought, he says, to be cautious in
rejecting any miracle ; for any possibly natural act *may* be
also a possibly supernatural act.   You may point out that in
the former instance there are two possible causes, arson or
lightning, distinctly before the jury ; but in the case, say,
of a man who speaks when his tongue is cut out by the
roots, and whose retention of speech has hitherto been
called a miracle, you may ask him, "If it should be proved
to your satisfaction not only that *some* men *do* thus speak

without their tongues, but also that, within a considerable range of experience, *no one has been known to be unable thus to speak*, will you give up the miracle then? What are your two possible causes there? Is not Nature the obvious cause?" But do you think you have driven him into a corner? "Two possible causes!" we can imagine him replying; "Is it possible that you are not aware that there are *always* two possible causes of anything? Do you not know that God may be *expected* to be continually intervening in His Church by means of miracles? that miracles are as much the characteristic, and (98) 'the most important of the characteristics, of sacred history,' as deeds of valour and enterprise are of profane history? and that to write the history of the Church without miracles, would be (98) 'to profess to write the annals of a reign, yet to be silent about the monarch'?" And then he might quote the last sentence of the *Essay on Miracles* (390), "This is ever the language men use concerning the arguments of others, when they dissent from their first principles —which take them by surprise, and which they have not mastered"; and finally he might tell you once for all that (*Apol.* 303) "no Catholic"—although of course recognizing that God does *sometimes* work through natural causes— "can *bind* the Almighty to act *only in one and the same way*, or to the observance always of His own laws." And so it comes to this—thanks to *Potentiality*—that Church property in portents is always safe; and that truth and evidence, in ecclesiastical suits about miracles, are never inconvenient to the advocates of the Church; for, "*Nullum argumentum occurrit Ecclesiæ.*"

But I have not yet done justice to the versatility of Newman's mind or the amplitude of his resources in emergency. Sometimes, for example, where the evidence for

supernatural agency is not very strong, Newman, with great
tact, will lay stress, not upon the necessarily miraculous
nature of the act, but upon the antecedent probability of the
miracle; as in the change of water into oil by Narcissus,
Bishop of Jerusalem, where he very briefly indeed just
touches upon the existence of oil wells known to the
ancients, and, instead of showing that there were no oil
wells in Palestine, he insists that (255) "it is favourable to
the truth of this account that *the instrument was an aged,
and, as was also the case, very holy man.* It may be added
that *he was born in the first century.*" But how differently
does he deal with the miracle of the Tongueless Martyrs,
mentioned above! In this case he feels that the necessarily
miraculous nature of the act, and the evidence of the fact,
constitute his strongest ground. "How can men speak without a tongue?" seemed a question that could be answered
only in the words, " In no way, and by no possibility." He
therefore spares no pains to prove that *no tongue was
left—no part of a tongue.* It is not often that he is so fond
of evidence; but he can be, on occasion, and he is so here
(381) : " 'He cut out the tongues *by the roots,*' says Victor
Bishop of Vite ; 'I perceived the tongue *entirely gone by
the roots,*' says Æneas ; 'As low down *as the throat,*' says
Procopius ; 'At *the roots,*' says Justinian and St. Gregory.
'He spoke like an educated man, without impediment,'
says Victor of Vite," and so on—calling up the same witnesses again to give evidence as to articulate utterance, and
clearly showing how he can appreciate really cogent and
complete evidence, *when it is on the right side.* Besides
this, he appeals to the variety of the witnesses, their consistency and unity and means of observation (380) : " out of
the seven writers adduced, six are contemporaries ; three,
if not four, are eyewitnesses of the miracle ; all seven were

living, or had been staying, at one or other of the two places which are mentioned," *i.e.* the abode of the Confessors on whom the alleged miracle was wrought. Again, we are asked to consider the different circumstances of the witnesses (380) : " One is a Pope ; a second a Catholic Bishop ; a third a Bishop of a schismatical party ; a fourth an Emperor; a fifth a soldier, a politician and a suspected infidel ; a sixth a statesman and courtier ; a seventh a rhetorician and philosopher." *O si sic omnia!* Could anything be fairer than this ?

All this is very strong indeed. It is by far stronger than the combined evidence for all the rest of Newman's miracles put together ; and he is quite right to lay great stress upon it. But then what is to be done if—as was hinted above— it should really be demonstrated that all this irresistible evidence as to the *complete absence of any portion of the tongue,* so far from proving the retention of speech to be miraculous, *proved, on the contrary, that the retention was explicable by natural causes ?*

Yet this was what was doomed to happen ; and Newman himself has to make the confession that it is so. In an Appendix to the second edition of his *Apology* published in 1865, and repeated in the latest edition (391, 392), he gives evidence which appeared in *Notes and Queries* (May 22, 1858) and which absolutely destroys the miraculousness of the story of the African Confessors. Colonel Churchill, in his " Lebanon," speaks of a certain Pasha as " extracting *to the root* the tongues of some Emirs," and adds, " It is a curious fact, however, that the tongues grow again *sufficiently for the purposes of speech.*" Sir John Malcolm, in his "Sketches of Persia," telling us of a certain Khan who was condemned to lose his tongue, says, " The mandate was imperfectly executed, and the loss of half this member deprived him of speech. Being afterwards persuaded that *its being cut close to the root would enable him to speak* so as to be understood, he submitted to the operation; and the effect has been that his voice, though indistinct and thick, is yet *intelligible to persons accustomed to converse with him.*" Strongest of all is the evidence of Sir John McNeill, who states, from personal observation, that *several persons* whom he knew in Persia, who had been subjected to that punishment, "spoke *so intelligibly as to be able to transact important business,*" and—after describing it as the *universal conviction* in Persia," that the power of speech, when lost by cutting off the tip of the tongue, can be partially *restored by farther amputation* —adds these emphatic words : "I *never had to meet with a person* who had suffered this punishment *who could not speak so far as to be quite intelligible to his familiar associates.*"

"*Never had to meet with a person who could not speak!*" What is to be done now? An ordinary man—a man who was not bound by some special rules of a Grammar of Ecclesiastical Assent not known to English laymen—would frankly give up this miracle. That, of course, for Newman, is out of the question. And yet Newman does not like here to fall back, in this instance, upon the reserve of Potentiality. So much stress has been laid upon the "cogent and complete" evidence in this case ; and the testimony from the Eastern experience of the three English witnesses is so strange and, as it were, so contrary to our common sense, that Newman feels that an immediate retreat to Potentiality is not perhaps necessary, and would certainly be humiliating. Potentiality he would prefer to reserve for cases like that of the Thundering Legion, cases of natural phenomena that *may be* supernatural interventions. So he resorts, in this instance, to another device—so ingenious that it deserves a separate section.

§ 5. *The Device of Indefinite Adjournment*

Hampden is praised by Lord Clarendon for resorting to this device with great tact in the House of Commons; but Newman does it much more effectually in proportion as his adjournments are for a longer period.   And there is besides —in the passage which I am going to quote and in which he, as it were, makes his formal motion for indefinite adjournment—a certain naive frankness in the plain way in which he lets us know that he does not really care for the bald, literal truth of fact in which laymen take an unaccountable interest.   His care is for the " system " of supernatural intervention into which he is "generously throwing himself," in comparison with which, facts are poor things; he is not seeking truth of fact; it is a war, not a search, in which he is engaged—a war against what he called "Liberalism" and against private judgment; and the laws of war will "fairly" allow him to resist evidence which non-theological laymen would find irresistible.   Here is the passage (392) :

"I should not, however, be honest if I professed to be simply converted by their testimony " [*i.e.* the testimony of the three English gentlemen above-mentioned] "to the belief that there was nothing miraculous in the case of the African confessor.   It is *quite as fair* to be sceptical on one side of the question as on the other; and if Gibbon is considered worthy of praise for his 'stubborn incredulity' in receiving the evidence for the miracle, I do not see why I am to be blamed if I *wish to be quite sure of the full appositeness of the recent evidence which is brought to its disadvantage. Questions of fact* cannot be disproved by *analogies* or *pre-*

sumptions ; the inquiry must be made into *the particular case* in all its parts as it comes before us.

"*Meanwhile*, I fully allow that the points of evidence brought in disparagement of the miracle are *primâ facie* of such cogency, that, *till they are proved to be irrelevant*, Catholics are prevented from appealing to it for controversial purposes."

Now let the reader carefully examine this passage three or four times, and word by word—many sentences of Newman require at least this, and some of them require a great deal more—and let him ask himself the following questions :—

(1.) To what purpose is the word " fair " introduced here, when the object is, or should be, to get at the truth, and there is no question of taking an " unfair " advantage in controversy ?

(2.) What is the meaning of " the full appositeness " ? And how does Newman hope to attain his " wish " of making himself " quite sure " of " *the full appositeness* of the recent evidence " ?

(3.) " Questions of fact cannot be disproved by analogies or presumptions." What is the meaning of " disproving a *question* of fact " ?

This is answered by referring to a previous page (*Apol.* 300), where we find that Newman " proposed three *questions* about a professed miraculous occurrence : 1. Is it antecedently probable? 2. Is it in its nature miraculous ? 3. Has it sufficient *evidence ?* . . . 1. The verisimilitude ; 2. The miraculousness : 3. The *fact*."

Obviously, therefore, " questions " of *fact* are to be distinguished from " questions of " *antecedent probability* and *miraculousness.*" The latter may depend upon " analogies or presumptions "; *e.g.* the *antecedent probability* (or *verisi-*

militude) and *miraculousness* of a cure by relics may depend upon the "analogy" of the miracle wrought (2 Kings xiii, 20, 21) by (*Apol.* 300) the "bones of Elisha," or upon the "presumption" that God would specially intervene in this or that important crisis, for this or that Saint. But the former, *i.e.* "questions of *fact*," imply the question asked in the last paragraph, "has it sufficient *evidence?*" and must depend upon "*evidence*" alone.

This being the case, the phrase "questions of *fact*" appears to mean really no more than "questions whether this or that happened"; and the sentence amounts to this : "Alleged facts cannot be disproved by analogies or presumptions." But who attempts, or has attempted, to *disprove the facts* about the African martyrs? Does any one even dispute the "facts"? Does not every one admit the *facts*, the only question being whether they can, or cannot, be explained by natural causes?

The meaning is so obscure that we must consider the last part of the sentence separately.

(4.) "By analogies or presumptions."

What is the meaning of this phrase? I believe it has been correctly explained in (3) above, as being the method of proof connected with antecedent probability, But lest it should be urged that the words are capable of another interpretation, I will give an alternative.

When we hear that a tower, *e.g.* the Tower of Siloam, fell in old days, we are in the habit of "presuming" that it fell in accordance with the Laws of Nature ; and some would say that this "presumption" was based upon an "analogy" with other cases of the fall of buildings. Is this the meaning here? Does Newman mean that we are not to "presume" that the sixty African martyrs retained their speech naturally, upon the "analogy" of the numerous

tongueless Persians who have retained it in modern
times?

If this were the meaning, it would be equivalent to saying
that we are not to "presume" that any act happened
naturally once because it happens naturally now ; *e.g.* we
are not to "presume," upon the "analogy" of a stone falling
to the ground *now*, that it fell to the ground naturally 1,400
years ago. If that were the meaning, *cadit quaestio ;* we
have no means of proving the naturalness of anything to
an antagonist who raises this objection. We have done with
him ; and we think he has done with common sense.

But, as I have suggested above in (3), I do not think this
is the meaning. If it is contrary to common sense, we have
no right to impute it to our adversary, unless we are forced
to do so by lack of other meaning. Besides, it is also
inconsistent with the phrase "questions of *fact*," not "of
miraculousness," but "of *fact.*" Lastly, it is not as though
we were driven to a nonsensical meaning, for lack of any
other. For there is the other meaning, pointed out above.
viz. : "Questions of *fact* cannot, like questions of *verisimilitude* and *miraculousness,* be disproved, or proved, by
analogies or *presumptions,* but must be proved, or disproved,
by evidence."

The worst of this interpretation is that it is so very true
as not to be worth saying. It is a truism, and not at all
to the point. But as I shall show elsewhere (221), it is
quite in Newman's manner to disarm his readers by con-
ceding to them, with a great appearance of moderation, at
a critical stage in an argument, something that is really no
concession at all ; and so the meaning here appears to be
this : "I wish to be convinced about the *evidence ;* surely I
am not to be blamed for this. On the contrary, I am
taking *your* view. You like *facts* and *evidence ;* so do I.

Let us have no speculative analogies here! Away with presumptions! Give me solid *facts*, and let us *inquire into the evidence all over again*."

(5.) " *The inquiry* must be made into *the particular case* in *all its parts, as it comes before us*."

When and how does Newman intend to make this important "inquiry," which, as he tells us, "must be made"? It appears to be an "inquiry" into the "facts." But what "facts"? Has not "the particular case "—viz. the case of the Tongueless Martyrs, already " come before him? Has not his " Inquiry " into " the particular case included "all its parts "? If not, why has he omitted any of the " parts "? And if he omitted any of the "parts " in 1842-3 (when he wrote the *Essay*), why did he not insert them in the edition of 1870, in which, with the exception of a few bracketed foot-notes, the only alterations are (viii) " of a literary character," and which was reprinted, without mention of any change at all, in 1890?

Lastly, what is the meaning of the words "as it comes before us"? They appear to suggest a reference to alleged miracles *in general*. But we do not want just now to think about miracles *in general*, but about *this* " particular case," and about the means by which Newman proposes to make that further inquiry into it " in all its parts," which, as appears from the next sentence, he is contemplating. Therefore, whatever may be the *intention* of the words —they serve no *purpose* except that of diverting the attention from this special miracle, which is the point in question, to a general and indisputable proposition which is not to the point.[1]

---

[1] It has been suggested to me that the words "as it comes before us" refer to the *circumstances* of the case. The present alleged miracle "comes before us," it is said, "not as a hospital case, but as a case of

All this is very bewildering and creates in us the uneasy suspicion that we may not be doing justice to our opponent. Let us make one last effort to enter into Newman's position and to imagine the strongest defence he might make for himself. He seems to have rebelled—and certainly it was natural for him to rebel—against the terribly hard conditions to which his tenure of miracles was subject :

"I have just frankly confessed—" we can imagine him saying to himself—"in the 303rd page of my *Apologia*, that 'the present advance of science tends to make it probable that various facts take place, and have taken place, in the order of nature, which hitherto have been considered by Catholics as simply supernatural.' Now if this 'advance' goes on, science will be always gaining, and religion will be always losing. Many years ago, for example, I 'bound' myself 'to the belief' (*Apol.* 300) in the miraculously medicinal effect of St. Walburga's oil ; but since I entered the Catholic Church I (*ib.* 302) found there is a difference of opinion. Some persons consider that the oil is the natural produce of the rock and ever flowed from it ; others thought it was miraculous now, or had been miraculous once. Consequently I have felt myself obliged to say above (*ib.*), 'this point must be settled, of course, before the virtue of the oil can be ascribed to the sanctity of St. Walburga.'

"Thus I am deprived, for the time at all events, of one of my best miracles ; and it really does not seem fair that science should be thus constantly capturing miracle

confession of Martyrs." Grant that this may be the meaning : then surely, so far as a knowledge of the "circumstances" is essential to a knowledge of the case, the "circumstances" are "parts" of the case, and included in the phrase "all its parts," so that the words "as it comes before us " would be superfluous—which I cannot believe.

after miracle from religion, while religion never captures a fact, nor even *re*captures a miracle, from science. Once give up a miracle and you never get it back again. Surely it is time to stop this losing game. Surely God *may* be working in a special way even through a natural fact. I value miracles simply as the signs of God's presence in the Church. Why then may I not give the name of a miracle, and ascribe some special Divine presence, to a fact so striking and so impressive as the articulate speech retained by sixty tongueless orthodox martyrs ?

" People want to persuade me that the case of these sixty orthodox martyrs is analogous to that of the poor wretches who now-a-days lose their tongues in Persia. But surely there may be a *miraculous explanation in the former, and a non-miraculous in the latter.* If those who believe in the non-miraculous explanation of the latter are justified in being sceptical about the miraculous explanation of the former, it is quite as *fair* for me to be sceptical about this new explanation as applied to the old fact. Consider *the immense antecedent probability of a miracle* in the former case, a probability which does not exist in the latter. I do not disbelieve in causes ; I simply believe that *more than one cause* may produce the same result. Because *x* is caused by *y* in one case, does it follow that it *may not be caused* by *z* in another ? So far therefore from resorting to the Device of Indefinite Adjournment, I am really only pleading quite justly and scientifically for the recognition of a scientific principle, the Plurality of Causes. Possibly some fresh light may hereafter be thrown upon these questions ; and I would have people meantime suspend their judgment."

To all which, we shall reply, " If you meant this, you should have said this ; and we should have done with evidence and argument. But you speak about an ' inquiry '

that 'must be made,' and about what you will do 'meanwhile.' Tell us, then, plainly *what you are going to inquire
into.* Into the ancient facts of the African martyrs? But
you know perfectly well you have exhausted them. Into the
modern facts, attested by the three English witnesses, and
the 'universal conviction in Persia,' attested by one of them?
But you do not even suggest where the evidence is faulty.
Into its 'appositeness'? What do you mean by that? Do
you mean that what is 'apposite' to 'poor wretches in Persia'
in the nineteenth century, is not 'apposite' to Athanasian
martyrs in the fifth? But in using that language, you would
be entering the region of 'presumption,' 'analogy,' 'verisimilitude,' 'antecedent probability'—which you appear to
have disclaimed, as having no bearing on 'questions of
fact'; and even if you mean that, how do you propose
to ascertain it?

"Then, as to your Plurality of Causes; you say that
'because x is caused by y in one case, it does not follow that
it *may not* be caused by z in another'—where, *by z you mean
'miraculous power.'* But, in the first place, the words 'in
one case' are misleading. You should have said 'in *all*
cases, so far as they have been examined'; it is the
'*universal conviction*' in Persia that x is *in all cases* caused
by y, *i.e.* articulate speech is restored *in all cases* by the
total (when lost by partial) extraction of the tongue. In the
next place, what proof will you accept that 'x *is* not caused
by z', knowing, as you do, that *by z you mean 'miraculous
power'*? You know that you will be satisfied with no proof
short of this : we must *use z, and show that x does not follow*'!
That is to say, we must *use 'miraculous power,' and show
that restoration of speech does not follow!* This will satisfy
you, this, and nothing else! Ordinary people will say that,
if we want to prove tongueless articulation to be always

natural, the best possible proof is to bring a number of men into a lecture room, and experiment upon them, cutting out the whole tongue in some cases and calling the audience to witness that these men *can* speak ; cutting out half the tongue in others, and showing that these *cannot* speak ; and then, in these last cases, cutting out the remaining half of the tongue, and showing that *now* they *can* speak.   Well this proof has been practically given you.   But this will not suffice.   Nothing will suffice to prove *for you* that the tongueless speech is non-miraculous, unless we enter the lecture-room, *armed with miraculous power, and disprove a miracle by means of a miracle !*

"Again, think for a moment, from the point of view of religious reverence, what is implied by your hypothesis that although a non-miraculous explanation covers the modern cases, yet a miraculous explanation *may cover* the ancient one ?   It implies this, that these tongueless martyrs, *if only God would have, so to speak, let them alone, i.e.* left them to the ordinary operation of His natural laws, *would have retained their speech ;* but that He intervened by a special act to make them *unnaturally dumb*, in order that afterwards He might make them *supernaturally articulate*.   In other words, you ask us to believe that God broke His Laws of nature (or, as I should call them, His Promises of nature) and took away from these poor wretches what may be called their natural right, in order that He might afterwards pose to the world as their supernatural Benefactor—much as a clever conjurer might pick the pocket of one of his hearers in order to give him back his purse again before all the audience, so as to extort their applause and make them clap him and cry, ' What a clever rascal ! '

"What we would urge is, that the truth in these matters should not be regarded as the prize of a game or of a war ;

and that you should not speak of what is ' fair ' but of what
is 'true.' If science, as you say, teaches us, century by
century, that many things supposed to be miraculous, can
happen by natural means, may not that be a warning that
we are to detach our faith in God from faith in miracles?
That kind of faith in a thaumaturgic God which you and
some of your former followers describe as the 'mediæval',
or as the ' aboriginal genuine ' [1] faith—are you so very certain
that, instead of being the 'genuine' faith, it was not a
rudimentary faith, intended to prepare the way for a higher
and more spiritual faith that does not contemplate material
but spiritual 'signs'? But even if you are not prepared at
present to adopt, or so much as to consider, that view, you
ought at least to deal fairly with yourself and us, and say
distinctly, as to this alleged African miracle, either what
proof you will accept as to its non-miraculousness, or else that
you will *accept no proof at all, except a proof that would
be itself a miracle.*"

It only remains to add that there is no reason to
suppose that Newman made the slightest attempt to gratify
his above-mentioned "wish to be quite sure of the full
appositeness of the recent evidence " which was "brought
to the disadvantage" of the African Miracle, or to conduct
"the inquiry" which needed "to be made into the particular case in all its parts." The evidence appeared
in *Notes and Queries* in 1858, and was inserted by Newman
in the second edition of his *Apologia*, in 1865. And yet
neither in 1870 nor between 1870 and 1890, is the slightest
attempt made to "prove" that the evidence *is*—or even
to indicate how the evidence *could be proved to be*—"irrelevant" !

Are we not justified in calling this by the name of the

---

[1] *Letters of the Rev. J. B. Mozley*, p. 175.

Device of Indefinite Adjournment? It is not—what it would be in any one else—deception, that is to say, direct deception of his readers; it is only self-deception; but indirectly it may deceive a good many who are willing, and some few perhaps who are unwilling, to be deceived. If Newman had openly said, " I never can believe that an event, edifying if miraculous, and long recognized to be miraculous, is not miraculous; and indeed any event, however explicable by natural causes, *may be* miraculous; so that further argument between us is really useless "—no one would have been deceived by that. We should then have understood that, as reasonable Christians refer many questions that are not questions of fact and do not come within the province of evidence and understanding, to a solution that cannot be reached on this side of the grave, so Newman indefinitely postpones questions that *are* questions of fact and matters of evidence, because the decision, upon evidence, is likely to be unfavourable to religion. Then there would have been no deception. But people may easily be deceived, when an honest man says, in effect, " This matter must be argued again after fuller investigation." They may actually suppose he *intends to investigate* it more fully. And therefore, in order that my readers may be upon their guard, let me give one more instance of the incredible, the almost superhuman consistency with which Newman, when convinced against his will, can remain still of the same opinion.

The instance given is of almost historic interest in the study of human nature. It deserves to go down to posterity with Galileo's famous instance of stubborn persistence in mental opinion, in spite of the coercion that forced him to make a lingual recantation. It is nothing less than a proposal to *defer the settlement of the question whether the earth is fixed or moves, till we have ascertained what is the nature of motion;*

and the reader will find it in what Mr. Wilfrid Ward [1] calls Newman's memorable Sermon on Development :—" Scripture says that the sun moves and the earth is stationary ; and science that the earth moves and the sun comparatively at rest. How can we determine which of these opposite statements is the very truth *till we know what motion is ?* " Is it not clear that, upon this system of Indefinite Adjournment, you are justified in declaring yourself unable to determine which of *any* opposite statements is true? All propositions, in their strictly logical form, may be reduced to statements with the verb *is* in them. Now if you cannot determine the truth of any proposition with the word " *moves* " in it till you know (in some new celestial objective shape) what *motion* is, why should you be able to determine the truth of any proposition with the word " *is* " in it, till you know what *being* is? And when will you know that? Never, this side of the grave. Thus, by the Device of Indefinite Adjournment, you can resist any logical assault, shelve any dispute, and remain convinced of anything you like, by putting off all inconvenient knowledge till the world to come !

I recommend honest and truthful young men who desire to remain honest and true to themselves, *not* to study such of Newman's works as bear upon Faith, on penalty of being tempted to dishonesty and untruth. Special pleaders ought to read them, and re-read them night and day. In the pages of the great Greek and Roman orators I have never met with such perfect and fascinating instances as are to be found in Newman's writings, of that subtle and delicately-lubricated illative rhetoric by which you are led downwards on an exquisitely elaborated inclined plane, from a truism to a probability, and from a strong probability to a fair pro-

[1] *Life of Ward*, p. 386.

bability, and from a fair probability to a pious but most improbable belief. Nowhere perhaps is Newman's knowledge of the weaknesses and imbecilities of the human mind, and especially of its liability to confused vision and its responsiveness to gentle guidance, more clearly manifested than in his graduated scale of demands upon our intelligence ; while he asks us, first, perhaps, only to consider something as fairly probable; then, not to reject it—since it may be possibly from the Lord, and we ought to " stand in awe and sin not " ; then, to ponder it as being what the Lord *may* have done ; then, to cherish it as what the Lord "*does* in secret" for our comfort and edification (though we are not to use it openly for controversy); and thus, ultimately and practically, to accept it into our mind and heart as true—though all the while it is almost certainly untrue, and to be rejected by any one who so far fears God as to believe that he must hereafter give account of the faculties received from Him for the attainment of the truth.[1]

Another great man, besides Newman, has given us a specimen of the Device of Indefinite Adjournment. When Francis Bacon, while Lord Chancellor, was ordered by Buckingham to cancel, in effect, one of his legal decisions, he adopted a similar plan to the method above described. He obtained a practically indefinite adjournment by giving orders for the appointment of a sham commission to investigate the case. Baron Heath, who, at Mr. Spedding's request, went carefully into the question,[2] after telling us how this sham commission was to be appointed, adds " I do

[1] See p. 243 below for this and other specimens of Newman's illative rhetoric.

[2] Spedding's *Lord Bacon's Letters and Life*, vol. vii. p. 587. The Investigation, being contained in an Appendix, has escaped the attention of all Bacon's biographers except Professor S. R. Gardiner.

not suppose anything was ever seriously meant by it except to ease the Lord Chancellor of his burden."

There is a similarity, but there is an important difference too, between Bacon's and Newman's "easing himself of his burden." The former knew what he was about ; the latter did not. The former knew perfectly well that he was not acting as a just judge should ; the latter, on the contrary, believed he was doing God service by upholding, at any cost, the inspiration of Scripture as to all matters of fact, and by maintaining against materialists the doctrine of frequent miraculous intervention. Bacon believed in the Laws of England and in the spirit of equity in which he was bound to administer them ; and he felt that his Indefinite Adjournment was a sham and a sin. Newman had no belief—no *practical* belief, no belief except where it was *convenient* to have it—in the Laws of Nature, nor in the rules of evidence, nor in the possibility of man's approximating to Divine truth by the use of his mental as well as spiritual faculties. Consequently to him the Device seemed—or at least may well have seemed—not only justifiable but pious and holy, a way out of temptation, a path appointed by God Himself. Newman does not believe that God intends us to attain to truth by using our mind and understanding as well as our heart and our soul, and that, about *historical facts*, we *are not* to use our heart, and *are* to use our intellect and observation. In effect, he is constantly asking, not, " How shall I find out, with God's help, the truth about this or that fact ? " but, " What does God wish me to believe, in some miraculous or quasi-miraculous way, about this or that fact ? "

Such conduct is not for us. Newman might think thus, and might act up (or down) to such thoughts, and might be, and remain to the end of his days, one who was always aiming at sincerity, and always, to the best of his ability, anxiously sincere ; but it is not given to ordinary men to do this. What he would call a battle against "Liberalism," common men would call a search after truth ; and where he would ask, "What is the harm?" common men are forced to ask "What is honest?" Hence his ways are not our ways. Such a *Grammar of Assent* as he practically acts on will be found to lead many ordinary men through credulity to atheism, through believing everything to believing in nothing whatever—neither in truth, nor in themselves, nor in God.

§ 6. *Distinction between the Theory and the Theorist.*

Nothing will be said in these pages against Newman as an individual ; and wherever he is described as deceiving and misleading others, it must be always understood that he is represented as doing this in perfect sincerity because he has first deceived and misled himself. But the very absence of charges against the man will constitute the severest of charges against the system which made him what he became.

It will also be understood that this treatise deals with Newman's theology only so far as it bears upon his theory of miracles. His sermons deserve all the admiration they have received for their grave and chastened beauty of expression ; but their literary merits ought not to overshadow their spiritual deficiencies. Many a teacher of youth may find in them, especially if he be optimistically inclined, the searching medicine of a bitter humiliation, profitable though depressing, and good for occasional use. But a young man loving Christ and striving honestly to serve Christ will find in them, so far as I can judge, little strength, little stimulus, little spiritual sustenance. They appear to exhibit a theologian who feared Christ far more than he loved

Him ; who regarded God as a centre of dogma rather than
as a loving Father; and to whom the Gospel brought news
not so much of hope as of terror. They contain exquisite
passages, speaking the language of the world yet most un-
worldly ; never stilted or inflated, yet never dull or prosaic
or falling below the level of a calm and natural dignity ;
displaying a subtle knowledge of the weaknesses, the tor-
tuosities, the self-deceptions of human nature ; recognizing
with an awe that approximates to dread the impenetrable
mysteries of the stupendous darkness amid which man
emerges for a moment to play his little part and vanish ;
capable, one may well believe, of leaving some impress
upon the callous worldliness of any but the most convinced
unbeliever ; and painfully penetrative to the very heart of
the anxious and inconsistent Christian. But they do not
seem to breathe Christian strength. They seem to speak—
except so far as ecclesiastical means of holiness, or "channels
of grace," are concerned—rather in the spirit of John the
Baptist than in the spirit of St. Paul. Take but one
instance. The virtue of thankfulness is inculcated on
almost every page of the Pauline Epistles ; in Newman's
Sermons, it seems conspicuous by its absence. "Are you
not a little hard on David?" writes Keble, criticizing
Newman's summary of David's mission which is described
in the *Lyra Apostolica* as being :—

> " on us to impress
> The portent of a blood-stained holiness."

And then Keble goes on to suggest that Isaac Walton
may have been right in explaining the saying that David was
"a man after God's own heart," by reference to that spirit
of "*thankfulness*" which is so clearly manifested in the
Psalms (Newman's *Letters*, ii. 85).

But how could Newman sympathize with this spirit if he had none of it himself? And how could he have it himself, if he felt nothing to be thankful for in himself, if his conscience was a horror, and his life a desolation from which he wished to be released as soon as might be? " Not that I am sorry so great a part of life is gone "—he writes to his mother shortly after his coming of age (*Letters* i. 58)— " would that all were over!—but I seem now more left to myself, and when I reflect upon my own weakness I have cause to shudder " : and afterwards, when his mother imputes this feeling to a morbid melancholy, he insists upon it that it represents his genuine and deliberate conviction : he can be " always cheerful," he says, in company; he is " ready and eager to join in any merriment"; but all this is mere surface-feeling, merely put on; "take me when I am most foolish at home and extend mirth into childishness; stop me short and ask me then what I think of myself, whether my opinions are less gloomy; no, I think I should seriously return the same answer, that I ' shuddered at myself.' " Does not all this explain why he was "a little hard upon David "? It was because he was very hard upon himself. If he "shuddered at himself," and had shuddered systematically for " five years," ever since his "conversion " at the age of sixteen, ought we to be surprised that he should "shudder at " the members of his congregation, and that a spirit of shuddering should pervade his teaching ?

It is a most vague and unsatisfactory explanation of these results to say that " the religious element was too strong for him." Such an explanation can satisfy none but those (though indeed they are not few) who are ready to accept any proposition that is sufficiently abstract and misty. " The religious element " may mean anything—intense love, hope, awe, trust, admiration, fear approximating to abject dread. In Newman's writings there are ample indications that Fear unduly predominated and that, in his estimation, Fear was not only, as he said it ought to be, "the prominent grace in the *beginning* of Christian life," but "prominent"—whether "grace, or not"—to the very end of his Anglican career.[1] Hence we can explain that "forlorn undertone now and then," in his sermons, which seemed to one of his hearers "at the time, inexplicable."[2]   It was not a mere thrill of intellectual misgiving in him as to the Anglican logical position ; it was a deeper pang of agonizing soul-piercing doubt as to whether he, the speaker, and they, the congregation, had *any position at all*, in the presence of the Supreme.

It is not now our business to discuss how he could reconcile this theory with such sayings as, "There is no Fear in Love," or "Perfect Love casteth out Fear," and the like.   No doubt he did contrive to reconcile them somehow.   But the important fact for us is that "Fear"— not in the high and pure sense of "awe" or "reverence," but "Fear" of a kind almost approaching to abjectness— assumed in his doctrine that prominent position which in St. Paul's and St. John's Epistles is generally occupied by Love.

The Love of God, as it is described in the New Testament, appears to have been either absent or quite latent in him : and he himself spoke of Love (see below, p. 223) as a "Preservative *Addition*" to Fear—a kind of after-thought in the scheme of the Christian religion.   Nor was the

---

[1] See p. 223 below ; also *Poems*, pp. 175, 123, 341, quoted with other passages, in the *Contemporary*, January, 1891, pp. 34-38.

[2] Professor J. C. Shairp, in Dean Church's *Oxford Movement*, p. 124.

absence of Love compensated by any profound trust in God's infinite justice and righteousness. There was not in Newman, as has been shown elsewhere,[1] any adequate sense of even human justice ; and, as for the justice of God, it was known to him only as a group of inferences from Scripture texts ; it was not bound to be like, nay, it was almost bound to be unlike, all human notions of what is ideally and perfectly just. Hence, he not only failed to attain that cheerful trustful faith which has characterized many Christians far less pious than himself, but he could not even rest in the lower and more rudimentary conviction that "the Judge of all the earth will do right." Thus the Image of God became for him the image, not of a Father, not even of a just Judge, but of a dread-inspiring Holiness ; a dazzling Splendour, dark with excess of light ; practically, a Darkness ; before Which he could but prostrate himself in abject awe, prepared for whatever lightnings and thunderbolts might come forth, and prepared to *call* them " just."

" You might be perplexed," writes Professor Shairp, from whom I last quoted, " at the drift of what he said, but you felt all the more drawn to the speaker." That might well be. Might he not have diffused around him an atmosphere of anxiety which made all men feel themselves neighbours with him in a community of trouble and desolation ? May he not have been a magnet of spiritual self-conviction drawing towards himself all that was responsive in the self-searching, self-condemning faculties of his hearers ? He was a Seer of a kind : and men perceived that he had seen something ; but what had he seen ? Was it not a Terror ? Might not men have thought they were listening to Isaiah,

---

[1] *Contemporary Review*, January, 1891, quoting *Fletcher's Short Life of Cardinal Newman*, p. 186, and *Expositor*, October, 1890, p. 305.

transferred from the Temple in Jerusalem to St. Mary's, Oxford, fresh from his vision of the Invisible King, *before* the seraph had touched his lips with the fire from the altar and had imparted to him the due prophetic peace and strength : " Woe is me, for I am undone ; because I am a man of unclean lips, and I dwell in the midst of a people of unclean lips ; for mine eyes have seen the King, the Lord of hosts"? The most callous soul could not but feel touched by such a cry as this.

"After hearing these sermons," continues our witness, "you might come away, still not believing the tenets peculiar to the High Church system ; but you would be harder than most men if you did not feel more than ever ashamed of coarseness, selfishness, worldliness ; if you did not feel the things of faith brought closer to the soul." Here are two things, quite distinct, confused together. "Ashamed of coarseness, selfishness, worldliness"—yes ; or rather not "ashamed," but more than "ashamed"; say "revolted," "horrified." But, as for "the things of *faith* brought closer to the soul"—that is quite a different thing. This indeed is another instance of a misleading abstraction, like "the religious element." For we must needs ask, " *What* faith?" Faith, chameleon-like, takes the colour of its surroundings. There are all hues of faith, from faith in a stock or a stone, to faith in Moloch ; and thence to faith in a just Judge ; and thence to Faith in God the Father as revealed in Christ the Eternal Son. If the last is meant, it seems scarcely possible that the things of *that* Faith—Faith in the perfect and ultimate triumph of the Fatherhood of God— could be brought closer to any soul by a Prophet of Fear, a magnet of spiritual anxieties.

Arnold once said that Newman was always thinking of himself when he was preaching ; and Newman, believing that the accusation implied a sense of superiority to his hearers, justly and firmly repelled it. But if Arnold meant that when Newman was analysing and convicting the thoughts of his hearers he was also analysing his own thoughts and condemning himself, he was not far wrong. Newman " never saw his congregation ";[1] when he preached at them, he was preaching at, or rather accusing and condemning, himself, in the sight of the Lord ; and it was this in part (besides his extraordinary versatility) that gave such a wonderful force and vividness to his utterances and caused him to appear to have so profound and sympathetic an insight into what were thought the depths, but were not really the depths, of human nature. Nothing could escape him that was conventional, or shifty, or inconsistent, or insincere, or half-hearted, or hollow, because he suspected his own single-heartedness and feared that he himself might be found hollow, if searched to the bottom.

"A sermon of Mr. Newman's," says Professor James Mozley,[2] " enters into all our feelings, ideas, modes of viewing things. He wonderfully realizes a state of mind, enters into a difficulty, a temptation, a disappointment, a grief. . . Every part of the easy, natural, passive process by which a man becomes a man of the world is entered into, as if the preacher were going to justify or excuse him, rather than condemn him. . . . He sets before persons their own feelings with such truth of detail, such natural expressive touches that . . . *he and the reader seem to be the only two persons in the world that have them in common.*"

How finely does this critic express the precise fact, and how innocently unconscious he is that he is expressing it !

[1] *Expositor*, September, p. 236, quoted in *Contemporary*, Jan. 1890, p. 48.
[2] Quoted in Dean Church's *Oxford Movement*, p. 121.

St. Paul's precept was, "*Rejoice* with them that do rejoice, *weep* with them that weep." But Newman seems to have confined himself to "weeping." He entered into only *one half* of the human being; he realized only *one half* of the human "states of mind," the "difficulties, temptations, disappointments, griefs," and the "easy processes by which a man becomes a man of the world." Search through the long and detailed criticism from which I have given a short extract, and you will find no recognition whatever that Newman "entered into" that *other half* of the human "states of mind," that element of purified "rejoicing," which is so prominent in the Epistles of St. Paul. He "entered into" the worldly self, the lower self, of each of his hearers, helping some of them to hate and loath and shudder at it, but, alas, tempting others to half-suspect that this after all was their true self, that they had nothing whatever of the image of God within them, nothing sound, nothing true, nothing honest; and forcing some towards the brink of that unutterably lonely, that God-forsaken precipice, to which Newman himself had come dangerously close when he sat down in the year 1834 and deliberately passed this sentence on himself, "I believe myself *at heart to be nearly hollow*."[1]

If this is even partially a correct estimate and explanation of some of the defects in Newman's teaching, it may explain much of the misdirection of the Tractarian movement. What is next best, often acts as a narcotic on the conscience, preventing it from compelling us to remain unsatisfied till we have achieved the best; and thus obedience is made to compensate for love, and anxious piety takes the place of faith, and authority supplants the spirit of life. So it seems to have been with Newman. The Church of his country

[1] Newman's *Letters*, i. 416.

lay half impotent at the Beautiful Gate, waiting for some
quickening Voice to say, as Wesley had said, but with tones
of a deeper and wider import than Wesley's message,
" Demonstrations and authorities have I none, but of such
as I have give I thee "—and then to bid her arise and walk
in the name of that Eternal Word Who rules, and will yet
hereafter more manifestly rule, in Nature, in Man, and in
the Church, and who is uniquely revealed to us in the Lord
Jesus Christ. But Newman's message was widely different.
It may not have meant this, but it sounded like this :
" Trust in Christ I have none, or not enough to inspire me
with fervent and hopeful conviction ; but you have the
sacraments ; and what the sacraments will do for you, may
be learned from the inspired Scriptures, and from the
authority of the Church, and from the traditions of the
Fathers, and from the writings of the great Anglican Divines :
try to walk with these."

Thus, what might have been a vital reform—and even, as
it was, had a spark of energizing vitality—degenerated too
often into a preaching of precedent, a religion of etiquette.
There were in the ancient and continuous history of
developed Christianity, realities of spiritual life, which the
Anglican Church had half or wholly forgotten. These
might have been spiritually revived. The doctrine of the
identity of the Universal Church with Christ ; the Remis-
sion of Sins by human agency ; the need of spiritual
Regeneration ; the transmission of the Spirit from Disciple
to Disciple ; the spiritual use of Prayer for the Dead ; a
spiritual doctrine of Purgatory very different from the formal
doctrine practically current in the Roman Church, and,
above all, the true and moral doctrine of Sacrifice (not
Bribing) as set forth in the Sacrament of the Holy Communion—all these, and the other highest truths of the

Christian religion, if they had been treated and taught as
spiritual realities, might have found access to the heart of the
nation without "movements" and "systems" and controver-
sies and factions of any kind. But as it was, these life-giving
truths were too often devitalized and degraded by the
Tractarians to the level of Ecclesiastical demonstrabilities :
instead of being preached from the heart, they were "got
up" out of books and repeated by rote ; thus they became
party cries, not truths to be felt and quietly and gradually
spread, but dogmas to be made into a "system" and fought
for, and wrangled about ; and Newman himself, and
Hurrell Froude, thought it no profanity, to write to one
another in their intimate correspondence about "cramming
their men" with the stock formularies needful for the
glib repetition of some of these momentous and sacred
mysteries.[1] Hence, a great work that might have been
greatly and fully done, was done but in part, with much
of pettiness and more of imperfection ; in some respects
so misdone that even now, much of it needs to be done
all over again.

From this digression—not needless, since it will show the
point of view from which Newman is regarded throughout
this treatise—I must not pass on without admitting that his
religious writings are too voluminous to justify one who has
only partially examined them in speaking with perfect confidence about their characteristic features, or at all events
in asserting a universal negative about them. Here, therefore,
I have preferred to rely largely upon the testimony of his
best admirers ; and even in commenting, with their aid,
upon this phase of Newman's teaching, I would speak under
correction, and should indeed be glad to be taught better,
and to be told of some of Newman's sermons that inculcate

[1] See p. 98 below.

thankfulness, strengthen faith, and stimulate and encourage us in a course of manly self-respecting [1] rectitude. But as to his theory of Assent, or Faith, I do not speak under correction, but desire without reserve to express my detestation of its practical working. For what indeed can be more detestable than a method of thought which converted an anxious and pious seeker after truth, into a misconceiver, ignorer, perverter and distorter of it ; which induced him conscientiously and habitually to say more than he meant in order to convince people that he meant what he really did mean [2] ; which blunted the sense of historical fact,

---

[1] In using the word "self-respecting," I had in my mind a dialogue between Mr. Ward and a friend, related in the *Life of Ward*, p. 217. Ward had said, " When we realize this" [*i.e.* the difference between Creation and the all-powerful Creator] "we feel that our attitude in the presence of God should be *abject*." To which the friend replied, " No, not *abject*, my dear Ward, not *abject*. Certainly it should be a *deferential* attitude, but not *abject*."

Mr. Wilfrid Ward has placed it on record that Ward found this reply "intensely *ludicrous*," and that "his *delight* and sense of its absurdity was unbounded." But is this subject one in which a mistake can be called "ludicrous," or can produce "delight"? "Deference" is certainly not the right word to express "devotion"; but is "abjectness" better? And ought not our conclusion about the whole matter to be that, whereas Jesus of Nazareth is generally supposed to have taught us to regard God with the feelings of a child looking in love and reverence towards an infinitely just and loving Father, Mr. Ward preferred to regard Him with the feelings of a slave?

I can hardly believe that Mr. Ward was serious in maintaining this. Yet I must admit that something approaching to "abjectness"—in the conception of the relations between man and God—appears to predominate in Newman's Anglican poems, and in his Anglican sermons so far as I have read them.

[2] See the letter to Sir W. H. Cope (Fletcher's *Life of Cardinal Newman*, p. 131) in which he says, "A casual reader would think my language *denoted anger*, but it did not. . . . It would not do to

paralysed the faculties which should have helped him to attain truth, and so transmuted his utterances that, although

be tame and not to *show indignation.*" I am perfectly aware that subtle distinctions might be drawn between "anger" and "indignation"; but I consider my statement is more than justified by Newman's avowal that he deliberately "*showed* indignation" although he did not really *feel* "anger."

No doubt, there were other causes—besides any "system of thought"—for Newman's extraordinary use of words ; and, among these causes, personal characteristics claim a prominent position. In a most interesting but too severe delineation of his own character (*Letters*, i. p. 416), Newman speaks of his own "rhetorical *or histrionic* power." Elsewhere (*ib.* ii. 441), in a very subtle and life-like description of his manner in rather awkward circumstances, "I seem," he writes to his sister, "if you will let me say it, to put on a very simple, innocent, and modest manner. I sometimes laugh at myself and at the absurdities which result from it ; but really I cannot help it, and I really do believe it to be genuine" : and a former pupil of his (*Expositor*, 1890, p. 231), has described the "extraordinary versatility" which he displayed at the rehearsals of Terence in the Birmingham Oratory, when he personated, for the imitation of his pupils, "a love-sick Roman or a drunken slave."

Other personal characteristics besides mere versatility of nature tended in the same direction. He had an exact knowledge of the superficial qualities of human nature—its inconsistencies, its vacillations, confusions, and insincerities, its self-deceptiveness and willingness to be deceived ; a profound sense of the great gulf between truth as it is and truth as the wisest of us conceive it—a sense not fitly tempered by the hope that through honest errors God is leading mankind toward the truth ; and a rooted distrust and contempt for the deceptive medium of words. Add to all these a most practical turn of mind, and a keen sense of *effect ;* and we can see at once why and how he was pushed towards "histrionism." He was constantly saying to himself, "What will be the *effect of my words ?* It is of little use to ask, 'What am I saying ?' ; men are such fools ; and words are such mere counters. I must always ask, 'What will be the *effect of my words ?*'" Consequently, he felt a more than usual tendency *to speak with a view to effect.* His anxious self-introspection led him, *at times,* to suspect this

we acknowledge that they proceed from one who was always striving with all his might to be honest, we are forced to recognize in them many of the phenomena that would characterize the most insincere of sophists?

tendency and to call it "histrionic." He was *often* on his guard against it; but the danger was *always* there. He was saved, however, from being seriously "histrionic" by being portentously self-deceptive.

CHAPTER I

§ 7. *Probability*

" BUTLER's doctrine that Probability is the guide of life, led me, at least under the teaching to which a few years later I was introduced, to the logical cogency of Faith " :— so writes Newman in his *Apologia* (p. 11), and by these words he leads us to consider what is meant by Probability ; how far it is the guide of life ; and in what way it is connected with Faith.

No one, of course, denies that we sometimes decide and act upon probability. Whenever we have to stop and think, the weighing of probabilities comes in. "What profession shall I choose?" "What school shall I send my son to?" "Will it rain to-day?"—as regards these, and a great many other matters, we have to act upon probabilities. But this admission is a very different thing from admitting that "Probability is the Guide of Life." In using the phrase "*the* guide" (not "*a* guide"), Newman apparently did not contemplate a spasmodic or occasional impulse, but such a continual and regular pressure as is implied when we say that God "will *guide* us with His counsel," or "*guides* the meek in judgment," or that the Holy Spirit "*guides* us into all truth " : and this seems to be confirmed by the supplementary phrase, " of *life* " as though he said, " Probability is to be our guide *through life*, not merely in rare occasions or important crises, but, *the guide of life*." This therefore is the question that first comes before us, " Are we to be always, or almost always, living, acting, and believing, upon probabilities ? "

All probability is, at bottom, of a statistical nature ; that is to say, it is based upon records of some kind. Sometimes the statistics are prominent and committed to paper, as in the business of an Insurance Office; sometimes less prominent, and rarely committed to paper, as when a farmer roughly conjectures the future weather from his mental records about past weather ; sometimes latent, as when a savage conjectures the weather much better than the farmer, but in so non-deliberate and unscientific a way that we feel inclined to call it instinct.

By Statistical Probability we can discover (from an experience, say, of one hundred or one thousand tosses) that a penny will turn up "heads " as often as "tails "; or, from a knowledge of the number of letters posted in London in 1890 without an address, we can discover roughly the number likely to be similarly posted in 1891₁; and, if we also know the whole number of letters posted with addresses in London in 1890, we can roughly infer the probability (which of course would be very small indeed and would be popularly called "improbability ") that a particular letter now being posted before our eyes this year (1891) by some stranger, would be without an address.

A moment's consideration shows that probability of this kind may be often difficult to calculate except on a large scale and with a vast amount of statistics. The business of

E

Life Insurance would be practically gambling if the interests of an Office were staked upon the life of one person, even though the probabilities of the duration of that one person's life had been calculated with mathematical accuracy ; but, when the risk is scattered over several hundreds of lives, the business is safe if the lives are correctly calculated : one insurer lives, so to speak, less long than he ought to have lived ; but another lives longer ; excess and defect balance each other ; and thus, over the whole mass of Insurers, the calculations of Probability made by the Office are verified by the results.

So much for Statistical Probability, which, as every one will admit, we are very far from consciously accepting as " the guide of life." But what as to our ordinary actions ? We get up in the morning, we breakfast, go out, catch our train, go to our business, keep our appointments, with scarcely any thought of probability, but in *faith*—faith that the sun will rise, faith (less, but sufficient) that breakfast will be ready and eatable, roads passable, trains (to some extent) punctual, our office not burned down, and so on. No thought of probability enters our minds about all these things.

Of course, if, as we are going down stairs, some one stops us and says, " Is it *certain* that you will have your breakfast to-day ? " we should perhaps—to be precise—reply, " Well, it's highly probable." But, whatever our words might be, we act in a practical certitude, derived (1) partly from our *experience*, knowing that the sun *has* risen, breakfast *has* been ready, roads *have* been passable, &c., and that no circumstances have arisen (within our knowledge) to break this course of things ; partly (2) from our *desire* that what has been shall be, or, we may almost say, from our feeling that a fixed order of things is so necessary to our existence that we *must* take it for granted, and that it is useless to speculate as to what would happen if that order were broken.   Really, and in truth, the routine of our life might be broken ; our place of business might be burned down, our trains all smashed in accidents, our roads rendered impassable by earthquake or by six feet of snow, bread might cease to be eatable, the sun might not rise, the laws of gravitation and friction might cease to act— all sorts of disturbances of our comfortable circle of circumstances might occur, some of them not very improbable, some very improbable, some so highly improbable that we are accustomed to call them impossible.   But even as regards these not very improbable interferences with our common course of life, our attitude is—and ought to be if we want to do our work well—one of *faith;* we do not spend our time in thinking of probabilities of interference, we assume that there will be no interference.

Of course when some of these interferences are reported to have actually occurred, we readily believe them, provided that the interferences are fairly common in our experience, and that there is no suspicion of deception, or of credulity, or of exaggeration in the reporter.   To such statements as, "Your office is burned down," "The train is smashed in an accident," we should give much more ready credence than to the statement that "every one of the sixteen persons with whom you have made different appointments is said to have died yesterday from heart-disease," or "the Bank is destroyed by an earthquake."   We do not therefore reject narratives of events, in themselves antecedently improbable, when they are reported on good evidence to have actually occurred. But the point is, that although all these interferences are possible, and some not in the highest degree improbable, we are so constituted by nature that, until they are alleged to

have occurred, we practically ignore all but those which are
of frequent occurrence.   To do this, is necessary for success
—which requires that our habitual basis for the immense
majority of the actions of life, should be, not probability,
but *faith* based upon experience.

Probability steps in, as we have admitted, when we " *stop
to think* how to act " ; but it is not the whole of life, it is
not the principal part of life, to " *stop to think* how to act." It
would not be to our purpose to consider whether, in borrow-
ing his doctrine from Butler, Newman has, or has not, altered
it.   Enough for us the common-sense conclusion that—if
the words " probability," " the," " guide," " life," have their
ordinary meaning—Probability is *not* entitled to be called
the Guide of life.

§ 8. *Is Faith based on Probability ?*

" But," it may be urged, " even though faith, and not
probability, be accepted as the ' Guide of Life,' yet this
faith itself—that is to say faith in the fixed order of things—
is based upon probabilities."

Is it so, as regards the most common actions of our life,
which depend upon our constant recognition of the laws
of gravitation, friction, and the like ? Can any one recollect a time when he thought that a stone would *probably*
fall, and that a wall would *probably* not yield to the pressure
of a finger, and that the sun would *probably* set ?   If
so, he can perhaps tell us how the accumulation of many
experiences of probability, blossomed, so to speak, into that
kind of certain faith which he now possesses.   But no one
can tell us the *how*, for no one can recollect the *when*—if
such a *when* ever was.   We are perfectly safe therefore in
asserting that as regards our most common actions and the

larger part of our lives, though we have passed from experience to what we call certitude, we have not passed to it
—*so far as we know*—over the bridge of probability. If
therefore Probability was really the guide of our lives in
leading us to these most important certitudes, Nature (or
God) has at all events covered up the fact, and may be
almost said to have hidden it from us lest Probability should
paralyse Faith.

Here however a speculative mind may raise an ingenious
objection. "You speak," it may be urged, " of the individual ; but what of the race? Race experience shows that
there must have been once this Bridge of Probability, of
which you deny the existence. The *tabula rasa* theory has
been abolished by that of hereditary and cumulative
experiences. There never was a time, we grant, in the life
of any now existing individual when it seemed *probable* that
the stone would fall, or that the earth would prove hard :
there was, and must have been, in the life of the race ; and
experiences of probability in the race have become a faculty
of faith in the individual—faith being thus *a priori* to the
individual and *a posteriori* to the race."

It may be so. I cannot myself feel confident that there
was ever a time when a race, human or destined to become
human, threw a stone up at acorns " upon a probability "that
the stone would go up but prepared to find it go down ; or
dropped a cocoa-nut from a branch upon the head of an
enemy below, on the chance that the nut would go down,
but prepared to find it go up. But still, for my purpose, I
welcome this objection. Grant that, as Æschylus says,
there was, first, a time, before the Promethean Advent, when
quasi-human creatures lived absolutely at random, " blending
all things at hazard " ; and then a second stage, when a more
highly developed race believed in the Law of Gravitation

upon a probability, and moved their legs and balanced their bodies on a life-long hypothesis : what follows ?   Why this : that Nature brought us through this lower stage and led us to a higher, where we have as completely forgotten the lower, as we have forgotten our first year's nursery annals. This being the case, why go back from the higher to the lower?   Let speculators assign probability, as a basis for belief in the fundamental laws of life, to the troglodytes, or if they will have none of it, to their primæval ancestors. But our business is with men.

And is it not manifest that man, as we know him, could not *constantly* live and act (consciously) by Probabilities ?   We could no more act upon probable laws of gravitation and probable laws of friction than we could worship a probable God.   As God must, so too must Nature's Promises (which are God's Promises, sometimes called Nature's Laws) be obeyed and trusted with all our heart as well as with all our mind.   To act *consciously and constantly* upon a calculation of probabilities would exclude the simultaneous co-operation of faith. Worry has been defined as unbelieving work.   Now the habit of consciously acting upon probabilities in all the relations of life, would tend to make all work faithless, and all life a succession of worries, beneath which the finest and strongest nature would speedily deteriorate and succumb.

" But," it may be urged, " we often act consciously, as well as unconsciously, upon the doctrine of Probability : more often, a good deal, than you have admitted above ; as for example, in taking, or not taking, an umbrella with us, upon the chance of its raining, or not raining.   Does not this one simple instance show how common the habit is ? "

Perhaps it is too common : but it is not very common.

One proof of its rarity is the invention of games.   In games we almost always act, and act consciously, "upon prob- abilities"; and the reason why this is so charming is, that our ordinary lives are full of dull routine ; in which we are so tired of acting, *not* upon probabilities but upon practical certainties, that we like, for a change, to act now and then "upon a probability," or, as we sometimes call it "upon the chance."   There is "no fun," we say, "no sport," in a game where there is not some element of chance. Hence too the love of war and enterprise, because they afford the rare and delightful stimulus of consciously acting upon probabilities.

It may be admitted however that even in ordinary life many of us act upon these grounds fairly often (though the frequency cannot be compared for a moment with the frequency with which we act on Faith).   But it is, or should be, *either where the stakes are small, or where there is more or less compulsion so to act.* Except in these cases, to act consciously upon nice probabilities is more or less demoralizing.   Even if Insurance Offices doubled the usual premium, a young husband, with a fair in- come but no fortune, would be right in saying, "My mathematical neighbour tells me I am a fool for insuring at such a cost : but when the question is whether my wife should go to the workhouse, I will have nothing to do with probabilities : give me certainties *there*." They are, of course, *not* real "certainties"; they are only comparative "cer- tainties," but "*certain*" *enough to release him from the strain of consciously acting upon probability.*

"Give me certainties"—yes, that is the right demand where the stake is *constant* as well as great. Generals and doctors and judges and juries—and all of us on rare occa- sions—are *forced* to act consciously on probabilities, and sometimes for high stakes ; and *the compulsion frees the action from the sense of gambling, and converts it from an excitement into a duty.* But the strain is severe and could not be long endured ; and, while we are under the strain, we are often obliged to reduce ouselves as far as possible to machines, suspending the play of the emotions ; and these facts, viz. the brief duration, the severe and, so to speak, unnatural tension, and the partial one-sided nature of this conscious " acting upon Probability," stamp it as being so exceptional as rather to confirm than weaken our assertion that Probability is *not* the guide of life.

Our contention is, then, that in the greater part of life, Faith and not Probability, is, and is to be, our guide. We also assert that this Faith—that is, Faith in the fixed and, in the main, beneficent order of things—though it is based upon experience, never, *so far as we know*, sprang from Probability ; or, if it did so spring, that Nature has so dealt with us as to forbid us to exhume, for the purposes of practical life, those base, distant, and forgotten antecedents which are, as it were, buried out of our sight.   But we seem to have been led on to a point where we perceive that this conclusion may also hold good for the nobler, as well as the "greater," part of our life.   For what can be a nobler task, and yet what task can involve a higher stake, than that of shaping an immortal soul ?   And we have seen above, that the greater the risk, the greater ought to be our aversion to acting upon Probability.   But this question has not yet been considered ; and it now demands our attention.   We have rejected Probability as the " guide " in the ordinary affairs of our material life ; are we to accept it as our guide for spiritual progress ?

CHAPTER II

§ 9. *Keble's Doctrine of Faith* [1]

IN attempting to apply his doctrine of "Probability as the Guide of Life" to belief in God and in Divine truths Newman confesses that he met a difficulty. How could a man pray to a *probable* God, or pray to God upon grounds of probability?

But, he says (*Apol.* 19), " I considered that Mr. Keble met this difficulty by ascribing the firmness of assent which we give to religious doctrine, not to the probabilities which introduced it, but to the living power of love and faith which accepted it. . . . In illustration, Mr. Keble used to quote the words of the Psalm : ' I will guide thee with mine *eye*. .' This is the very difference, he used to say, between slaves, and friends or children. Friends do not ask for literal commands ; but from their knowledge of the speaker, they anticipate his half-words, and from love of him they anticipate his wishes."

This profound truth, thus simply expressed, demands our

[1] The following remarks refer to Keble's "Doctrine " simply *as stated by Newman in the present passage.*

close attention; for it may explain the gradual divergence and ultimate parting between Keble and the man who thought himself at that time his follower. Newman fancied that he agreed with Keble; but he did not and could not, because he had not the same conception of God. Keble—or Keble as here represented—loved God as a Father, and was content to remain as a child, trusting and believing; Newman feared God as a Judge, and was consequently always "asking for literal commands," either direct from God, or indirect, through authorities appointed by Him. Between two theologians, thus differing, however unconsciously, in the fundamental principle of Christianity there could be no ultimate harmony.[1]

Again, for a man of Newman's disposition—not only timorous of error, distrustful of his own feelings, and anxiously prone to lean upon authority, but also endowed with a strong dialectic faculty and a keen sense (keen when not dulled by prejudice) of logical difficulties—it would soon seem unsatisfactory to have to defend his belief in a great mass of "religious doctrine" by a mere metaphor about the guidance of the Divine *eye*. Our personal trust in God our Father may enable us to understand sympathetically and to grasp firmly such doctrines as tell us that Christ authoritatively, and in some real, objective, and possibly natural way, forgave sins; that He, in some real, objective, and possibly natural way, rose from the dead; and that He in His last will and testament bequeathed Himself, His real and personal presence, for ever, to His disciples. But it is only a few very simple and fundamental doctrines that flash, as

---

[1] It may be urged that "the fundamental principle" is the *recognition* of the *existence* of God. But though that may be the fundamental principle of some religions, it is not the fundamental principle of Christianity, which is to *love* God as a *Father*, in Christ, as the Son.

it were, conviction upon our hearts, as though our Father Himself were, with a glance, expressing in them His will, and helping us at the same time to do it. How could the *eye* of God, or " living trust and faith," help a believer to accept—what Newman felt not only bound to accept, but bound to justify himself in accepting—the truth and divine origin of the " doctrines " that set forth the stopping of the sun by Joshua, the human utterance of the ass of Balaam, and the destruction of the swine by our Lord Himself? Probably Keble believed all these things, and, somehow, connected them with "faith." But how was the connection "logical"? How was Newman to defend the whole mass of Biblical "doctrine" against those who would assail it with the doctrine of private judgment? For this purpose Keble's metaphor gave him no assistance ; and therefore we ought not to be surprised at his half-complaint, that this view of the matter was (*Apol.* 20) " beautiful and religious, but *it did not even profess to be logical.*"

Yet this objection ought to prepare us not to be altogether surprised if Newman misconceives the nature of Christian Faith. A " logical view " of Christian Faith is, no doubt, a justifiable expression—just as, I suppose, we might speak of a " logical view " of parental, filial, or conjugal love, meaning a view that is not inconsistent with facts and that can connect a certain number of facts as effects and causes ; but it sounds as though it *might* be misleading. However, we can say no more about this till we have determined what Christian Faith is. And, to begin with, let us clear our minds by asking what is Faith ?

§ 10. *What is Faith?*

Faith, like love, takes its colour from its object, and is as
often bad as good : we may have faith in ourselves, in our
luck, in tact, in audacity, in money, in advertising; or we
may have faith in good men, in our friends, in honesty, in
the influence of good character, in justice. Faith always
implies desire : we never say " I have faith that my audacity
will fail," " I have faith that honesty will not prove the best
policy"; in such cases we should use the word "belief."
Faith differs from hope, in that the latter, generally, having
to do with particular cases, is more readily verifiable than
the former : " I have a hope (not ' a faith ') that I shall make
£100 by advertising," but, " I have faith (not so often ' hope,')
in advertising generally," that is, " I believe that advertising
generally succeeds, and I have a sort of liking that it should
succeed."

It is a great pity—for it is the source of great confusion—
that faith should be used in so many different senses.   Faith
in money or advertising is—we feel—quite a different thing
from faith in our father, wife, children, or friends.   The
former implies little more than a belief in sequence, viz.,
that the use of money or advertising will be followed by
certain results, and a desire, selfishly strong in particular
cases, but weak and little more than acquiescent in general,
that this sequence should be preserved.   But in the latter,
the belief in sequence is quite subordinate.   The mere
intellectual anticipation that the exercise of will on the part
of one's father, wife, or children, will be followed by certain
moral actions and not be followed by immoral actions, is
wholly swallowed up in an *affectionate desire* that this sequence
shall be observed combined with an *affectionate certitude* that
it *will* be observed.

Perhaps some people will tell us that it is nonsense to speak of an "affectionate certitude," certitude being an intellectual condition : "How," they will ask, "can you be affectionately certain that your son will tell the truth, any more than you can be affectionately certain that you will catch your train? In both cases you are simply (what you call) 'certain'; and the certitude is, in both cases, a high probability based upon evidence. So far as it is thus based, it is likely to be right ; so far as it is not, it is likely to be wrong. 'Affection,' if it interfered at all, would disturb the judgment. Affection for your dining-room clock will not more certainly make you lose your train than affection for your children (unless held in abeyance) will make you miscalculate and miscredit their actions."

This is clever ; and I have heard a still more clever objection, to the effect that, if you want to know a man really well and to anticipate his actions, you cannot do better than hate him ; for then, not a weakness of his will escape you, and you will probe every corner of his nature. Judging men, and hating men, crinanthropy[1] and misanthropy—in theory these are admirable means for knowing men ; but we are speaking of practical life. And in practice we find that affectionate certitude answers better—at least as regards that very large and important part of our human course in which the influence of the family is shaping and moulding the character.

Think for an instant how that critical attitude which I have called crinanthropy would answer in family life.   I

[1] Dr. Murray's Dictionary has not reached the stage at which it could be ascertained whether this word as yet exists.   In any case, I hope the reader will pardon the word because of the commonness of the thing.   For one *misanthropist* there are a thousand or ten thousand *crinanthopists*.

have admitted above that our faith in the ordinary course
of material things is so far modifiable that if we were
suddenly asked, "Is it *certain* that this, or that, will
happen?" we might have to reply, "Well, no, not
certain; but at all events highly probable." But supposing such a question were put to us about *persons;* suppose
the questioner were to begin from the end of the Deca-
logue and work upwards, asking us "Is it certain that
your parents, your wife, your children, will not do this, or
that?"—who would endure, in some of these contexts, to
answer with the word "probable"? We simply decline to look
at the matter in that light.   Regarding it physiologically, we
should say that to entertain questions of this kind tends to
insanity; Biblically, we should say it leads to Hell.

Thus far we seem justified in asserting that affectionate
certitude works better than crinanthropy for ourselves, that
is, for our moral welfare and sanity, in family life.   It might
also be maintained, we think, that, in the end, it works better
for our own intelligence; because it enables us to understand
phenomena, quickening our sympathetic imagination, and
helping us to throw ourselves into the position of others, to
feel as they feel, and to know what they need.   Lastly, even
a man of the world will admit that this way of looking at, or
feeling about, persons, works well for the persons themselves.
For it is a common-place that such affectionate certitude, such
trust as this, often makes a man trustworthy—a spiritual
result that no one would attribute to crinanthropy or misanthropy.   So, seeing that our illogical practice of affectionate
certitude works on the whole well, and certainly better than
the theories of our critics, we cannot surrender it to them.

The only concession we can make to our critics is, perhaps
the word " certitude," which makes them uneasy because it
has an intellectual sound.   If the word does indeed suggest

any prominent intellectual element, it certainly is deceptive; for the highest kind of faith, though suggested by knowledge, and therefore indebted originally to the understanding, does not appear to be, in itself, intellectual but emotional. The intellectual factor in it, if it exists, is quite subordinate; and perhaps "factor" is not the right word. The Faith of which we are speaking does not, perhaps, *contain* an *element* of reason, but is only *accompanied* by a sense of *consonance* with reason. Let us therefore substitute for "affectionate certitude," either "faith" or "trust." Where this "trust" is spread over a long period, and is not likely to be confirmed or confuted at any definite time, the intellectual factor in faith (if there is such a factor) is more than ever subordinated and forgotten (say, like a scaffolding, stowed away when the house is built); and most of all where the final verification is not expected on this side of the grave.

§ 11. *What is Christian Faith?*

So far, we have seen that this very deceptive word faith—though it always implies more or less of desire, and a belief in some kind of sequence—varies from what is little more than an intellectual belief with a spice of desire, good or bad, up to an intense, affectionate, desire, producing all the certainty of conviction although any intellectual factor that may have once existed is either latent or absent.

In what sense, then, do we propose to use the word. It is not enough to say, "religious faith," nor even "Christian faith," unless the phrase is defined. For there are several kinds of so-called "Christian faith"; (1) "faith" that the Bible is verbally, historically, and morally inspired; (2) "faith" that there is a true, visible, and authoritative Church of Christ upon earth; (3) "faith" that oneself and a "few" are to be eternally saved and the "many" to be eternally damned; (4) "faith" that God will judge the world in Christ, *without regard to the justice of that judgment;* (5) "faith" that there are three Persons in one God, *without regard to the nature of those Persons and the moral goodness of that God:*—all these five faiths are quite different from (6) faith in God as the Father, revealed in Christ, as the Son. Hence, whenever we hear a proposition about "faith"—even in the phrase "Christian faith"—we must treat it as we should treat a statement about "property" bequeathed to us, where we have good reason for doubting which will be the larger, the debts or the assets. In that case we should have to say, "'Property'; yes, but for what amount, positive or negative?" And so, "'Faith'; yes, but in what object, good or bad?"

The following then shall be our definition. The object of Christian Faith is that invisible order of things which is described in the Gospels as the Kingdom of God, or the Kingdom of Heaven. Our belief is that God, *as revealed through Christ in the character of a Father,* is already, in some sense, and will be seen to be hereafter in a sense beyond our present apprehension, *the ruling Power of the Universe;* and our desire is that this should be so. But, by its very nature, this *belief,* in the *existence* of a God thus revealed, is absorbed by a *trust* in the God thus revealed. This will be best seen from an instance.

I am drowning, we will suppose; and I suddenly catch sight of a man who has plunged into the water and is by my side to save me. Reasonably or unreasonably I trust him; I am (we will suppose) at once possessed with the conviction that he will save me. Now is it necessary that I should see him first, as a man, and trust him afterwards as a deliverer? Or may I not see him and trust him *simultaneously,* seeing him, *from the first*—as soon as I see him at all—*as a trusted saviour?*

In the same way, mankind is—from the Christian point of view—struggling in an ocean of sin ; and God, when *revealed to us in Christ*, is revealed as a *Helper from the first.* Until He is *thus* revealed, *He—the Christian God*—is not revealed to us *at all ;* and any other conception that we may have formed of God is *not the Christian conception.* As regards our visible rescuer in the water, it *might* be true to say that we saw him as a man first and trusted him as a rescuer afterwards ; but as regards our invisible Saviour, this cannot be true ; for *until we see and trust Him as a Saviour*, we do not see Him (*as He is in Christ*) *at all.*

But it follows from the nature of this revelation that the intellectual and logical process which might lead us to form propositions, such as God *is*, God *helps*, are altogether subordinated to the emotion of *trust.* Nor need it be supposed that the Author of the Epistle to the Hebrews, in defining Faith as "the assurance of *things not seen*," contradicts our statement that Faith is not belief about *things*, but trust in a *Person ;* for what "things" has the writer in his mind ? Clearly, the same that St. Paul has when he speaks of "Jerusalem that is above"; he means that invisible order of things by which humanity is to be conformed to the Divine image ; and this may be described as the invisible history of humanity as represented and predicted and summed up in the Life, the Death, the Resurrection, the Ascension, and the Reign of Christ. Thus Faith as defined in the Epistle to the Hebrews is practically identical with Faith defined in the Epistle to the Romans ; it is trust in an Eternal Order, summed up and represented in an eternal Person.

What part does Reason play in the formation of this faith ? Reason classifies phenomena and infers their prob-

F

able causes ; does Reason lead us to God in Christ through the phenomena of the world, the family, the Bible, and the Church? We shall have a difficulty in answering this question as long as we retain the ambiguous "us." What does "us" mean? Does it mean (1) those who, in the full maturity of manhood, are converted to Christianity; or (2) those who are born and bred amid the influences of the Spirit of Christ?

To take the former case, first. It would seem that here there must needs be a weighing of probabilities. In the play of Euripides, we see Ion, ignorant of his parentage, scrutinizing his old cradle, and minutely examining the swaddling-clothes, and the tokens of his babyhood, and pondering over his mother's answers before recognizing that he is indeed her son, and flying into her arms. The suspense is terrible, the strain is unique. Much more might it seem at first sight to be so in the case of the recognition of a heavenly Father by a long-estranged and fatherless soul.

But the parallel is not perhaps quite a fair one. For it omits the influence of family likeness, which, even in some human "recognitions" on the stage, plays no unimportant part, and which, in the spiritual recognition of souls—the wandering soul of man turning towards the great fixed and loving World-soul—ought to be (one may well think) almost powerful enough, of itself, to convert suggestions of kinship into demonstrative proof. And this anticipation is in some degree confirmed by the records of the earliest conversions handed down to us, in which we seem to see that Reason from the first plays a subordinate part, and soon retires quite into the background. Evidence was brought forward : " Christ rose from the dead ; *I* saw Him "; or, " He was seen by so-and-so " ; with some brief account, perhaps, of what Christ was and did. This seems slight testimony ; but at this point there entered in the influence of the "family likeness," and this, in two ways. The message was brought, not only *about* a Father, but also *by* a brother. If it was not, it failed. The " I " in the "*I* saw Him," was a most potent element, the element of an inspired and inspiring personality, giving forth part of that life and power which it had received from the Giver.

The heart of the believer recognized the invisible Father, in part through the recognition of the visible brother who breathed as it were a spirit of sonship which made the message seem, first, credible, then, natural, then, so sublimely glorious that it was felt that it *must* be true. And thus these two Spirits of the " family likeness "—or shall we not rather say, the Three Spirits of Father, Son and Brother ?—combined in an irresistible alliance which converted what else would have been a mere verbal message, into a Spirit of Power. That Christ, being what He was, *could not* be holden by death ; that He was, as it were, *bound* to triumph over sin and death, these words of fire—even without the marvels of faith-healing which often accompanied the Good News— carried the Spirit of Power into the very heart of the hearer and compelled him to feel that he was in a region not to be fathomed or verified by verbal logic, and that, apart from the exact accuracy of this or that fact, God *must* be such a one as Christ, and Christ *must* represent the Ruling Principle of the world.

At this juncture, therefore, when Reason would fain weigh the *pros* and *cons*, and decide the question in her own systematic way, faith puts her gently aside. " If this were a question of simple fact, I should have to bow to you ; but it is now mainly a question of the unverifiable *causes* of fact. You did your work when you laid the evidence before me and helped me to judge of the honesty of the witness and general consistency of the testimony. That is now over. It is *right* for me to believe that God is our Father; I *need* to believe, and it is *right* to believe, that Christ in some sense rose from the dead and triumphed over sin. We are here in a region where what is *right* is true ; and to test the *right* is my faculty, not yours."

There is nothing unreal, then, or dishonest, or contrary to facts, or of the nature of a make-believe, in all this. Dr. Martineau, describing Newman's theory of faith, says, "an uneasy wonder comes upon us when we are told that in early times men became Christians, not because they believed but *in order to believe (Arians*, p. 78 ; *Loss and Gain*, p. 343) ; and that the characteristic doctrines of the Gospel were not offered to them till they had bound themselves to the Church by baptism."[1]   Certainly it would be an entire misrepresentation of the facts to say that the early Christians "believed *in order that* they might believe"; they believed *because they could not help it ;* because conviction came rushing upon them, and conscience threw open the gates and surrendered at discretion.   They did not believe, "upon a probability." The probability, the harmony, of the evidence, *arrested their attention ;* but it was the sense of affection that did the deed ; it was the "family-likeness" between man and God self-asserting itself in the heart of the converted ; it was the spirit leaping up to welcome the Father towards whom it had long been blindly groping.

We pass to the consideration of those brought up from infancy under Christian influences. What part does reason play in shaping their faith, and where does probability step in ?

To such a child, unable to conceive of anyone better, wiser, and more powerful than his parents, faith in God

[1] *Essays*, vol. i. p. 240.

means, at first, simply trust in his parents, and then, trust in One above to whom even his parents look up with reverence. "Is this, then, 'belief on authority'? And does a child believe that there is a God, simply on the authority of his parents; just as he believes that there are red men, and *would believe that there are green men*, upon their authority?" No; it is not so. If he believes that there is a God *in the same way* in which he believes that there are red men, he has a wrong conception of the term God; he must *trust* in God through his parents, if he is to be said, with any truth, to "believe in God." They must be, as it were, mediators between him and God; otherwise God is a mere Name to him, or something worse than a name, something not good but bad. The evidence, or authority, of his parents, places the truth before the child's mind and heart; and so far as the spirit of the household has prepared him to welcome that truth by imbuing him with the love of goodness and justice, so far, and no further, he takes in the truth.

But, in either case, whether he believes in God or not, he does not believe, or disbelieve, upon a probability. He accepts the proposition in either case as a certainty; but it either remains upon the surface of the soul as a theory that does not practically affect him—perhaps because he sees that it does not practically affect his parents—or else it penetrates the soul for good or ill. If for good, then there is the germ of the faith in a heavenly Father. If for ill, then there is the germ of the dread of a hard Judge or capricious Tyrant, or a vague sense of a mysterious Restrainer of pleasures and Meddler with innocent amusements. In no case, does a child believe in God "upon a probability."

But perhaps it may be argued that the conscious "belief upon probabilities," enters later on; at the point where, for example, the child, or youth, or man, passes from his false

belief about God as a Tyrant to a true belief in God as a
Father.   Do the records of religious experiences justify such
a supposition?   *Does* a man pass from dreading God as a
domineering Interferer, to loving and trusting Him as a
Father, by some nice weighing and pondering of probabilities which leads him perhaps to discover that, whereas
he had believed that there were three chances for a Tyrant
and two for a Father, he now discovers there are three
for a Father, and only two for a Tyrant?   Surely such a
hypothesis needs only to be fairly and fully stated in order
to be unhesitatingly and irrevocably dismissed with the
words of the Apostle : " Ye have *not so learned Christ.*"

It is the beauty and the glory of the Righteousness of
God in Christ that turn us from thoughts of darkness and
from self-brooding fears, and captivate us and constrain us to
trust in Him.   Some glimpse or other of the truth obscured
in childhood—and often obscured by well-meant religious
teaching—brings home to us the reality of Christ ; that,
after all, He *was* a man, though Divine ; that He *did*
indeed bear the sins and carry the iniquities of all mankind, as, on a small scale, men are now bearing one
another's sins and carrying one another's iniquities :
that He *did* indeed introduce a new power of forgiveness
into the world ; that He *did* indeed bequeath His very being
to be our food and the sustenance of our souls for ever ; and
then, gradually or suddenly, we find that our dread of Christ
as a Judge, or our dim and far-off reverence for Him as a
mysterious amalgam of the human and divine, has become a
passionate certitude that He, and no other thing or person,
expresses the ruling principle of the Universe.   Then almost
all things become clear ; and Sin itself, though it can never
become quite clear in this life, looms through the half-
dispelled mist no longer as a "stone of stumbling," but as a

step, an altar-step leading to a higher Righteousness than
could ever have been achieved by an innocent world. This
is Faith ; and Faith, we willingly admit, derived help from
Reason, which did its good work in discerning and classifying
the operations of the Divine Word, working in many shapes
and with various results ; but still there is no room in this
Faith for Probability.

Nor does Probability step in at any later stage. 'Probability' means 'proveableness.' But no man now-a-days,
that is to say, no educated man, believes that he can *prove*
the truth of Christianity. Once people thought it could be
proved by miracles alone; no one thinks that now. If a
man worked a miracle in heaven to *prove* that Christ was an
impostor, we should not believe him : then how can we ask
sceptics to believe that Christ was God because, it is said,
He worked miracles on earth ? We did not approach Christ,
we do not remain in Christ, on the strength of such proofs
as these.

There are certain facts—facts of the nursery, of social
life, of history, of science, of the Church, of the Bible—which
suggest that God is the Father of mankind ; there are others
that point in a contrary or different direction, suggesting that
Evil, or Nothing, rules the Universe. The honest Christian
does not tamper with either class of facts ; but he allows his
mind to rest more on the former, because he loves them and
finds them helpful. Some of the facts that prepared him in
his childhood to accept God as a Father—*e.g.* his trust in
parental goodness and perfection, and perhaps his trust in
the historical accuracy of some parts of the Bible—he finds,
as he grows older, to be not so fully true as he supposed ;
but meantime, his increased spiritual experience and his
enlarged knowledge of human nature have combined to
build up the structure of Faith within his heart. Then,

the structure being complete, some of what he thought
facts—which were but as a kind of scaffolding and not
a part of the building itself—can be dispensed with, not
only without injury, but even with benefit to the building ;
and the Faith remains, cleared from much that was once a
help but is now an encumbrance.

In a painfully curious passage written by a man of ability,
but much given to "views," and perhaps more versed in
books and views than in the higher possibilities of human
nature, a kind of patronage is extended to the rational
" view " of Faith, as put forward by the late Dean Church :
" Also that view of Faith has so much in it that you
ought to make more of it, some time or other. *I could
fancy its working up to something.* The same of the view
of 'the powers which God's wisdom has in these last days
placed in the hands of men.' They are views which seem
to explain our present state of things—the former, as showing *that mediæval faith was not so much better than ours as,
in some aspects,* it seems ; the latter, as showing that *our want
of that aboriginal genuine faith has something to say in its
defence,* and can point to a new dispensation of things
which *in some measure justifies or explains it.*" [1]

It is lamentable that from a professed theologian there
should have come forth such an avowal of ignorance of the
first principles of the Christian religion.　As though anything
whatever could " justify " our want of "genuine " faith ! But
no "justification " at all is needed. *The modern faith is the
more "genuine" of the two.*　It is faith in Christ for His
own sake and not for the sake of His supposed thaumaturgic powers.　Dean Church's " view " (or, as I should call
it, statement of facts that should be patent to all Christians)
is this, that Christian faith should be faith in God's Eternal

[1] *Letters of the Rev. J. B. Mozley,* p. 175.

order as revealed in His Eternal Son : " Search as we will, we can find nothing to rest upon, nothing that will endure the real trial, but the faith of the Psalmists in the eternal kingdom of God—the faith of the Psalmists lit up by the ' grace and truth that came by Jesus Christ.' " [1] It is only theological viewists who would dream that such faith as this required justification or apology because it found its nourishment less in wonders such as the articulate speech of Balaam's ass, or the liquefaction of the blood of St. Janu-arius, than in the spiritual, the naturally-spiritual experience of Christian souls and Christian societies.

The weakness of such a Faith—if it is a weakness—is, that it does not embrace a large number of dogmatic propositions. The strength of it—besides that it has no quarrel with Reason and incurs no danger of fanaticism—is, that it is under no temptation to deal dishonestly with facts. Recognizing that there is an opposing Evil in the world, it confesses that our trust in the ultimate triumph of Goodness is sometimes, and is intended to be, of the nature of an effort. Christian Faith is a victory; but it is *not a victory over facts, in the sense of dishonestly denying facts.* It is a victory over selfish ignoble desires, brooding melancholies, bestial passions that tempt men to think themselves meant to be beasts; it is not a victory over the mind, the understanding, the observation and the judgment, with which faculties, as we conceive, man has been endowed by God in order that he may seek and approximate to truth. If the Devil were to paint the sky to-morrow with the luminous letters THERE IS NO GOD, Christian Faith would still believe in a God ; but it would not try to blink the NO or say it was meant for an A.

[1] Church's *Advent Sermons,* p. 28. Macmillan. 1885.

§ 12. *Newman's Inclined Plane of Probabilities*

Such a Faith however seemed too weak and too illogical for Newman. He tells us that, though he made a partial use of Keble's theory, yet he was (20) "dissatisfied, because he did not go to the root of the difficulty." What "difficulty"? He means the "difficulty" of assenting firmly to a vast mass of Biblical statements as to facts, concerning some of which there is not very strong evidence ; and the evidence—such as it is—we sometimes have little means of investigating. In other words, Newman quarrels with Keble's theory of Faith because it does not logically enable him to take up some "system" of fact and thought, and to adopt it whole, and to say, "All these facts and statements I have not investigated and shall not investigate ; but I am certain they are all accurate." This is the "difficulty" which Keble's theory of Faith does not meet and which Newman's theory is intended to meet.

He therefore attempts, as he expresses it (*Apol.* 19), "to *complete*" Keble's theory by "considerations" of his own, to be found in his *University Sermons, Essay on Ecclesiastical Miracles*, and *Essay on Development of Doctrine.* The advantage of his theory is that it attaches to all statements in the Bible, to all the miraculous narratives therein contained, and even to all the alleged miracles of Ecclesiastical History, something of the sentiment that we attach to faith in God Himself. The disadvantage is, that it attaches to our fundamental faith in God that taint of the *simultaneous* feeling of Probability from which Faith and Love shrink as from a leper's touch. Belief in God and belief in the liquefaction of the blood of St. Januarius are both made beliefs of the same kind, though

differing in *degree ;* one is at the top of the inclined plane
and represents a "transcendent" Probability; the other,
perhaps half-way down, is believed in upon a medial Probability; then perhaps the belief in the Miracle of the
tongueless Martyrs, mentioned aDove (p. 18) might come
at the bottom representing the lowest degree of Probability.
The Probability at the top we may call "certitude"; that
in the middle, "a belief," or "a pious belief"; that at the
bottom "a pious opinion" or "a religious conjecture."
From Newman's point of view, this is a very useful theory
which he might call the "Inclined Plane of Probabilities."
If you have certitude about God, upon grounds of
Probability, why not, upon similar grounds, have a "pious
belief" in the Liquefaction of the Blood of St. Januarius,
and a "religious conjecture" about the African Martyrs?

In his *Apologia* (p. 21) he stated his theory thus :—

"That, as there were probabilities which sufficed for [1] certitude, so there were other probabilities which were legiti-
mately adapted to create opinion : that it might be quite as
much a matter of duty in given cases and to given persons to
have about a fact an opinion of a definite strength and consistency, as in the case of *greater or of more numerous probabilities it was a duty to have a certitude ;* that, accordingly,
we were bound to be more or less sure, on a sort of (as it
were) graduated scale of ascent, viz., according as the probabilities attaching to a professed fact were brought home
to us, and, as the case might be, to entertain about it a pious

---

[1] Both here, and on p. 20, the original edition has "to create,"
instead of "for." The reason for the change is this : Newman believes
that "probabilities" do *not* "*create*" certitude ; but, when they have
accumulated so far as to "suffice," *God* steps in and *creates* certitude.
On p. 22 of *Apologia*, "to *create* certitude," is still left—no doubt, by
a slip. Notice, in the next line that "probabilities" *may* "create"
opinion.

belief, or a pious opinion, or a religious conjecture, or at least, a tolerance of such belief, or opinion or conjecture, in others." He adds that, " in other cases " (but he does not define whether they are " cases " of intellectual improbability or moral repugnance) we are *not* to believe, opine, or conjecture.

Here it is *implied* that, just as we believe in a fairly probable miracle upon a fair amount of probabilities, so *we believe in God upon those " greater or more numerous probabilities " in the case of which it is our " duty to have a certitude."* But still, as Newman does not expressly say that we *believe in a God on a ground of probability*, it will be best to quote at full length the passage in which he at last commits himself to these very words. Although nineteen years had elapsed between the Essay on *Development* (1845) and the *Apologia*—giving him ample time to formulate his theory—he nevertheless considerably altered, in subsequent editions, the exposition contained in the first edition of the latter. Where they diverge, I give both versions :—

(1864 *and* 1890).

(199) " I am not speaking theologically, nor have I any intention of going into controversy, or of defending myself ; [1] but, speaking histori-

---

[1] I have inserted the words, " I . . . myself " as the omission of them might seem unfair to some who may see their bearing on what follows. But I fail to see it. I do not understand the difference (here) between " speaking theologically " and speaking secularly. At the conclusion of the passage he says (200) : " But, let it be observed, that I am stating a matter of fact, not defending it ; and *if any Catholic says in consequence that I have been converted in a wrong way*, I cannot help that now." Possibly, therefore, Newman means, by this introductory *caveat*, no more than this, that some of his expressions may not seem *technically* accurate in the light of authoritative Roman theological principles.

cally of what I held in 1843-4, I say, that *I believed in a God on a ground of probability, and that I believed in Christianity on a probability, and that I believed in Catholicism on a probability*, and that

1864. (p. 324).	1890. (p. 199).
"all three were *about the same kind of* probability,	"these three grounds of probability, distinct from each other, of course, in subject-matter, were still, all of them *one and the same in nature of proof*, as being probabilities—probabilities of a special kind,

(1864 *and* 1890).

"a cumulative, a transcendent probability, but still probability ; inasmuch as He who made us has so willed, that in mathematics indeed we [should, om. in 1864] arrive at certitude by rigid demonstration, *but in religious inquiry* we [should, om. in 1864] arrive at certitude by accumulated probabilities :—

1864. (p. 324).	1890 (p. 199).
"—inasmuch as He who has willed that we should so act co-operates with us in our acting, and thereby bestows on us	"He has willed, I say, that we should so act, and, as willing it, He co-operates with us in our acting and thereby enables us to do that which He wills us to do, and carries us on, if our will does but co-operate with His, to

(1864 *and* 1890.)

"a certitude which rises higher than the logical force of our conclusions."

Reserving for the next section the question *how* we are to co-operate with God so as to *gain* this "certitude," let us for the present briefly consider whether there is not a terrible possibility of *losing* it. Imagine a pious believer brought up

upon the principle of this Inclined Plane of Probabilities :
entertaining a " pious belief" about this miracle, a " pious
opinion" about another, a "religious conjecture " about a
third, and a "certitude " about God ; and recognizing that
all these mental conditions, viz. certitude, pious belief, pious
opinion, and so on, are similar in kind, but different in
degree—the certitude being our "duty"in the case of "greater
or more numerous probabilities " but the pious belief being
equally our "duty " where the probabilities are less great
and numerous—and that all alike are based upon probability.
And imagine—a thing by no means impossible—that the
evidence against first one, then another, of these miracles,
compels him at last to give them *all* up.

What follows ? He has been taught and trained to believe
in these and other miracles as special revelations of God's
Personal attributes, the "most important characteristics " of
the records of His reign ; he has been habituated to regard
these royal manifestations with something of the solemnity
and awe with which he regards the invisible King Himself ;
they are, so to speak, a holy region, the precincts and outer
courts through which we pass to His immediate presence ;
precincts that bear the impress of His immediate touch,
His handiwork ; so personal to Him as almost to be—if God
had parts—veritable parts of God. And now, step by step, he
is forced back by evidence and common sense and honesty,
surrendering a first, a second, a third, of the sacred enclosures ;
never gaining ground, always losing it ; losing as it were
Divine ground, losing the tokens of the Divine presence. Why
ask what will be the end ? When a soldier begins to look
behind him, do we not generally know, without asking, what
the end will be ? Giving up this, and that, and the other, of
beliefs once held "upon probabilities," will he not presently
be tempted to ask himself whether he may not be compelled

at last to give up that highest belief of all, which he was taught to regard as *resting on the same basis of proof*—call it, as in 1864, "about the same kind of probability," or call it, as in 1890, "one and the same in nature of proof," call it "cumulative," call it "transcendent," call it "certitude"; still, at bottom, and in fact, *nothing more than "probability" after all?*

And further, besides the danger of *losing* a "certitude" tainted with this conscious thought of probabilities, there is also the danger of *never gaining* it at all by these means. Bishop Butler, from whom Newman says he borrowed (whether in Butler's sense, or not, I will not stop to enquire) this Doctrine of Probability, when lying on his death-bed, is said to have confessed to his chaplain that he was afraid to die. "'My lord,' said the chaplain, 'you have forgotten that Jesus Christ is a Saviour.' 'True,' was the answer, 'but how shall I know that He is a Saviour for me?' 'My lord, it is written, *Him that cometh to me I will in no wise cast out.*' 'True,' said the Bishop, 'and I am surprised that, though I have read that Scripture a thousand times over, I never felt its virtue till this moment; and now I die happy.'"[1]

Stories of this kind are often false and almost always exaggerated; but, true or false, this story exemplifies what might be expected from one who has always believed in Christ "upon a probability." Somehow or other the simultaneous thought of "probability" paralyses affection and trust. Faith implies an *action* of the soul, a stretching out of the hand, or an opening of the eyes, to receive God's proffered love; but the sense of probability implies, *not* action, but

---

[1] This story is related "on the authority of Mr. Venn," in the Introduction to *The Analogy of Religion*, edited by the Rev. Dr. Angus, p. xii.

"*stopping to think.*"   Hence it comes that a belief in God
held upon probabilities—even though we call them by the
finest titles, "cumulative," "transcendent," and the like—
rests upon the mere surface of the heart ; and the longer we
become familiarized with it as a probability, the harder it is
to recognize it as a certitude.   We read or repeat our Creed,
"a thousand times over," but we "never feel its virtue."

§ 13. *How to attain Religious Certitude*

We now have to consider the question, How are we to
"act," according to Newman's scheme, so as to attain certitude in religious inquiry?   The earlier and shorter version
of the scheme (which I prefer to quote because the later
seems only to make the process a little less clear and a
little more mysterious) tells us that we are to "act";
and then God "co-operates with us in our acting, and thereby bestows on us a certitude which rises higher than the
logical force of our conclusions."   But *how* has God
"willed *us to act*"?   Going back for our answer to the
previous words, in the passage quoted above (p. 77) "willed
that we should so act," we find ourselves once more carried
back (after Newman's fashion) to what again precedes,
"God has willed *that in religious inquiry we should arrive
at certitude by accumulated probabilities.*"   Our "acting," then,
is to be "arriving at certitude by accumulated probabilities."   We obtain therefore—upon an exact and grammatical
interpretation of the passage—this inane and futile result,
that we, on our side, are to "*arrive at* certitude" by
accumulated probabilities, and, *if* we do this, God, on His
side, will "*bestow* on us certitude."   Obviously Newman
does not mean this.   He means that we are to *attempt*
to arrive at certitude.   But *how?*   By "accumulated

probabilities"; and if we go on patiently "accumulating probabilities," God will at last step in, as it were, and, with a magic touch, convert our heap of probabilities into a "certitude."

This is Newman's theory and this appears to have been—at least occasionally—Newman's practice. It exactly describes what he himself did in 1845 while he was waiting for some intimation of the Divine will, some "sign" that might make it clear to him that it was his "duty" to join the Church of Rome. His heap of "accumulated probabilities" may be found in his *Development of Christian Doctrine* in which he supplied himself with a logical basis for his proposed action. We are therefore justified in believing that this passage really does represent his deliberate theoretical estimate of the right means of obtaining religious certitude. The emotions Hope, Love, Faith, seem to be altogether out of court, and to have no place, no right to say a word, in the formation of religious certitude; nor is the "acting" to be moral action, beneficent action, that kind of action which appears to be contemplated in the words (John vii. 17) "If any man will do his will, he shall know of the doctrine, whether it be of God." It is to be a piling up of probabilities; a supplying oneself with a logical basis. We are to believe in God and in Christ on the same grounds as we are to believe in the liquefaction of the blood of St. Januarius; only in the former case the probabilities are by some mysterious process (not illustrated by anything in nature) to be converted into a "certitude," whereas in the latter case they remain untransmuted, merely "beliefs," or "pious opinion." The former is transcendent probability, the latter is medial probability; still, both are probabilities.

Practical atheism being that state of mind in which a man believes in God without a basis of Love, Newman—if

G

he had really in his heart of hearts adopted this theory —
would have been a practical atheist : and indeed we should
be driven to that conclusion if we felt obliged to receive as
true the following pitilessly cold and cruel self-judgment
passed by himself upon himself in 1834 (*Letters*, i. 416) :—

"Indeed, this is how I look on myself; very much (as the illustrations goes) as a pane of glass, which transmits heat, being cold itself.
I have a vivid perception of the consequences of certain admitted
principles, have a considerable intellectual capacity of drawing them
out, have the refinement to admire them, and a rhetorical or histrionic
power to represent them ; and, having no great (*i.e.* no vivid) love of
this world, whether riches, or honour, or anything else, and some
firmness and natural dignity of character, take the profession of them
upon me, as I might sing a tune which I liked—loving the Truth, but
not possessing it, *for I believe myself at heart to be nearly hollow*, i.e.
with little love, little self-denial."

Such a sentence as this a lost soul might pass upon itself
on the Day of Judgment. It makes us shudder to the very
depth of our being. It contains so much that is subtly
true, so much well-balanced praise, so much half-justified
self-suspicion, that we are disposed to exclaim, "Can it be
really true? Was he indeed 'nearly hollow'?"

That it was not true, is proved by these same letters that
supply the accusation. It was Newman's way, in his self-
introspective mood—ignorant as he was of human nature
at its best and of its glorious possibilities, and versed, like
any diplomatist, in its intricate weaknesses—to distrust and
shudder at himself, as he shuddered at "the world" around
him. In his *Apologia* he tells us that when he renounced
his brother in 1833, he "put his conduct upon a syllogism."[1]
He was not so cold-blooded. He renounced his brother,

[1] *Apol.* p. 47, "I would have no dealings with my brother, and I put
my conduct upon a syllogism. I said, 'St. Paul bids us avoid those
who cause divisions ; you cause divisions ; therefore I must avoid you.'"

with one-half of himself, as a prophet, or, if you will, as a fanatic; and afterwards, with the other half of himself, he justified his action as a logician.

Now, just as we refuse to believe Newman himself when he accuses himself of being "nearly hollow," and of renouncing his brother "upon a syllogism," so we are justified in refusing to believe that he trusted in God upon a probability—even upon a transcendent probability. It was, perhaps, through fear of himself and distrust of a basis so subjective as the emotions, that he was induced to impute to logic and probability a feeling of certitude that really sprang from nobler sources. There must have been, somewhere or other in the formation of his religious certitude, the elements—though inadequately present—of Hope and Love. But if we refuse to call a man so blind as he makes himself out to be, it does not follow that we should at once go into the other extreme, and say that he is fit to be the guide of others. Even to himself his theory must have been most injurious; but on some of his followers—who had less reverence and less knowledge than he had—this theory of "going by the greater probability" must have acted like poison, destroying such germs of honest faith as they once had, and forcing them back upon the sole duty of believing whatever was safe.

The following letter, written by one of Newman's followers to Mark Pattison, will give an instance of the danger here indicated. Every line of it is infected with the Newmannian spirit, which occasionally breaks out in what may be described as the Tractarian cant of " going upon grounds " (only that the writer calls it "*facing* grounds ") and "going by probabilities." It is an invitation to join the Church of Rome, and though it sounds dispassionately and almost mathematically reasonable, it is really and radically immoral. For it practically urges the reader, for the sake of saving his soul, to say that he believes what, *in his heart, he does not believe.* This letter does indeed justify Dr. Martineau's accusation quoted above (p. 68) that the tendency of Newman's teaching was to lead people to " believe in order to believe "; that is, in this particular case, to take the plunge into the Roman Church in the hope that, when you have once said that you believe what you don't believe, you will feel delightfully certain about it for the rest of your life :—

" MY DEAR PATTISON,

I hope you will excuse my earnestly pressing upon you the duty of *facing your grounds* for remaining a Protestant, and of *going by the greater probability* as to which is the Church. You seemed to me to be getting quite towards scepticism last time I had a talk with you, and that is one reason why I urge you not to delay. Depend upon it that *you cannot expect more than probability out of the Catholic Church,* and that you really ought to act on that, whether you feel inclined to do so or not.

" People say that converts are 'cocky'; but that impression arises in part from the fact that they who have it have no more than doubtful evidence for what Catholics have certain proof [of]. This is not a conviction arising from my own case, but from all I see around me. It would be ' cocky ' in me to say so : but I don't care what it is, so as I may urge you not to be slow about the ' *unum necessarium* ' of caring for your own soul." [1]

This letter was written in 1846, a year after Newman had joined the Church of Rome. The writer (if we may accept the testimony of Mark Pattison's *Memoirs*) appears to have thought it consistent with his honour, while still remaining a member of the Church of England, to lose no opportunity of reviling her as a "stepmother," and to avow—in such Virgilian quotations as "Tendimus in Latium"—the determination of his party to approach the Roman Church. We have therefore no right to attribute his unquestionable "cocki-

[1] Mark Pattison's *Memoirs*, p. 222.

ness " to the Church of Rome. But Newman cannot be so easily acquitted. If this "cocky" creature had learned from his leader some sense of the nobility of those natural emotions whereby alone we can approximate to God, he could hardly have written, on so solemn a subject, a letter so frivolously shallow and so contemptibly mean : but what else can be expected from a man, naturally light-minded, who has been taught by his spiritual guide that we are to arrive at Faith in the living God "by accumulated probabilities "? [1]

Is it surprising that more manly characters were so repelled by this artificial notion of a special and ecclesiastical Faith that in their reaction from it they were driven to say, "If this is what Faith means, we will have nothing to do with it nor with anything that calls itself by such a name "? Such was the attitude of J. A. Froude : "What was faith ?" is the question suggested to his mind by Newman's doctrine. "And on what did it rest? Was it as if mankind had been born with but four senses by which to form their notions of things external to them, and that a fifth, sight, was conferred on favoured individuals, which converted conjectures into certainty? I could not tell. For myself, this way of putting the matter gave me no new sense at all, and only taught me to distrust my old ones." [2]

---

[1] At the same time it ought to be said, in fairness, that Newman himself had been scandalized, even in 1839, by the absurd audacity of his follower (*Letters*, ii. 291) : "What does he do on St. Michael's day but preach a sermon " [occupying Newman's pulpit in St. Mary's] "not simply on angels, but on his one subject, for which he has a monomania, of fasting ; nay, and say that it was a good thing, whereas angels feasted on festivals, to make the brute creation fast on fast days . . . The next Sunday . . . he preached to them " [*i.e.* the Heads of Houses] "the Roman doctrine of the Mass. . . . To this he added other speculations of his own still more objectionable."

[2] *Life of Ward* p. 396.

CHAPTER III

§ 14. *What is " Legal Proof " ?*

"SOME infidel authors," says Newman (231), "advise us to accept no miracles which would not have a verdict in their favour in a court of justice; that is, they employ against Scripture a weapon which Protestants would confine to attacks upon the Church ; *as if moral and religious questions required legal proofs, and evidence were the test of truth."*

What is "legal proof"? It is simply proof of the ordinary kind, by evidence direct and indirect, but stronger and stricter. Legal proof, being seldom required except where facts are affirmed and denied by interested parties, requires (in a greater degree than ordinary proof) that the evidence shall be deliberate—hence, the use of the oath ; free from exaggeration or misunderstanding—hence, the rejection of hear-say evidence ; consistent and truthful— hence, the demand that every witness shall undergo cross-examination ; free from suspicion—hence, the preference of evidence as to character (and even of evidence as to facts) coming from witnesses who have no interest, one way or the other, in the ultimate decision. Occasionally, in the excessive desire to serve order, law has unfairly favoured despotism ; and, in the excessive desire to be fair to the accused, it has foolishly excluded evidence that might have fairly helped the accused. But on the whole, it may be said that legal proof is of the same kind as ordinary proof, only superior in degree.

What then do people mean when they say, " Our knowledge of our friend so-and-so *gives us a proof far stronger than any legal proof*, that he *never* committed such and such a crime "? Whatever they may mean, they talk sophistically ; for there is no such thing as a *legal proof* that " so-and-so *never* committed such and such a crime ; " law never attempts to *prove a negative of this general kind*. But if these people mean that their knowledge of their friend gives them a proof, far stronger than any legal proof, that he did not *commit a definite crime at a definite time and in a definite place*, then they talk sentimental nonsense,—pardonable, but still nonsense. For "legal proof" could show on the testimony of a score of competent witnesses that their friend was a thousand miles away from that definite place, at that definite time, engaged in some occupation which made it physically impossible that he could commit that definite crime. But their knowledge of their friend could not show that he might not have suddenly developed kleptomaniacal or suicidal, or homicidal, tendencies ; or that he might not have been drugged, or hypnotized, or otherwise coerced, into doing something wholly alien to his nature ; or that he might not of himself, have experienced some sudden lapse into an isolated act of evil.

" Then here "—it may be said—" you are arguing *for* probability (since probability is all you can get out of legal proof), and against the feelings—just the opposite to your former line." Of course I am. For I am speaking now of historic *facts*, where one's feelings, so to speak, are to be put in one's pocket, being useless and indeed worse than useless, in weighing evidence for fact—except so far as they may constitute testimony to character, which, of course, may be sometimes of great weight as evidence. I said, above, that, as regards the *future*, if the suggestion were made to us that those whom we loved best might not very improbably commit certain abominable crimes, we should do well to refuse to "look at the matter in that light" : that this way of looking at things did not *work;* that it was not good for physical or moral health to contemplate such con. tingencies in such a cold-blooded way ; that it was against nature, and therefore unnatural. And to that I adhere. But I have never contended that probability was not to be our guide, on those comparatively exceptional occasions when we have to inquire into the truth or falsehood of *what actually happened.*

Is there, then, no such thing as "moral proof" as to facts ; and may not a father say—without laying himself open to the charge of folly—"I am morally convinced that my son did not do, and could not have done, this or that defin- ite act at a definite time and place "? There is not the least harm in the phrase, provided that, in the first place, it be *confined to negatives*, and, in the second place, it be remem- bered that "moral proof" is *a mere non-legal phrase for witness to character."* If the father says, "I am morally convinced that my son must have *done* this or that," he is wrong ; for all sorts of accidents, having nothing to do with morality, may have prevented the action. The moral con- viction of a father, that his son could *not* have done this or that, arises from a great mass of evidence, facts small and great, which, if they could be put before a jury in court by a number of disinterested and independent witnesses, would have great legal weight. Because (1) this evidence coming from a father, who is interested in the decision, has —and ought to have—comparatively little weight in a Court of Justice; and because (2) it is, by its nature, very lengthy; and (3) because it is often so subtle that it cannot be easily reproduced in Court, we have come to think of it, and to talk of it, as though it were quite distinct, in kind as well as in degree, from "testimony to character:" but it is identical in kind, though not in degree.

The phrase "moral proof" or "morally convinced," is sometimes used of the future, *e.g.*, "I am morally convinced that so-and-so will pay his debts, or, will not neglect his parents, will not ill treat his wife," and so on. Here, of course, "legal proof" is out of the question, because the law seldom, if ever, recognizes proof as to what *will be*, but what *has been*, or *is* (*e.g.*, as to my *present* reasonable fear that my neighbour will assault me—a fear that must be shown to be reasonable by evidence as to the past). There is no great objection to the phrase "moral conviction" with reference to the future, except that it has two words, and "faith"— which is one word—means the same thing. However there is a shade of difference between them ; and there is room for both in the language. But in any case we are not to ground upon this application of "moral proof" to the future, any vague inference that "moral proof" can dispute with "*legal proof*" in the peculiar province of the latter, that is to say, *the region of historical fact.*

§ 15. *Is Evidence " the test of Truth " ?*

Now we return to Newman's dictum : "as if moral and religious questions required legal proofs." To this we must reply, "If, by 'moral and religious questions,' you mean, such questions as, whether there is a God or not; whether He is just; whether He will ultimately conform man to His image; whether Good will ultimately triumph over Evil—then we agree with you. For these questions are in the region of hope, aspiration, and faith; and, as we should allow no facts to disprove these beliefs, so we must admit that no facts could prove them, though facts *can* help us, and have helped us, to shape, and to develop, and to identify with our inmost being, those hopes, those aspirations, and those beliefs. But if you mean, by 'moral and religious questions,' the question whether God stopped the sun (relatively to the earth) at the prayer of Joshua, and the question whether our Lord killed two thousand swine, who at the worst had done no greater harm than belong to a Jewish owner, and more probably belonged to a Gentile—then we must reply that you enter the region of historical fact; and here faith has no place, and, 'legal proof' is the best possible proof; and if you cannot get it, you ought to try at least to get something as much like it as possible; and if you cannot get something very like it, you must be content to say, ' This fact is not proved.' "

Against this, Newman would have two rejoinders. In the first place he would reply that although the truth or falsehood of the stopping of the sun at the command of Joshua, or the slaying of the Gadarene swine, is not *of itself,* a " moral and religious question," yet it becomes so, through its inclusion in the canonical Scriptures. The Scriptures he accepts as inspired—at least so far as questions of fact—and so heartily accepts that he will even wait to find out the meaning of motion (see above, p. 32), and, for the present, suspend his belief that the earth moves, rather than say that the Scriptures err in asserting that the earth is still. On this point we need not dwell. We should have to agree to differ. He, on his side, would tell us that it was at our peril that we rejected a single scriptural statement of fact on our private judgment; we should reply, on our side, that it was at his peril that he swallowed the Scriptures whole, doing violence to his mind and understanding. He would say we must not "pick and choose"; we should rejoin that we must "test and discriminate" the true from the false, and hold fast that which is true. He would warn us that we might not find ourselves "safe" on the Day of Judgment if we rejected God's word in the Bible; we should warn him that he was "unsafe" already, and probably would be still less safe hereafter, since he deliberately rejected God's word in Science. And so we should part, with mutual warnings, but still with hopes, perhaps on both sides, certainly on ours, that in the end, if we were both honest, there might be found "safety" of some sort for both of us.

But Newman's second rejoinder would be, "You say, 'This fact is not proved': granted, but (177) 'a fact is not disproved because it is not proved,' and I must repeat what I said just now, that 'evidence is not the test of truth,' Thousands of people in Central Africa have no 'evidence' of the existence of ice, and would deny its existence; yet ice exists."

The answer to this, is, that people *practically deny, and are quite right in practically denying, the existence of everything of which they have no evidence, direct or indirect.* There *may be* regions of four, five, or fifty dimensions; there *may be* bipeds in the sun, each as big as the moon; there *may be* in the earth at this moment a diamond a hundred times as big as the Koh-i-noor; there *may be* an instance in which the law of gravitation has been suspended. But we are so constituted as not to act on any "may be" that is not at least suggested by some evidence. Until thus suggested, the "may be" is non-existent relatively to us; it is "nothing"; and of course every one knows how many neat and sophistical truisms can be elaborated about "nothing." But, if we are to be serious, we must say that, in practice, although millions of facts are daily occurring of which we have heard nothing, and for which conse-quently we have no evidence—yet still *no truth is a truth for us unless an alleged fact has borne the test of evidence* —evidence direct, or indirect, but always evidence of some kind.

Of course a man may make a mistake now and then in rejecting some truth for which, though there exists ample evidence, none but inadequate evidence has been submitted *to him.* But, still, rejection, under these circumstances, is the right course. A Central African ought to be praised, not blamed, for rejecting the existence of ice, if casually mentioned—or even deliberately attested—by some Euro-pean whom he has repeatedly detected in *exaggeration,* and *embellishment,* and sometimes in deliberate *falsehood.*[1] The right rule is, to regard as non-existent all alleged facts for which there is no evidence direct or indirect ; and to regard as *antecedently* false, or highly improb-able, *all statements that contradict our knowledge of the fixed and orderly course of things.* Observe we do not

---

[1] Comp. (171): "it is doubtless the tendency of religious minds to imagine mysteries and wonders where there are none, and, much more, where causes of awe really exist, will they unintentionally misstate, *exaggerate,* and *embellish*" ; also, (*ib.*) "certain others, *i.e.* miracles," are said to be "rejected on all hands as *fictitious* and *pretended*"; and (239), "*false* miracles at once *exceed* and conceal and prejudice those which are genuine"; and (*ib.*), it is implied that the *true* are as much fewer than the *false,* "as the elect are fewer than the reprobate, and hard to find amid the chaff." These passages justify our illustration of the "European" who *exaggerates, embellishes,* and sometimes *lies.*

say they *are* false ; but, being practical people, with a
limited amount of time at our disposal, and having been
taught by repeated experience that innumerable similar
stories have originated from nothing but misunderstandings,
or exaggerations, or deliberate impostures, and that very few
of such stories have been based on truth, we shall say to an
alleged fact of this kind, "Statistical Probability is 100 to 1,
or 1000 to 1, against you ; pass on ; we have no time to
think of you. Other propositions have higher claims."

This practical, reasonable, and justifiable quasi-prejudice
against the extraordinary—though it ought not to prevent
us from examining a case here and there where the evidence
is particularly strong—is absolutely necessary for a truth-
seeker, because it prevents him from wasting his time upon
the myriads of marvellous lies which have abounded in all
ages, and leaves him leisure for serious investigation. It is
not really prejudice ; it is only a kind of selective Suspension of Judgment, whereby we select some, and dismiss
other propositions, that claim to be considered, because
some are more worthy than others, and we have not time to
hear all. The practical conclusion, then is this : since, for
all the purposes of life, no "truth" of fact can, so to
speak, exist for a man of sense, until it has presented some
proof that it has passed a preliminary test of evidence, we
may say, roughly and popularly speaking, that evidence *is*
"the test" of truth as regards fact, and that truth of fact
does "depend upon evidence."

But if any one chooses—not without a touch of pedantry,
as we think—to insist upon it that "Evidence is *not the
test of truth ;* for truth may exist without our knowing
anything about it," we submit and acquiesce at once ; for
we deny, as firmly as he does, that "Man is the measure
of all things." Only we venture humbly to remind our

adept in this nice use of words to be on his guard lest, if he should apply this maxim to the investigation of historical facts, *where he has an interest in this or that conclusion,* he may find that from freely and familiarly using it against antagonists, he has sometimes come to act as though he believed that "Evidence is *of no use for testing truth.*" That Newman has acted thus, has been, in part, and will be, more fully, demonstrated.

§ 16. *Belief " on Authority "*

"But does not the experience of childhood show that belief based on parental authority must be with all human beings one of the stepping-stones to the knowledge of facts; and does it not hence follow that the demand for 'legal proofs' as to facts is against nature?"

Nothing of the kind follows. "Legal proof," as every one knows, includes the opinions of experts. To the child, the father is an expert as to the big world outside the nursery. Suppose a father tells his child that there are red men and black men : that is, to him, "the evidence of an expert," and he accepts it as a judge and jury would accept the evidence of four physicians declaring that such and such a condition of a dead body was produced by strychnine.

Indeed the experience of childhood, so far from showing that it is against nature for men to demand "legal proof" as to facts, shows just the opposite. It is natural for children not only to receive, but to digest information, comparing it with their pre-existing knowledge, and, in a rude way, classifying it. Now they cannot classify or digest a piece of information that gives the lie to their experience. For an intelligent child, to be told that the sun does not move, and to be told no more, is a morsel of indigestible news, which disorganizes his mind, dulls the mental palate, and enfeebles the appetite : " What is the use of one's eyes "—he unconsciously, or consciously, says to himself—" if there is no trusting them ? I give it up." No father, of any sense and sympathy, would ever tell a child that the sun does not move, without at least attempting to show him how the deception of the senses can arise ; nor would he feel angry, but rather pleased, with the child, for feeling dissatisfied with the contradiction between the evidence of the expert and the evidence of his own senses, and for desiring to find some reconciliation between the two.   And if we admit, as I think we should, that the wisest and best father will be most desirous that his children should be led steadily onward to use their senses and faculties, and to examine facts, for themselves—not lazily taking on trust what they themselves have the means of ascertaining for themselves by a little patient labour—then it would seem to follow that it is not against nature to expect that the Supreme Father should take the same course and even more apparently.

Thus, it seems in accordance with Nature, (1), that, from the very beginning, the infant should take in its largest store of fundamental truths as to facts, from *his own experience*, amplified and helped by *a faith in the fixedness of the order of Nature ;* and that this should constitute in the human being a definite habit of trusting to what is called "the evidence of his senses," so far as concerns things that come within this province : (2), that he should, afterwards—but not at first—*take upon trust the evidence of experts*, whose experience extends to things beyond his ken : yet (3), that he should not rest quiet where the evidence of experts contradicts his own experience, but should seek to reconcile the discrepancy : (4), that, as his own experience is enlarged, he *should gradually believes less and less upon authority, so far as concerns the common things of life,* such as the simplest laws of the material and of the moral world. These are Nature's Laws for healthy human growth; and any one who should continue, past childhood, to rest upon authority for those simple and fundamental truths which are necessary to material and moral welfare, would be in a condition so dwarfed and undeveloped as to deserve the name of an idiot.

On the other hand we concede to the advocates of " belief on Authority " that as civilization developes, we— and by " we " I mean not children now, but men—shall find ourselves forced to believe more and more, upon the authority of specialists—such specialists, that is, as tell us the metals of which the sun is composed, and instruct us how to construct phonographs and telephones, and to lay electric wires so that they shall do their work effectually and safely. But, then, civilized mankind will accord this belief to experts, only because—as the very word " expert " shows— that belief is in accordance with experience and can be justified by experiment. And let it be repeated that this " belief on Authority " seems to be gradually retiring, as humanity moves upward, and to be destined still further to retire, *from the simpler and more fundamental truths,* which once were inexplicable, but are now recognized as the property of the common intelligence. Our astronomers may specialize and claim belief as specialists ; but every educated person now knows the marvellous Law that keeps the Universe together ; our physicians still claim, as of old, obedience to their authority, but we obey more intelligently because we ourselves have some knowledge of the Laws of health, which will, we trust, soon become familiar to every child in our elementary schools.

Thus, instead of trying to repair and perpetuate the worn-out yoke of Authority in matters of belief, we ought rather to assist those tendencies which are preparing us for the time when it will drop away, and when men "shall teach no more every man his neighbour, and every man his brother, saying, ' Know the Lord ' ; for they shall all know me, from the least to the greatest." Experience, if it teaches us that authority may be sometimes cast aside too soon, teaches us with equal emphasis that it may be sometimes retained too long, and that it must be at some time cast aside by all who are to attain to the stature of full-grown humanity. Better to learn through mistakes than to remain ignorant by never placing ourselves within the possibility of error.

Our Lord, indeed, is said to have " taught with authority," but it was with the "authority" of the Living Truth, the great World-Conscience, so to speak, appealing to the "authority" of the kindred consciences of His several hearers. He did not wish to be believed or accepted as an external authority. No belief pleased Him, except that of a reverent affection which took Him into the heart of the believer, and assimilated the Voice of the individual conscience to His own.

The Scribes and Pharisees taught also, after their fashion, "with authority," that is to say, with constant reference to external "authorities." The religion of the Authority of conscience will become, as the centuries roll on, more powerful and less voluminous ; the religion of "authorities," more voluminous and less powerful. The one grows more spiritual and less embodied, more vital and vitalizing, but more independent of any special and external integuments or surroundings ; the other grows less spiritual and more corporeal and material, scattering and diffusing in outward manifestations the force that should have been spent on inward growth.

The teaching of the Scribes and Pharisees, of every age and in every religion, will always constitute a solid, substantial, and imposing "Body of Divinity," a "system" into which a Pupil of Authority can "throw himself generously," teaching nothing that is not "consistent," and leading the souls of men steadily onward from mist to fog, and from fog to utter darkness, a darkness that may be felt—a darkness that may be, so to speak, cut into squares and measured out in rations of quasi-spiritual pabulum.

All Scribes are essentially crammers. Newman himself tended by degrees to become a Scribe, and unblushingly avowed his readiness to condescend to cramming of the most pernicious kind. "It would be much," he writes to his most intimate friend Hurrell Froude (*Letters*, ii. 124) "if we could *cram* our men" [meaning "our faction," "the Tractarian party"] "in one and the same way of talking upon various points, *e.g.* what the Church holds about heretical baptism, about ordination before baptism, about the power of bishops, &c. This is a strong point of Romanism; they have *their system so well up.*" "*Cramming*" and "*being up to*," or "well *up in*," are terms that the Tractarians apparently think it no profanity to apply even to so awful a subject as the nature of God Himself: "As to Sabellianism and facts," writes Froude (*ib.* 141), "I fear you have been unable to *cram* me with your views." Children were to be "crammed" in the same style; and enthusiastic Tractarians, destined in due course to become theologians of repute, went out to Littlemore, to hear the great Tractarian crammer who could contrive to make the children of his church-school "have their system *so well up*." "I heard him last Sunday," writes Dr. James Mozley, "and thought it very striking; done with such spirit, and the children so *up to it*, answering with the greatest alacrity. It would have provoked some people's bile immoderately to have heard them all unanimous *on the point of the nine orders of angels ; the definiteness of the number being, in itself, a great charm to the minds of the children.*"

"Provoked some people's bile immoderately"! Might it not have provoked some thoughtful parents reasonably, that their children should be "crammed" with such "*definite*" doctrine about things doubtful or baseless? If, in after years, one of these children, led by knowledge and thought to reject—"upon probability"—his old belief, so authoritatively inculcated by a respected and honoured teacher, in "the nine orders of angels," were consequently led on still further to reject—again "upon probability"—the belief in God Himself, would not our minds instinctively turn to that tremendous warning which speaks about "little children" in connection with "a mill-stone"? Would it hereafter avail for the teacher to say in the Great Day of Summing Up, "I had no deep convictions of my own, and therefore I thought it best and safest to teach upon authority"? Surely the reply would come, "If you could not teach upon conviction, you should not have taught at all"; and there would be a terrible danger that such "cramming" might "provoke"— not "immoderately," but most justly—the great Friend and Advocate of "the little ones," in spite of the "definiteness" of the doctrine.

The teaching of Jesus was not, and never will be, of this definite character : it will be only half-satisfying ; it will ever lead us to desire more ; it will be continually resisting our efforts to systematize it and to throw ourselves into systems ;

it will resolutely refuse to satisfy our petition, "Tell us what to believe, that we may believe it"; it will sometimes take us into the wilderness apart, and there, with a searching Eye fixed on our heart of hearts, it will bring Jesus before us, saying, "Whom say *ye* that I am?" and, when we glibly reply, '*Some* say that thou art 'Man,' and *some* say 'God,' and *some* say, 'a Fable,' and *some* say, 'We know not what'—it will waive aside these idle delayings, and say again, in words that admit no evasion, "But whom say *ye* that I am?" Sooner or later—in death, or after death, if not in life—this question must be answered : and then how hollow will seem the answer of "*Some* say," how vain our tremulous reference to "the *best authorities*"!

CHAPTER IV

§ 17. *Newman's " First Principle "*

THE manner in which Newman was led to apply his Doctrine of Probabilities to Ecclesiastical Miracles, is thus stated in the *Apologia* (p. 21) :

" Considerations such as these " [*i.e.*, of graduated probability above described] " throw a new light on Miracles, and they seem to have led me to reconsider the view which I had taken of them in my Essay 1825-6. . . That there had been already great miracles, as those of Scripture, as the Resurrection, was a fact establishing the principle that the laws of nature had sometimes been suspended by their Divine Author, and, *since what happened once might happen again, a certain probability, at least no kind of improbability, was attached to the idea taken in itself, of miraculous intervention in later times ;* and miraculous accounts were to be regarded in connection with the verisimilitude, scope, instrument, character, testimony, and circumstances, with which they presented themselves to us : and, according to the final result of those various considerations, it was our duty to be sure, or to believe, or t o

opine, or to surmise, or to tolerate, or to reject, or to de-
nounce."

This important passage contains what Newman elsewhere
calls "the first principle" upon which Romanists accept,
and Protestants reject, Ecclesiastical miracles (*Apol.* 1st ed.
Appendix, p. 49) : "Both they and we start with the miracles of the Apostles ; and then their *first principle* or presumption against our miracles, is this, 'What God did once,
He is *not* likely to do again ; ' while our *first principle* or
presumption for our miracles is this ; 'What God did once,
He is likely to do again.' "

Educated Protestants, so far as I know, recognize no
such "first principle" as is here imputed to them. They
deny Ecclesiastical miracles because they are proved, so far
as they have been investigated, to be either natural, and no
miracles, or else false. But that may be passed over. Let
the reader however observe that the latter of the two quotations is less guarded and cautious than the former. The
latter states that the recurrence of miracles "*is* likely " ; the
former, more cautiously, says that it "*might* happen again,"
or that there is a " *certain probability*," or " at least, *no kind
of improbability*." In reality there are a great many com-
binations of things that are continually happening *once*, but
will almost certainly *never* happen again. The mere routine
of yesterday, which happened *once* to the reader, will never
befall him, nor any one else, again, as long as the world lasts
—not in all its precise details, occurring at precisely the
same times, and in precisely the same circumstances. Innumerable things that we accept as having occurred *once*, we
think extremely unlikely ever to occur again.

But it may be replied that Newman is speaking not of a
combination of things, but a *thing*, viz., Divine intervention
by suspension of the laws of nature. I should conceive

that (upon the miraculous hypothesis) if God for a special purpose, at a special time, really gave to special agents the power of suspending the Laws of Nature, not capriciously but by Divine impulse, so as to act, for example, upon the bodies of other men in healing diseases—all this *did* involve a combination of things which (like the very rarely occurring " break " in Babbage's calculating machine) may occur hardly ever, and perhaps never again ; and therefore even if it be assumed that God did " intervene " miraculously when He created the world anew in Christ, it is illogical to infer that He consequently was " likely " to thus " intervene " in later times, or even that such an intervention was " not improbable."

Another logical objection—from Newman's own point of view—is this, that he himself admits the Scriptural miracles to *be so very different* from the Ecclesiastical Miracles, that to argue from the fact that He performed the former to the probability that He will perform the latter, is, in effect, to argue thus : " Because God once did something *for a special purpose*, therefore it is likely that He will hereafter do something *quite different, and for no purpose, or at all events for no discernible purpose !* " Lest the reader should suppose that I have exaggerated the difference recognized by Newman himself between the two classes of miracles, I must repeat what I have already quoted, in his own words (99) : " Ecclesiastical Miracles, that is, Miracles posterior to the Apostolic age, are, on the whole, *different*[1] *in object, character and evidence*, from those of Scripture on the whole, so that the one series or family ought never to be confounded with the other ; " and similarly (115), the " Scripture Miracles are for the most part evidence of a Divine Revelation, and that, for the sake of those who have not yet been instructed

[1] In 1843, " *very* different."

in it . . . . ; but the Miracles which follow have sometimes *no discoverable or direct object, or but a slight object;*" and, still more emphatically, they were sometimes (141), "*so unlike the Scripture Miracles,* so strange and startling in their nature and circumstances as to *need support and sanction themselves, rather than to supply it to Christianity.*"

It is on the ground of the radical *difference* between the Ecclesiastical Miracles and the Scriptural Miracles, as a whole, that Newman explains the repeated statements made by Chrysostom, Augustine, Isidore, and Pope Gregory, who declare that in their days *Miracles no longer existed* because they were no longer needed (135—146). In answer to the Protestants who point to these disclaimers of Miracles, committed to writing by the highest authorities, *in centuries to which tradition subsequently attributed Miracles without end, of the most startling, wild, grotesque and purposeless character,* Newman replies in effect, "These Fathers really meant, not that there were *no* miracles in their days, but that they were *quite different* from the old Scriptural miracles ; they were *often not* (116) 'grave, simple and majestic,' as the Scriptural miracles were ; they *often* had a (116) 'wildness and inequality' and partook of (116) 'what may not unfitly be called a romantic character'; they have 'sometimes no discoverable or direct object, or but a slight object.' Hence, on the whole, they were so different from the Scriptural Miracles that the Fathers, having the Scriptural Miracles in their minds, were quite justified in saying that miracles *no longer existed* in their days, as, for example, Chrysostom says (136) 'Argue not that, because miracles *do not happen now*, they did not happen then . . . . In those days they were profitable, and *now they are not.*'"

What then will become of Newman's "first principle," in behalf of a miraculous intervention in Ecclesiastical History.

the great anti-Protestant aphorism, that "What God has done once, He is likely to do again"? He disguises its fallacy from himself, with his usual skill in self-deception, in the following homely metaphor (*Apol.* 1st Ed., Append., p. 51), "If the Divine Being does a thing once, He is, judging by human reason, likely to do it again. This surely is common sense. If a beggar gets food at a gentleman's house once, does he not send others after him?"

This is a Metaphor. May not an absolute contradiction of this proposition be expressed in almost the same words, with a little change of Metaphor, and with far more truth? "If the Divine Being does a thing once, it is very unsafe, judging by human reason, to say that He is likely to do it again. This surely is common sense. If a landscape-gardener and a florist get employment at a gentleman's house when he is laying out a garden, will they expect to get it again next year when the garden is laid out and the gentleman is waiting to see the plants grow?" Our analogy between the planting of the Garden and the planting of the Church, is surely far more to the point than the daily relief of beggars. If our adversary denies it, we shall quote against him his own quotation from Pope Gregory (138): Miracles, we may say, were "necessary in the beginning of the Church . . . just as *when we plant shrubs, we water them till they seem to thrive in the ground,* and as soon as they are well rooted *we cease our irrigation.*" To which we shall add, "Is not this *common sense?*"

There is also the additional retort that, under that ambiguous pronoun "what"—"*What* God has done once, He is likely to do again"—*there are really latent two nouns meaning quite different things.* Scriptural Miracles, we have been told, were so different from Ecclesiastical Miracles, that although, says Newman, the latter existed from the fourth to the sixth centuries, yet the Fathers in those centuries were justified in saying that *practically there were no miracles at all.* Then, in the face of this admitted and essential difference, is it not a manifest absurdity to argue that " *What* God has done once, He is likely to do again," when you really mean, " Because God did *a certain thing* once for a special object, therefore it is likely that He should do something *quite different* a great many times for no discoverable object " ; and, if there can be a still higher height of absurdity, is not the climax reached in dignifying this fallacy with the title of a " first principle " ?

§ 18. *Detailed Incongruities of the Doctrine*

Similar absurdities pervade the rules at which Newman tries to arrive as to the probable times, seasons, and agents, of Ecclesiastical Miracles. He considers it (*Apol.* 23) "a natural and on the whole, a true anticipation " that miracles attend " transcendent sanctity," and, since (23) there have been centuries of disorder and of revival, and "one region might be in the mid-day of religious fervour and another in twilight or gloom," it did not follow that (*Apol.* 23) " because we did not see miracles with our own eyes, miracles had not happened in former times, or were not now at this very time taking place in distant places " ;[1] he adds (*Apol.* 298) that primarily they were granted to Evangelists, especially to the Apostles as Evangelists, in attestation of the Gospel ; hence to such later Evangelists as St. Gregory Thaumaturgus and St. Martin ; and (*ib.*) "in less measure to other holy men " ; and (*ib.*) " since, generally,

---

[1] Although the following quotation is separated by a great interval from this one, yet the two are connected in a foot-note (*Apol.* 23) referring the reader from the former to the latter.

they are granted to faith and prayer, therefore in a country in which faith and prayer abound, they will be more likely to occur, than where and when faith and prayer are not." But he himself tells us that (130) " in the second and third centuries "—when converts needed more to be made, and the Gospel needed more to be attested, than in the fourth or fifth centuries—not only are the accounts of miracles much less detailed than those of the fourth century, but also those kind of operations which are " the most decisive proofs of a supernatural presence, are but sparingly or scarcely mentioned." In other words, when the Christian Faith was struggling against Paganism, and needed miracles badly, there were, so far as we know, scarcely any miracles of a striking nature ; but as soon as Christianity had become the established religion and could afford to do without them, the most startling miracles began to abound ! It is as though the candle-light of Ecclesiastical Miracles were denied to " regions of twilight and gloom," and lavished on those who sit in " the mid-day of religious fervour." This seems a very grotesque contradiction of any reasonable doctrine of Antecedent Probability ; but perhaps it may be fairly said to be in accordance with that common characteristic assigned above to Ecclesiastical Miracles, that they often have " no discoverable object."

Another important difference between Scriptural and Ecclesiastical Miracles is that the latter largely partake of an element of imposture. No educated sceptic, so far as I know, imputes fraud or imposture to the narrators, or agents, of the New Testament Miracles : but Newman himself repeatedly admits, in various forms of admission, that no one should inquire into (229) the " miracles reported or alleged in Ecclesiastical History, without being prepared for *fiction* and exaggeration in the narrative, to an indefinite

extent"; (117) "in Ecclesiastical History true and *false*
miracles are mixed, whereas in Scripture inspiration has
selected the true"; the narratives (116) "often . . seem to
betray exaggerations or *errors.*"   Incidentally we find references to denunciations made by Romanist authors indicating (236—7) that impostures were extremely common ;
but as to their number, Newman himself is generally reti-
cent; we find however that (171) "as a matter of course,
on many accounts, where miracles are really wrought,
miracles will also be attempted, or *simulated*, or imitated, or
fabled"; that (171) it is "no real argument against admitting the Ecclesiastical Miracles on the whole, or against
admitting certain of them, that *certain others* are rejected on
all hands as *fictitious or pretended*" : that (229) "*so many
others* on the contrary are certainly *not true*" : but not till
the very last section of the general discussion are we suddenly brought face to face with the admission that *the great
mass of Ecclesiastical Miracles is false* (239) : "as the elect
are fewer than the reprobate, and *hard to find amid the chaff,
so false miracles at once exceed and conceal and prejudice those,
which are genuine.*" The reference of course implied in "the
elect," is to the statement that "*many* are called but *few* are
chosen;" and it is hereby admitted that, while true Ecclesiastical Miracles are *few*, false Ecclesiastical Miracles are
many.

§ 19. *The Statistical Probability of an alleged Miracle*

Now of course, from the point of view of statistical
Probability, this is a most damaging admission. What it
amounts to cannot be well perceived without some use of
numbers ; for, as I have said above, Statistical Probability
implies numbers.   But here we ought perhaps to take

warning from Newman himself, who used numbers without much reflection; and hence, having first called on men to believe in Christ (see p. 221 below) upon a probability of "three to two," he then found it necessary to substitute "a dozen to two."

However, if it is clearly understood that the numbers are only hypothetical, there can be no harm in them. And indeed we have some guide to a rough estimate of the total number of miraculous stories to be expected in the History of the Church from the passage in which he tells us that (*Apol.* 299), "Miracles are the kind of facts proper to ecclesiastical history, just as instances of sagacity or daring, personal prowess or crime, are the facts proper to secular history." Now from the secular history of Europe during the period of Christianity, we could easily pick out one or two hundreds of thousands of "instances of sagacity, daring, personal prowess or crime." If therefore "miracles" are equally "proper to ecclesiastical history"—and we well know how copious is the literature of saintly biography as well as the public history of the Church—we seem justified in expecting a very large number indeed of miracles, especially since we are including all kinds, the false and the doubtful, as well as the true.

Suppose, then, for argument's sake, the *total number* of alleged Ecclesiastical Miracles to be one hundred and twenty thousand, a number probably very much under the mark; and suppose the number that are *certainly false* (which, as we have seen, Newman himself admits to be *decidedly the majority*) to be, say, a hundred thousand; and the number that are *certainly true* to be one thousand. This last estimate is very much over the mark; for Newman himself maintains (229) that only a "*few*" can be so proved as to "demand acceptance"; and he himself only alleges *nine*,

for all of which the evidence will seem to many to be by no
means sufficient to "demand" their "acceptance." But still
take this very one-sided estimate, so much too favourable to
Newman ; then there will be left nineteen thousand Ecclesiastical Miracles that (229) "are *neither certainly true nor
certainly false.*"   Now, what follows, according to his own
admission ?   All these nineteen thousand miracles are (229)
"*recommended* to his devout attention by the circumstance
that others of the same family have been proved to be true,
and all *prejudiced* by his knowledge that as many others, on
the contrary, are certainly not true."   What then will be the
proportion of the "prejudice" to the "recommendation"?
It will be the same proportion as the number of "certainly
false" miracles to the number of "certainly true" ones, *i.e.*
a hundred thousand to one thousand, or *a hundred to one.*
In other words, the statistical probability that any one of
these neutral and doubtful miracles will prove false will be
a hundred to one !

And this result, be it observed, is based on an estimate
most unfairly favourable to Newman.   I can scarcely believe
that Newman himself—surrendering as he does one of his
Nine Miracles (393), admitting another to be (254) "*probably
not through miracle,* in the philosophical sense of the
word," and saying of another (259) that "we cannot
bring ourselves to say positively that we *believe* it "—would
imagine that he had ninety-one other miracles at hand
supported by evidence so cogent and complete as to "demand their acceptance."   In real fairness we ought probably to rate the "few" provable Ecclesiastical Miracles
at, say, under a hundred (from Newman's point of view).
Give him a hundred.   This would leave, as before, one
hundred thousand of these miracles that are certainly false,
and a hundred that are certainly true ; and then the proba-

bility that any doubtful Ecclesiastical Miracle would be false, would be one hundred thousand to one hundred, or *a thousand to one :*

Does it seem quite fair, in the face of such considerations as these, that Newman should have written the words quoted above (171), it is "no real argument against admitting *the Ecclesiastical Miracles on the whole, or* against admitting *certain* of them, that *certain others* are rejected on all hands as fictitious or pretended "?[1] How could he bring himself to write down the words "admitting the Ecclesiastical Miracles *on the whole,*" when he knew that the great majority of them are false?   He corrects the phrase with an "or"; but even an "or *rather*" would not suffice. The words ought not to have been written, and, having been written, should have been cancelled.   And, even after the cancelling, is the sentence fair?   We do not know which of the three classes (see p. 12 above) of Ecclesiastical Miracles is here meant by "certain" in "*certain* of them." But suppose he means the intermediate class which is "neither certainly true nor certainly false," of which we give him 20,000, while the "certain others" are, say,

---

[1] (1) It has been suggested that, by the words "the Ecclesiastical Miracles on the whole," Newman may have meant, "Ecclesiastical Miracles, *as a principle,*" or "the principle of miraculous intervention in post-Apostolic times." But Newman could have used either of these phrases if he had meant it; or he could have said "against *miracles generally* in the ages after the Apostles," as in (102); or "against *Ecclesiastical Miracles generally,*" as in (103); or (*Apol.* 21), "the *idea taken in itself of miraculous intervention* in later times." But the "*the,*" as well as the "*on the whole,*" shows that he does not mean this.

(2) It has been suggested that by "on the whole," he may mean "apart from" the "certain others" mentioned below. That is possible ; but the "certain others" are the *immense majority,* say, 100,000. "On the whole" is a most misleading expression to denote, say, 20,000, out of, say, 120,000.

100,000. The sentence will then run, " It is no real argument against admitting *twenty thousand* doubtful Ecclesiastical Miracles, that *a hundred thousand others* are rejected on all hands as fictitious or pretended." Is that " no real argument "? We have just quoted his own admission (229) that this intermediate class of Miracles is "*prejudiced*" by our " knowledge that so many others on the contrary are certainly not true." And he himself, when Christianity is in question, imperiously calls upon us to go upon probabilities even though they may be little more than evenly balanced, and once told us that we cannot be Christians, " if we will not go by evidence in which there are (so to say) *three* chances for revelation and only *two* against."[1] Then what is to become of us if we neglect facts which show that the probability of falsehood is *ten*, or a *hundred*, or a *thousand* to *one*?

The truth seems to be that, though Newman talked so much about, and set such store upon, probabilities, he had very little notion indeed about them, not having any practical conception of induction—an ignorance which one might indeed infer from the recklessness with which he first wrote " three " and then substituted a " dozen " in the sentence last quoted. An interesting instance of this, is afforded by the answer which he gives in an orthodox foot-note, appended to a heterodox attack made by him in 1826 upon the Roman Church (77) : " The notorious insincerity and frauds of the Church of Rome in other things are in themselves enough to throw a strong suspicion on its testimony to its own Miracles." To this he replies (77) : " There have been frauds among Catholics, and for gain, as among Protestants. . . or among antiquarians, or transcribers of MSS., or

---

[1] *Cardinal Newman*, by Mr. R. H. Hutton, p. 57. In a later text, Newman substituted a " dozen " for " three."

picture-dealers, or *horse-dealers*. . . but that does not prove
the Church to be fraudulent." His own amusing climax,
"horse-dealers," is, in itself, almost sufficient to make
retort unnecessary. Yet he does not seem to see that we
shall at once reply, "True: and therefore, if the frauds
among Romanists about miracles are as numerous as the
frauds among horse-dealers about horses, we are sure you
will not blame us if we treat the former, *in re* miracles, with
the same suspicion with which we should treat the latter, *in
re* horses. In fact you will not be surprised if we are even
a little *more* suspicious about a Romanist miracle than about
a horse-dealer's horse; for you will hardly say that *most* of
the horses sold by horse-dealers are unsound; and yet
that is what you yourself have told us about the miracles
reported by Ecclesiastical writers."

§ 20. *Rhetorical Charge against Protestants*

And yet, after all these admissions of error, exaggeration,
fiction, fabling and imposture, Newman ventures to reproach
Protestants with the general suspicion—which he himself
entertained in 1826—of the "notorious insincerity and
frauds of the Church of Rome" (*Apol.* 1st ed. Appendix.
p. 50): "*The whole mass* of accusations which Protestants
bring against us under this head, Catholic credulity, imposture, pious frauds, this vast and varied structure of im-
putations, you see, all rests on an assumption, on an opinion
of theirs, for which they offer *no kind of proof.* What then,
in fact, do they say more than this, 'If Protestantism be
true, you Catholics are a most awful set of knaves'?
Here, at least, is a most sensible and undeniable position."

This passage is not creditable to Newman's logic or
charity, and hardly even—I venture to think, for once—

I

to his rhetoric. In the first place, the "opinion" for which Protestants are said to "offer no kind of proof," is, as I have shown, simply this, that "It is unsafe to argue that, because God did a thing once for a special purpose, He will therefore do again, repeatedly, something quite different and often for no discoverable purpose at all"; and unquestionably the burden of disproving this "opinion" rests with those who would reject it. In the next place, Newman himself—including, as he does, "credulity" in his supposed list of Protestant charges against Romanists—destroys his own accusation that Protestants call Romanists "a most awful set of knaves." From the Protestant point of view, this is as much too unfavourable to the morality, as it is too favourable to the intellect, of Romanists. It takes many fools to make, so to speak, a living for a single knave; and therefore no Protestant of sense—although he might possibly call some Romanists "a most awful set of," say, simpletons—could possibly call Romanists "a most awful set of *knaves*."

Newman ventured to classify Romanists with "horse-dealers." Protestants would say that in some respects such a classification is unfair to Ecclesiastical writers ; in others, unfair to horse-dealers. A horse-dealer knows a sound horse from an unsound, and cheats when he sells the latter for the former. But the reporters of Ecclesiastical Miracles were very often so ignorant that they could not tell what was natural from what was miraculous; and often, quite innocently, reported the former as being the latter. Thus, though they were intellectually inferior, they were morally superior to "horse-dealers." But their morality was all the more dangerous for posterity because their very innocence helped them to deceive. Nevertheless, there are abundant instances —as Newman himself has been found (see above, p. 108) to admit—where miraculous narratives in the History of the Church cannot be explained on any but the theory of imposture.

§ 21. *Did Impostures "abound" in the Apostolic Church?*

Nothing shows more clearly at once Newman's rooted conviction of the prevalence of imposture in the region of Ecclesiastical Miracle, and his sense of the damaging nature of the argument derived from this fact against Ecclesiastical Miracles as a whole, than the desperate remedy to which he resorts in order to meet this objection. Directly, he could not meet it. He therefore attempts to meet it indirectly, by analogy, and by touching on (173) "the impostures of various kinds, which *from the first hour*, abounded *in the Church.*" The implied argument is, that, as the Scriptural impostures prove nothing against the Scriptural Miracles, so neither should the Ecclesiastical impostures prove anything against the Ecclesiastical Miracles. We naturally ask, in some amazement, "What are these 'impostures'?" In answer, he gives no direct information; but he inserts in the midst of his sentence a reference to a foot-note, and then adds a fine rolling passage which is certainly misleading to a careless or indolent reader, and perhaps even to one who is neither careless nor indolent, if he is too busy to look out references. Text and foot-note are so characteristic that they shall be given in full (173) :

"'The impostures then of various kinds which *from the first hour* abounded *in the Church* [1] prove as little against the truth of her miracles as against the canonicity of her Scriptures. Yet *here too* pretensions on the part of worthless

[1] "*Vid.* Acts viii. 9 ; xvi. 17 ; xix. 13. *Vid.* Lucian. Peregr. etc. ap. Middlet. Inqu. p. 23."

men will be sure to scandalize inquirers, and the more so if, as is not unlikely, such pretenders manage to ally themselves with the Saints, and have an historical position in the fight which is made for the integrity or purity of the faith ; yet St. Paul was not less an Apostle, nor have Confessors and Doctors been less successors, because, 'as they have gone to prayer,' a spirit of Python has borne witness to them as 'the servants of the most high God' and the teachers of 'the way of salvation.' "

What is the meaning of this grand sonorous period ? Is it intended to crush some argument of straw, such as this, that " St. Paul could not have worked true miracles, because on one occasion a 'damsel possessed with a spirit of divination' cried out testifying to his Divine mission ? " Is this poor mad " damsel " included by the writer in the "*pretenders* managing to ally themselves with the saints"? But what sceptic could be so inconceivably foolish as to set up such an argument? As if the demoniacs and lunatics who are said to have recognized our Lord as "the Holy One of God" in the synagogues of Galilee were "*pretenders* managing to ally themselves with" Him! Who but a lunatic would argue thus? And is it worthy of the subject that a sane man trying to meet a serious difficulty, should set up insane arguments in order to play at knocking them down ? And even if any sceptic were disposed to argue in this absurd fashion, what analogy is there between this and the errors, fables, fictions, false miracles, pretended miracles, imitated miracles, in Ecclesiastical History, many of which were fabled or circulated not by lunatics but by deliberate impostors ?

Again, where, in the New Testament shall we find *in the Church* "pretensions on the part of worthless men" that will " scandalize inquirers "? Can it be that Newman means Simon Magus? But Simon Magus was *not in* the

Church when he made these "pretensions." He was outside the Church. When he was admitted into the Church,
it is true that he is said to have offered to *buy* miraculous
powers from an Apostle. But to offer to *buy* miraculous
powers, so far from being identical with "making *pretensions*"
to them, implies on the contrary that at that time, while he
was in the Church, he did *not* "make pretensions" to them.
This being disposed of, what other "worthless men" are
there who made "pretensions" while "*in* the Church," and
"from the first hour"? There are none—that I know of,
and apparently, none that Newman knows of except persons, *not in* the Church, but "vagabond Jews" *outside*
the Church, who tried to practise exorcism in the name
of "Jesus whom Paul preacheth."

What then was the meaning of this fine rolling sentence?
The *result* of it, whatever the object may have been, is to
sweep us onward upon the stream of rhetoric—past the
references inserted in the middle of the first sentence,
"*Vid.* Acts viii. 9 ; xvi. 17 ; xix. 13. *Vid.* Lucian. Peregr. &c.
ap. Middlet. Inqu. p. 23 "—and to leave a lazy reader under
the impression that "*if* he had time to look out the references
in the *Acts*, which were *appended to the first sentence*, he
would probably find that there were three more instances of
imposture, *besides those alluded to, but not referred to in the
second sentence*, so that after all, it would seem as if there
were *something to be said* for Newman's theory. And then
besides, there is ' *Vid.* Lucian, Peregr. &c. ap. Middlet. Inqu.
p. 23.' " In fact, however, the three references in the Acts
refer simply to *the same* cases, afterwards mentioned, viz., the
lunatic, who was *outside* the Church ; the vagabond Jews, who
were *outside* the Church ; and Simon Magus, who was in the
Church, but is said to have been speedily cast out, and who,
while "in the Church," made no pretensions to miraculous

powers. Lastly, the mysterious reference (as it would probably seem to most of Newman's readers) to " Lucian. Pergr. &c.," is to one of Lucian's dialogues in which that sceptical sneerer scoffs at a man, Peregrinus by name, who was said to have publicly burned himself in A.D. 165, and who, *from being a Christian, had turned Cynic*—surely a strange authority (though it must be confessed, not ill matched with the other three) for proving that " impostures, *from the first hour, abounded in the Church* " ! [1]

What is the explanation of this abuse of language ? It seems to have been caused by an incredible self-deception springing from theological zeal. Convinced that there *must be* some way of defending these personal characteristics of God which are set forth in Ecclesiastical Miracles, Newman seems to have drifted into exaggerations, thinking his way as he wrote, somewhat after this fashion : -

" Whatever is in the post-apostolic Church must have had something corresponding to it in the apostolic. To doubt this would be to doubt the unity and continuity of the Church. This therefore being an axiom, I have to find in the apostolic Church something corresponding to those impostures which I have repeatedly acknowledged as existent in the post-apostolic. Now I cannot find in the Scriptures that any one, recognized as being in the Church, perpetrated such an imposture. That is unfortunate ; but what can I find next best to that ? I find that (1) a girl, said to have been possessed by an evil spirit, called Paul a follower of the

---

[1] Those who wish to see how absolutely baseless is the superstructure built by Newman on this Satire of Lucian, should refer to Bishop Lightfoot's *Apostolic Fathers*, i. pp. 322-4 ("Christian and Cynic, *Ignatius and Polycarp*, unite in one "), where it is shown that, so far as Lucian is scoffing at any particular Christians, he appears to be aiming at *Ignatius* and *Polycarp*, whom Newman would hardly call " impostors," or even " bystanders."

Most High God ; (2) that some vagabond Jews who did not believe in Jesus tried to exorcize in His name, and were roughly handled by the man on whom they experimented ; (3) that Simon Magus, while in the Church, offered to buy the power of performing miracles—though unhappily, the Scriptures do not enable me to say that, while he was in the Church, he performed any miracles, or even tried to perform them.

"This is all the evidence I have. By analogy, this evidence might go some little way toward justifying me in preparing my readers to expect that in the history of the post apostolic Church, Jewish and Pagan exorcists, jugglers, and magicians, attempted to imitate the miracles of the Church. But this is not at all what I want. Notoriously, the great mass of fictitious or pretended Ecclesiastical miracles were feigned or pretended by those who were *within the pale of the visible Church*. I have repeatedly implied this, both in the quotations I have given from other authors, and in my own statement (238), 'It as little derogates from the supernatural gift residing in the Church that miracles should have been *fabricated* or exaggerated, as it prejudices her holiness that *within her pale* good men are mixed with bad,' where I have certainly implied that as the 'good' and 'bad' men, so the workers of true miracles and 'fabricators' of false miracles, are, both alike, ' *within her pale.*' " Besides, if I ventured to argue, 'these fabricators of miracles were not in the *true and invisible* post-apostolic Church,' my antagonist would at once reply, ' But they were in the *visible* post-apostolic Church. Never mind the invisible : we will let you say what you like about that. But show us the same phenomena in both the *visible* Churches. If your analogy is to hold, there ought to be, *in both cases*, people *within the pale of the visible Church, feigning or pretending miracles.*

In the *pale of the visible* post-apostolic Church there are, say, 100,000 such miracles ; show us in the *pale of the visible* apostolic Church, 1,000 ; show us 100 ; show us 10 ; show us 1.'

" This looks a bad business. If only Demas, or Ananias, or Sapphira, had pretended to work miracles, that would have been just what I want. However, no doubt it will work out all right on paper. I can begin by saying that we find in Scripture (172) 'bystanders '—I am safe, so far ; for that word will apply to Simon Magus, who was as it were a looker-on upon the Church ; that is one instance ; and the vagabond Jews will make another. That makes two in all. But probably these were not their only impostures ; I may therefore describe their impostures conjecturally, as being ' of various kinds.' But now, I *must* have these impostures *in* the Church. Well, they *are, as it were, in the* Church, for they are *in connection with* the Church, *in the history of* the Church. Under the pressing circumstances, then, of the case, I think I may venture to say that, if not the impostors, at all events the *impostures*—that will be a capital distinction—took place *in the Church.* ' *Took place* ' however is a trifle tame—and it will not do to be tame—for the conclusion of a period. There were, I admit, only *two* instances ; but having called them ' impostures *of various kinds*,' surely I may go a step further now, and say that they ' *abounded.*' That will make a very pretty climax, not much inferior to Falstaff's men in buckram, 1st, ' *two* '; 2nd, ' *of various kinds* '; 3rd, ' *abounded* ': and then the sentence will run very neatly thus :—

(172) " Moreover, as Scripture expressly shows us, wherever there is miraculous power, there will be curious and interested bystanders who would fain ' purchase the gift of God ' for their own aggrandizement," [*that is, Simon Magus :*

instance number one ; but note that Simon does nothing ; he would only "fain" do it ; call this, then, half an instance] "and 'cast out devils in the Name of Jesus," [*that is, the 'vagabond Jews' ; instance number two*] "and who counterfeit what they have not really to exhibit, and gain credit and followers among the ignorant and the perverse. The impostures then of various kinds" [*that is, one and a half*] "which from the first hour abounded" [*being one and a half in number*] "in the Church" [*being not in the Church, but outside the pale of the Church*] "prove as little" &c. &c.

These last words, "prove as little," are the only words in the whole of this artistic passage that contain a particle of truth ; and even they are not really true. The "one and a half" instances do not "prove little" ; they prove absolutely nothing—except the nature of the logic and the character of the logician who would make them "prove" much.

Thus this terrible remedy of Newman's—which must surely seem to conservative Protestants well to deserve the name of "kill or cure," attempting, as it does, to reconcile us to the fact that the great majority of Ecclesiastical Miracles are impostures by demonstrating that impostures also "abounded" in the Apostolic Church—is found to be a bubble that vanishes into whatever space may be reserved for fallacies that perish as soon as they are created, beneath the touch of any painstaking reader who will take the trouble to verify four references.

This inanity being out of the way, Newman's defence of Ecclesiastical Miracles has nothing further to fall back on. The two intelligible lines of defence were these : first, that because God suspended the Laws of Nature when He planted the Church, He must therefore continue to do so while it is growing (the fallacious assumption which Newman called a "first principle") ; secondly, that (173) "it is no real argument against admitting the Ecclesiastical Miracles *in the whole, or* against admitting *certain of them*, that *certain others* [*say* 100,000 *out of* 120,000] are rejected on all hands as fictitious or pretended." I will not say that these two lines of entrenchments have been captured; they have merely been defined; and it needed nothing but clear definition and concrete illustration to compel an immediate surrender at discretion.

There now remains for assault, only what was described above (p. 14) as the position of "Potentiality," the fortress of "may-be," to which hard-pressed Credulity flees for refuge when "is" and "was" are taken by storm. This citadel is, of course, logically impregnable. Let a "pious believer" resolve to say, when he sees a stone fall down or a spark go up, that the one *may* descend, and the other *may* ascend, by Miracle, and what logic can prevent him? Arguments cannot shake him, for they cannot show that it is false; and he will rather enjoy being demonstrated to be silly. But perhaps he will ask us with a smile—indeed, Newman *does* ask us—" What is the harm of this belief?" To that question the next chapter will endeavour to make a reply.

CHAPTER V

§ 22. "*A Church without Miracles is a Reign without the Monarch*"

WE have been unable above to find any but fallacious bases for Newman's theory of the probability of Ecclesiastical Miracles; but we know that he retained it. We have seen him indeed once correct himself when he had used, apparently with approval, a phrase that implied the *general* acceptance of Ecclesiastical Miracles. Once, but only once, has he frankly admitted the great mass of these Miracles to be false. But his general attitude is that of one who accepts Ecclesiastical Miracles "on the whole," and thinks it good and safe and pious not to be disposed to reject *any* Ecclesiastical Miracle (however slight the evidence) unless it is immoral, or, though moral, wrought by a heretic. What were the reasons that made one who was by nature keen-witted and subtle, put on such, as it appears to us, superfluous fetters?

The answer is not difficult, and Newman himself leads us to it. He had been impressed, as a boy, with the belief that (*Apol.* 22) "upon the visible Church came down from above at certain intervals, large and temporary Effusions of Divine grace." The author, Joseph Milner, from whom he had accepted this theory, expressly deprecated the inclusion of miraculous operations in the " Effusions" of post-apostolic ages. But Newman, later in life, accepted the theory without the deprecation. To maintain that these " Effusions" were, in modern times, simply outpourings of love, joy, peace, long-suffering, and those other moral qualities which St. Paul calls "the fruits of the Spirit," seemed to him an arbitrary and narrow limitation of the Divine power. Acts of faith-healing had unquestionably accompanied the first preaching of the Gospel ; and, although St. Paul seems to set comparatively little store upon them, they seem to have had great power in aiding the attainment of a special object, viz. the evangelization of the first generation of Christians. To Newman—who, after his twenty-first year, seems to have become uneasy in his faith, and to have been always " seeking for a sign "—these, and other much more striking and marvellous acts, seemed fit to be continued, as personal characteristics of God, even without that object, yes, and even "for *no discoverable object.*" This was what he *said* to himself ; but in his heart of hearts he seems to have felt that there *was* always a "discoverable object" for them, because they supplied proofs and "Notes" of the true Church.[1]

[1] A somewhat similar belief in mediæval and modern miracles appears to be required by the theory of Dr. James Mozley, *Letters*, p. 262, where he gives Dean Church a sketch of his proposed Bampton Lectures on Miracles. The "evidence part" he finds—not unnaturally— "tiring" ; and he thinks that he "will try to bring out . . . the argument that the practical force and success of Christianity has depended on certain motives, which motives have been *supplied by certain doctrines,* which doctrines *could not have been proved without miracles.*"

According to this theory, a man in the nineteenth century may say, " I am unfairly treated. You say, 'Christian doctrines *could not have*

Naturally in this aspect—regarded as proofs and demonstrations—love, joy, peace, and the like, seemed intangible,

been proved without miracles': no miracles have been vouchsafed to me ; therefore you cannot consistently blame me for rejecting what has not been, and—by your own admission—'*could not have been,*' proved to me."

Perhaps we may reply : " We did not say ' the doctrines could not *be* proved *now,*' but, ' the doctrines could not *have been* proved *to the first generation of Christians.*'" But he will retort, " How do you know that ? It is always hard to prove a negative. Even if you take it upon yourselves to limit what human nature ' could have done ' in the way of trusting an incarnate God, you must be venturesome indeed to lay down in Bampton Lectures a limit to what the incarnate God Himself ' could have done.'" And what shall we say to that ?

Perhaps we may take up another position. " There is no unfairness," we may say ; " you have evidence showing that miracles *were wrought* 1860 *years ago,* and you have also the proof afforded by the history of the beneficent operations of the Church. *These two together* are equivalent to the ocular demonstration of such a miracle, for example, as the Destruction of the Two Thousand Swine." " No, they are not," he may reply, " I very much prefer the ocular demonstration ; I *agree with you as to the importance of miraculous proof ;* but a miracle *to my great-great-grandfather* is not the same thing as a miracle *to me ;* nor are Christian doctrines *proved to me* because they are alleged to *have been proved miraculously to my progenitors. Demonstrations of this kind cannot be received by proxy. They require to be repeated for each generation in its turn.* I am therefore defrauded, according to your own admission, of my just proof. The history of the Church will not make up for the deficiency. I take you at your word that Christian doctrine ' *could not have been*'—only I go further and add that it ' *cannot be*'—*proved without miracles.* And if the Church of England denies me modern miracles, I must go to the Church of Cardinal Newman which does not deny them."

The real truth is that Christian " motives " are not " supplied by doctrines " at all, but by Christ Himself ; by the Spirit of Christ passing from the heart of the believer to the heart of the unbeliever ; and, although belief in the miraculous did, as a historical fact, originally —and still does to a very large extent—help the human heart to take into itself the germ of the true conception of Christ, yet it is by no means necessary that this should be the case in all the ages of the Church.

vague, and unsatisfactory in comparison with striking sus-
pensions of the Laws of Nature. Consequently he did not
look at the question as one of fact and evidence, but as one
of "natural" belief (*Apol.* 22) : "it was *natural* for me, admitting Milner's general theory, and applying to it the principle of analogy, not to stop short at his abrupt *ipse dixit*,
but boldly to pass forward to the conclusion, on other
grounds plausible, that, as miracles accompanied the first
effusion of grace, so they might accompany the later." This
conclusion agreed also with his interpretation of one of the
two great Maxims of his religious life (*Apol.* 5), viz., "Holiness," or Sanctity, "rather than Peace"; for (*Apol.* 23)
"according to the ancient Catholic doctrine, the gift of
miracles was viewed as the attendant and shadow of transcendent *sanctity.*" Thus Newman's belief in Ecclesiastical
Miracles was really a necessity of his nature and position.
When he had lost the assurance of "final perseverance"
which (*Apol.* 4) "gradually faded away" after his coming
of age, and when he had passed through that brief phase of
"Liberalism" which could not long satisfy his cravings, it
became imperative that he should obtain some substitute
that might still his religious fears; and the only possible
substitute was the safeguard of the true Church. How then
could he exist in uncertainty as to what the true Church
was? And what "signs" could he find, better calculated
to dispel his uncertainty than a continuous dispensation of
miracles? He could not believe that the peaceful development of the moral qualities and the emotions was the best
sign of the true Church; and consequently he accepted
as "natural"—and could never give up when he had once
accepted it—the belief that God *must* continue to work
miracles in the true Church.

It is true that elsewhere he quotes with cordial approval

the sayings of the Fathers who declared that the Church attested the Ecclesiastical Miracles, not the miracles the Church ; but, in practice, he accepts the miracles as "signs" of holiness, as "Notes" of the Church, as being necessary in order to break "the *prestige*" of the Laws of Nature, and, in a word, as being so antecedently probable—whenever God is supposed to be specially acting—that (190) "*the main point* to which attention is to be paid is the proof of their antecedent *probability*."

Newman's practical view, then, of Ecclesiastical Miracles is that, though supernatural, they are, in the true Church (190), "the natural effects of supernatural agency." He has admitted that false miracles are far more common than true ones ; yet still (191) "the history of miracles . . . . is, at first sight, almost 'to be admitted of course, without a strong reason to suspect it.'" Miracles are as much characteristic of sacred History as natural acts are characteristic of profane History ; and they are so much (98) "the most important of its characteristics that to treat the History (98) "of the Catholic Church without taking them into account is to profess *to write the annals of a reign yet to be silent about the monarch*—to overlook as it were his personal character and professed principles, his indirect influence and immediate acts"; or again (*Apol.* 299), "Miracles are the kind of facts proper to Ecclesiastical History, just as instances of sagacity or daring, personal prowess or crime, are the facts proper to secular History." Just as a mother, poring over a letter from some far-distant son and missing the usual message of affection might find it (though it is not there) perhaps in some blot, or say, "It is the fault of my eyes ; it *must be* there, somewhere," so we, yearning for Miracles in God's History, are to accept them on little evidence, and almost upon none.

Even among those who clearly recognize the baselessness
and unfairness of this theory, some may be disposed to think
that, after all, in practice, it can do no great harm. "A little
excess of faith," they may say, "in a somewhat sceptical
age, may be perhaps a fault on the right side." But they
are confusing faith in goodness, or faith in God, or faith
in men, with *faith in past facts*. There can indeed be
no excess in the faith that goodness will ultimately triumph
over evil, or in the faith that God is good; for these faiths
justify themselves by their moral and spiritual results; and
as they do not enter the region of proof and disproof, they
can never lead us into hypocrisy or falsehood. Again, as to
faith in men, there may certainly be an excess in our faith
that a particular person is good; but such faith as this
sometimes justifies both itself and us, *by making some one
whom we have trusted trustworthy by reason of our trusting
him*; and, at the worst, if it never leads us to *contradict facts*,
but only to trust a man sometimes too much in spite of
them, an occasional failure can do little harm in proportion
to the good that results from the general habit. It may
make us seem slightly foolish; but it will be folly of that sort
which, as Plato tells us, is almost essential to the highest
nobility; and it can never make us liars, nor ever such
absolute fools as men of the world are sometimes made by
utter trustlessness.

But faith *in facts, against evidence*, is quite a different
thing. It is an insult to those faculties which God has
given us for learning the truth about facts; it is a faithless *distrust* of His gifts, and therefore, so far as we recognize these gifts to be from Him, it is a distrust of
the Giver Himself. Such faith is a fault; and an excess of
it is an excess of fault. And surely, if we regard the actual
results in Newman's case, we must conclude that the fault is

neither little nor harmless when we find him, for example, using on so sacred a subject such exaggerated special pleading as this (*Apol.* 1st ed. Append. p. 56) : "As regards the miracles of the Catholic Church, if indeed miracles never can occur, then, indeed impute the narratives to fraud ; *but till you prove that they are not likely, we shall consider the histories which have come down to us true on the whole, though in* particular cases they may be exaggerated or unfounded." "*True on the whole* "—and this though he has himself practically admitted (see p. 108 above) that the false are "*many*" and the true "*few*"!

§ 23. *Newman's Standard of Credulity*

The importance attaching to Newman's admission of the preponderance of false miracles over true depends of course upon his standard of credulity. If he was only moderately credulous, the admission does not amount to much ; but if he was immoderately credulous, the admission is enormous. Now the extent of his credulity may be *indirectly* inferred from his implied defence of such miracles as he had condemned in the days when he was drifting towards Liberalism, the miracle of " the exorcised demoniac camel," the miracle of the "fowl petrified" because it had been dressed at a season of fasting, and such other portents as have been described above, pp. 7, 8. But lest any of my readers should suppose that there is no *direct* evidence of the de-intellect-ualizing influence of this resolute faith in miracles as "the kind of facts proper to Ecclesiastical History," let me enu-merate a few to which Newman yields express assent.

He (*Apol.* 1st ed. p. 57) "cannot withstand the evidence which is brought for the liquefaction of the blood of St. Januarius at Naples, and for the motion of the eyes of the

K

pictures of the Madonna in the Roman States ;" and can
" see no reason to doubt the material of the Lombard crown
at Monza ;" and does " not see why the Holy Coat at Trèves
may not have been what it professes to be " ; and " firmly "
believes " that portions of the True Cross are at Rome and
elsewhere ; " and that " the Crib of Bethlehem is at Rome."
The multiplication of the wood of our Saviour's Cross
(as well as its discovery) seems to him fit to be included
among those miracles (134) " which have an historical
character." He can record, with apparent acceptance, the
appearance and vanishing of (123) "a large plate of silver "
before St. Anthony in the wilderness ; and relates, in the same
spirit of acquiescence, the miracles of St. Martin who, in
answer to a heathen's challenge, received a falling pine-tree,
and caused it to (128) " reel round and fall on the other side "
by making the sign of the cross, and stopped a whole
procession of heathens by the same means, and warned
off a fire from the building which it is on the point of
consuming.

" Why not? Did not St. Martin 'believe'? And is it
not written that ' these signs shall follow them that believe ' ? [1]
If therefore you venture to deny that St. Martin wrought these
miracles, you, in effect, deny that St. Martin was a believer"—
such is the style of argument that an apologist for St. Martin's

---

[1] Of course, we must not expect Newman to take into consideration
the fact that these words (Mark xvi. 17) are considered by the most
competent authorities, upon the most cogent evidence, not to be
genuine (see Westcott and Hort's *Greek Testament*, ii. 51). Newman
neither had, nor pretended to have, any critical knowledge whatever of
the text of the New Testament. I have noticed only one passage (34)
in which (writing in 1826) he calls attention to a possible interpolation
in the Received Text ; and *in his controversy with Kingsley, in* 1864,
he uses (Apol. 301) *that same passage* (John v. 4) *without any mention
of the possibility of interpolation.*

miracles might "almost" make, and apparently "almost" with Newman's approval. Else, why, after quoting from St. Mark's Gospel the spurious verse above mentioned, does he append the following foot-note (209); "Sulpicius *almost* grounds his defence of St. Martin's miracles on the antecedent force of this text. He says of those who deny them, *Nec Martino in hac parte detrahitur, sed fidei Evangelii derogatur. Nam . . . qui Martinum non credit ista fecisse, non credit Christum ista (Mark xvi. 17) dixisse*"! A very large number of Protestants will accept not "almost" but altogether—the challenge here thrown down by Sulpicius : and will declare that, sooner than believe in St. Martin's portents, they will believe that Christ did not utter the words imputed to Him in this spurious interpolation. But surely Newman's very mention, without condemnation, of such an imbecile and uncharitably aggressive argument, is sufficient to show that some moral as well as intellectual deterioration must result from "throwing oneself generously into a system " of thought which requires a man to believe that (*Apol.* 292) : " Miracles are the kind of facts proper to Ecclesiastical History ; just as instances of sagacity or daring, personal prowess or crime, are the facts proper to secular History."

Yet immediately after the sentence just quoted, the writer naively adds " What is *the harm* of this ? " The question is characteristic. He does not say, " What is *false* in this ? "— for truth of fact is not, in his mind, so prominent as what is spiritually profitable and edifying. I have tried to show that it is *false*. I will endeavour now, briefly and summarily, to show that it is *harmful*, referring for the details of the proof, where needed, to the sources where they may be found.

§ 24. *The Six Harms*

(1) The first harm, then, is that the belief tends to make us cowards, by making God strange, and terrific, or perplexing, to us.

For indeed, to recognize God chiefly and mainly as breaking that natural order of material things in which men find their material security, and to say that, unless He does this and does it perpetually, He is a *roi fainéant*, and His kingdom is "a reign without a monarch"—what is this, at the best, but to ignore in blind ingratitude the glorious harmony of His works, and to convert Him from His real character of a wise Father training His sons for manhood by silent influences, into the semblance of a fussy and meddlesome nurse who can never let children alone, but must be always at them, spoiling their pleasures, stunting their mental growth, and dwarfing their characters, for the purpose of perpetually vindicating her authority? Or take it at its worst, and we shall find that such credulity metamorphosizes God into a Tyrant resolved to show his slaves that they exist but upon sufferance; a Tyrant, not the less terrible because, at times—if we are to accept the Ecclesiastical Miracles "on the whole"—with their "petrified fowls," and "weeping-stones," and "exorcised demoniac camels,"[1] he appears, like Nero, to take a pleasure in affecting the character of an antic before an audience who must needs profess a reverent astonishment at his grotesque surprises or perish if they venture to show a symptom of disgust.

Men cannot thus degrade God, or make Him unknown, without making themselves more or less timorous in such a Being's presence. And Newman's whole life attests this

[1] See pp. 7, 8 above.

timorous attitude.[1] "The fear of the Lord" was, with him, the end, as well as "the beginning," of his spiritual "wisdom."

(2) The next harm is, spiritual blindness.

By thus laying stress on mere violations of the material order of things, as the chief indications of God's "personal character," a man degrades God's love, justice, forgiveness to a position where they become mere dogmatic unintelligible fictions, wholly detached from the natural human virtues corresponding to these names. This was Newman's fate. I have already said that his sense of the love of God was swallowed up in fear. But, further, he had no adequate sense of justice in man, and no sense at all of justice in God.[2] He confused human forgiveness with foolish and arbitrary forgetfulness.[3] He converted God's forgiveness of sins into an "economy" which makes God say *what is not true*.[4] And while doing all this, and while thus supremely blind to God's supreme attributes and to the gifts and graces which He is bestowing on the Church, he nevertheless accuses those who reject the Ecclesiastical Miracles of the very blindness under which he himself is suffering : they

[1] See *Contemporary Review*, Jan. 1891, p. 34, also the notes on p. 38 above, and p. 223 below ; also the *Letters*, passim, *e.g.* i. 58. Comp. also Fletcher's *Life of Cardinal Newman*, p. 162, "He was anxious about his own soul ; he thought that he had done nothing unless he had succeeded in making others anxious." "*Fear*," he said (*Letters*, ii. 128), "was what *Cambridge* wanted." It is the absence of such "fear," and the presence of a reverence incompatible with such "fear," that, above all other differences, distinguish Maurice from Newman.

[2] *Contemporary Review*, Jan. 1891, pp. 45, 46.

[3] See Mr. R. H. Hutton's *Cardinal Newman*, p. 85.

[4] *Ib.* p. 84, where Mr. Hutton quotes *Lectures on Justification*, 3rd ed. p. 78, "By a merciful economy or representation, *He says of us as to the past, what in fact is otherwise than what He says it is.*"

are, he says (188) "expressing their own disbelief in the
Grace committed to the Church; and of course they are
consistent in denying its outward triumphs, when *they have
no true apprehension of its inward power.*"

How much more spiritual is the utterance of one of his
own authorities! "*The miracles of the soul,*" says Pope
Gregory (139), "are *the greater because the more spiritual;*
the greater, because they are the means of raising, not
bodies, but souls: these signs then, dearest brethren, by
God's aid, ye do, if ye will."

(3) The third harm is a recklessness in statement which,
beginning with inaccuracy, may end in actual falsification.

Sometimes this inaccuracy may spring from honest fear.
Those who have not forgotten their first book of Cæsar's
Gallic War (xxii.) may remember the cold contempt with
which that most practical man tells us how the craven
Considius came galloping back to him at dawn, with the
false news that the Helvetians were beforehand with him
on the hill-side—thus spoiling all his plans for a surprise. The
great man does not waste a word on reproach: "Late in the
day," he says, "Cæsar ascertained. . . that Considius, *in
mere panic, had reported that he had seen what he had not
seen.*" Such panic, such resultant mischief, such consequent
contempt, must always be in store for those who allow themselves, when judging facts, to be influenced by "fears of
rejecting" this or that, and by notions of the "safety" or
"unsafety" of accepting that or this. The strain is too
great. They *must sometimes* "report that they have seen
what they have not seen"; they will probably sometimes go
further and report that they have felt what they have not
felt; they may occasionally go further still and declare that
they believe what they do not believe.

Of course, this last condition of mind, though distinguishable, is not far removed, from dishonesty. I once knew a child who was told that he could not have an impending holiday unless he could say that he was sorry for something he had done. He replied that he did not at present feel sorry and could not say so. But the holiday was not to come for a week ; and in the interval the child persuaded himself that he really was sorry, and said so, and got his holiday. My impression is that the act was one for which he really ought to have been genuinely sorry ; but it is also my impression that, under the circumstances, it would have been better, far better, for that child, either not to have felt sorry, or if he felt so, not to have said so. Whatever tendency to insincerity he may have felt in later life, must have been increased by that expression of a too timely and too profitable penitence. And how much greater is the danger for those grown-up children who call themselves men, when they are told that unless they can say that they believe in this or that, they shall not have *their* holiday—after death ! The stake being so very great, will not the temptation to dishonest self-deception be proportionately great? Will not many people say to themselves " I *ought* to believe," " I really *ought* to believe," so very often that they will end in *saying*, "I *do* believe "— yet all the while not really believing at all, or, if at all, with a half-belief and half make-believe ?

For the proof of inaccuracy in Newman's case, I refer my readers to the following analysis of his Nine Miracles, (pp. 152—196) as well as to the Introduction.

(4) The fourth harm is a logical fatuity, which, though it leaves its victim an adept in the skilful shifting and turning of words, and in the cut-and-thrust of rhetorical polemics, takes away from him all real reasonableness, all rational views of probability, and all trust in common sense.

Of this, there will appear abundant instances hereafter. But it ought almost to be sufficient to have exhibited the advocate of Ecclesiastical Miracles practically accepting them "on the whole" while admitting that by far the greater number are false ; declaring that, because God is supposed to have performed something once, it is therefore "a first principle " to believe that He will probably do something quite different again ; and then asking us " What is the harm ? " of asserting that miracles in Ecclesiastical History are as much to be expected as deeds of prowess and adventure in profane History, while he alleges no basis whatever for his assertion, except, first, the exploded "antecedent probability " just mentioned, and, secondly, a statistical probability derived from the supposed demonstrable truth of, say, Nine Ecclesiastical Miracles,—or say even nine hundred—as compared with the universally recognized falsehood of, say, a hundred thousand !

(5) The fifth harm is laziness ; which is all the more vividly illustrated in Newman as he was by nature one of the most painstaking and laborious of men.   But he took pains in the wrong way, and laboured at the wrong things.   Instead of collecting and classifying evidence, he busied himself with " accumulating probabilities," that is to say, antecedent probabilities based upon analogies—mere verbal pyramids balanced on their tops.

From his point of view he was quite right.   " Antecedent Probability," being with him (190), "the main point,' why should he toil to no purpose about the collection of evidence which, when collected, could not make him—or those who thought with him, or most of those whom he hoped to make think with him—a whit more convinced than they were before ?

I have illustrated this consistent indolence in the Introduction, but will do so more fully hereafter in a separate chapter treating of the Oil of St. Walburga.   One instance however may be given here.   Newman is writing about the luminous letters written in the sky, said to have been seen by Constantine and his army.   Now there are other cases where meteoric phenomena have been interpreted as letters, and for the full discussion of an alleged miracle it would be necessary to collect such cases.   But Newman, who always regards the natural explanation of a Miracle as a stratagem of Liberalism and not as an attempt to get at the truth, says (272), " Since *any extraordinary appearance* at such a juncture, whatever be its physical cause, or whether it have one or no, *is undeniably the result of an immediate Divine superintendence*, it is not easy to see what is *gained* by an hypothesis of this nature.   If, in matter of fact, our Lord was then really addressing Constantine, it seems *trifling* to make it a grave point *to prove that he did so in this way and not in that*."

(6) The sixth harm is a loose employment of words, By "loose" I do not mean slovenly ; for, on the contrary, it is highly (though unconsciously) artistic ; but "loose" in the sense of "verging on immoral shiftiness."   This mischief arises from a disbelief in the use of words as a means to the attainment of truth.

It is this habit in Newman that, more than any other, has given rise to the impression that he is not entirely sincere.   But the main basis for the charge of insincerity is afforded by his own confession,[1] that sometimes he said a little more than he meant in order that he might be supposed to mean what he really did mean ; and, after all, if a man does his best to make you understand his real meaning, although he may take a crooked path towards

[1] Introduction, p. 45.

his end, he cannot be accused of real insincerity, but only of contempt for his readers and of contempt for language in general. This loose employment of words generally manifests itself in what I have described above as a kind of "illative rhetoric,"[1] whereby Newman leads on himself and his readers from one step to another by an illogical and merely verbal descent, which by its smoothness, and by the delicate juxtaposition of graduated shades of thought, carries us from a premise that is always true and often a truism, to a conclusion that is often in the highest degree improbable. Such a result in a professed rhetorician would be artistic ; but in Newman it cannot be so described without an important qualification. The art is unconscious and the artist is deceiving himself more than he deceives others. It is the playing with words and logic by one who despises both, yet feels bound to use both, in order to show himself that he is not afraid of them ; it is a thinking out of thoughts by one who has already determined upon his conclusions and who wishes to "supply himself with a logical basis," though all the while quite ready—but for the shame of the thing—to believe without any logical basis at all. In his *Apologia* (p. 113) Newman gives us an interesting extract from his *Prophetical Office*, in which, at the conclusion of his treatise, he expresses "a sort of distrust of" his "theory altogether." It deserves quoting in full ; for nothing could better express Newman's general attitude towards the verbal discussion of things that appear to him beyond and above all words : "Now that our discussions draw to a close, the thought, with which we entered on the subject, is apt to recur, when the excitement of the inquiry has subsided, and weariness has succeeded, that *what has been said is but a*

---

[1] For instances see chapters viii. and ix. below.

dream, the wanton exercise, rather than the practical con-
clusions, of the intellect."

This is the explanation of Newman's apparent sophistry.
He does not wish to deceive you, nor himself; but he
speaks as though he did. He throws out words, and when
he thinks over them, they seem "a dream;" but he lets
them stand, for they will do as well as anything else; are
not *all words* "a dream"? He publishes to the world what
upon reflection appears to him "the wanton exercise of the
intellect." But why not? He does not deceive the world.
He tells them plainly and himself that he does not believe
in himself nor in them, nor in his intellect, nor in theirs, nor
perhaps in the possibility of approximating to truth by any
human faculties without some special and quasi-miraculous
aid from God. So let it pass.

These then are the "harms" that we should allege in reply
to Newman's question, What is the *harm* of my theory about
Ecclesiastical Miracles? —(1) religious timorousness, (2)
spiritual blindness, (3) recklessness of statement bordering
upon falsification of facts, (4) the loss of reasonableness,
(5) intellectual laziness, (6) a loose employment of words
verging on immoral shiftiness.

CHAPTER VI

THE OIL OF ST. WALBURGA

THE allegation concerning St. Walburga (*Apol.* 300–302) is that oil flowing from her remains has wrought miraculous cures. This alleged miraculous action differs from all others alleged in Newman's Essay, inasmuch as this is said to be still in operation : so that in this case there was room for a special and careful investigation, which was impossible as to the "historical" Miracles of the Thundering Legion, the Multiplication of the Cross, and the rest. We shall see how far Newman avails himself of this special opportunity, and what may be learned from his treatment of this subject concerning his attitude towards evidence and facts in their bearing on the question of a miraculous or non-miraculous explanation of an alleged miracle.

A great number of other miracles are recorded as having been wrought by the intercession of this Saint concerning which Newman says (*Apol.* 300), that without denying that numerous miracles had been wrought by her intercession, he felt that he had not "grounds for binding" himself "to the belief of certain alleged miracles in particular." "I made, however," he says, "*one exception :* it was the medicinal oil which flows from her relics." He then proceeds to state (*Apol.* 300) the proof of " (1) the *verisimilitude ;* (2) the *miraculousness,* and (3) the *fact,* of this medicinal oil."

First as to the *verisimilitude,* he thinks it sufficient to show that Scripture narrates a miracle performed by the relics of a dead Saint, viz. Elisha (1 Kings xiii. 20, 21), and other miracles wrought by an inanimate substance which had touched a living Saint, viz. St. Paul (Acts xix. 11, 12). He also mentions that a pool wrought miracles, quoting John v. 4, "An Angel went down, &c." [1]

But conservative Protestants will reply that, unless there is *some proportion* between St. Walburga and Elisha, or St. Walburga and St. Paul, and between the objects to be attained by the Scriptural miracles, and those to be obtained by St. Walburga's miracles, they cannot admit the *verisimilitude.* In the whole of the history of the Chosen People, and of the Primitive Church, only one instance is even alleged of a cure effected through the relics of a Saint ; is it then antecedently probable that *several* such miracles should be wrought by a single obscure Saint in the eighth century ?

2. As to the *fact.* He has said above (*Apol.* 300) that though he did not deny that numerous miracles had been wrought through St. Walburga yet "neither the Author of her life nor I felt that *we had grounds for binding ourselves to the belief of certain alleged miracles in particular. I made, however, one exception ;* it was the medicinal oil which flows

---

[1] Yet in earlier days (1826) Newman had stated about this very verse (which is omitted in our Revised Version) that it (34) "*is wanting in many MSS. of authority and is marked as suspicious by Griesbach.*" He had also said : " There is a difficulty in the narrative contained in the first verses of John v. ; because we cannot reduce the account of the descent of the Angel into the water to give it a healing power, under any known arrangement of the divine economy."

from her relics." This he again emphatically repeats. As
to St. Walburga's other alleged miracles, his position was
this (*Apol.* 301) ; "they *might* be true, but they *were not
proved* to be true, because there was not trustworthy testimony. However," he continues, "as to St. Walburga *I
made one exception, the fact of the medicinal oil, since for that
miracle there was distinct and successive testimony.* And then
I went on to give *a chain of witnesses.*"

It seems impossible to mistake the meaning of all this.
He has " grounds for *binding himself to the belief*" in this
one exceptional miracle. The others, though possible, are
" not proved to be true," but this, being "the one exception,"
is, we must infer, "*proved to be true* "—*at least to his
satisfaction*—by "trustworthy testimony" of a nature "distinct and successive." And he accepts it as his duty to
"prove" it, *i.e.* to prove, first the fact, and secondly, the
miraculousness of the fact, and to "give *a chain of witnesses.*"

How does he prove it? What is the "*chain*"? He
gives, in full, such evidence as he can procure, showing
(301) "that such miracles are said to have commenced about
A.D. 777. Then," he continues, " I spoke of the medicinal
oil as having testimony to it in 893, in 1306, after 1450, in
1615, and in 1620. Also I said that Mabillon seems not to
have believed some of her miracles ; and that the earliest
witness had got into trouble with his Bishop. *And so I left
the matter, as a question to be decided by evidence, not deciding
anything myself.* What was the harm of all this?" What
harm? Why, practical (though, no doubt, unintended)
tergiversation—that was "the harm." Just now, he led
us to understand that he had distinctly decided that the
miracle was true ; and here he leaves it " *to be* decided,"
and "decides nothing" himself! He told us above that
he was "*bound to* this " one exceptional miracle ; and that

he intended to prove it by a "*chain*" of "*successive*" testimony. And we are waiting for the proof; and asking whether the "*chain*" is broken off in the seventeenth century—surely a very natural question! Yet he actually insults Kingsley for asking it (302) : "My critic muddled it together in a most extraordinary manner, and I am far from sure that he knew himself the definite categorical charge which he intended it to convey against me. One of his remarks is, 'What has become of the holy oil for the last 240 years, Dr. Newman does not say.' *Of course I did not*, because I did not know ; *I gave the evidence as I found it ; he assumes that I had a point to prove, and then asks why I did not make the evidence larger than it was.*"

What words are fit to characterize so insolent a contempt of facts—all the more unpardonable because, as we shall see, facts would have greatly strengthened his case? *No* "*point to prove*"! We thought he intended to prove the miracle by "successive" testimony. "*Of course I did not, because I did not know*"! As if it was not his business to "know"! And then the rhetorical distortion, "he asks why I did not *make* the evidence *larger* than it was,"—a phrase that suggests that his antagonist wished him to *exaggerate* the evidence ; whereas what Kingsley was really asking him amounted to this, "Why did you not fulfil your promise of making the '*chain*' of evidence for the miracle '*successive*'—if there was indeed a succession of cases down to the present time—instead of snapping off the chain in the seventeenth century?' And finally he puts down poor Kingsley's complaint as his twenty-fifth "blot [1]"!

[1] The offence is all the greater in the first edition of the *Apologia*, (Append. p. 42) in which he lays stress upon the continued and *present* existence of the oil : "The main question then . . . . is *the matter of fact :—is* there an oil *flowing* from St. Walburga's tomb which is medi-

Then follow words which, as they were originally written, are a positive aggravation of the previous offence (302) : "I can tell him more about it now ; the oil still flows ; I have had some of it in my possession ; it is medicinal ; *some* think it is so by a natural quality ; *others* by a divine gift. *Perhaps* it is on the confines of both."

And here, in the first edition of the *Apologia* (Append. p. 44) the subject ends—without one word of information as to the " medicinal " results ; and whether those results were producible on non-Romanists, as well as on Romanists ; and what was the proportion of the failures, if any, to the successes. And not one word as to the nature of the " some " who think it flows " by a natural quality "—whether chemists, or physicians, or ecclesiastics, or peasants, or Romanists, or non-Romanists—nor as to the nature of the " others," who think that it flows " by a divine gift " !

What he does therefore in the first edition of *Apologia* amounts to this : he first shows that there is no reason why St. Walburga's relics *should not have* worked miracles since there is Scriptural authority for similar facts ; then he adds (*Apol.* 1st ed. Append. 42) "the main question then (I do not say the only remaining question, but the main question) is the *matter of fact :—is* there an oil flowing from St. Walburga's tomb which is medicinal?" in other words he assumes that the *miraculousness* of the fact, *if* it is a fact, is so nearly obvious as to be quite a subordinate consideration ; then he repeats that he gave distinct and successive testimony to show that there *was* such a medicinal oil up to the seventeenth century ; then he sneers at his opponents

cinal? To this question I *confined myself* in the Preface to the Volume." If the " main question " was whether *the oil is still flowing*, why does he blame Kingsley for asking—instead of blaming himself for not stating—what had become of the oil in the last 240 years?

for asking for information as to the "successive testimony" in the eighteenth and nineteenth centuries, which might have proved that there *is* such an oil; then he suddenly gives up the decision as to its being miraculous or not, by adding "*some* think it is so by a natural quality, *others* by a divine gift. *Perhaps* it is on the confines of both"! Is not this what, in other people, we should call tergiversation of the worst sort—running away after you have hit your adversary below the belt?[1]

Of course this would not do, when all readers came to review the controversy deliberately. The gross unfairness would then be too patent, and they would ask for proof of the *miraculousness* as well as proof of the fact. Accordingly, in the second edition of the *Apologia*, Newman formally recognized the three heads above mentioned (1) *verisimilitude;* (2) *fact;* (3) *miraculousness*. But, on this last head, here is all he has to say (302):

"3. Its *miraculousness*. On this point, since I have been in the Catholic Church, I have found there is a difference of opinion. *Some* persons consider that the oil is the natural produce of the rock, and has ever flowed from it ; *others* that by a divine gift it flows from the relics ; and *others*, allowing that it now comes naturally from the rock, are disposed to hold that it was in its origin miraculous, as was the virtue of the pool of Bethesda.

" *This point must be settled, of course,* before the virtue of the oil can be ascribed to the sanctity of St. Walburga ; for myself, I neither have, nor ever have had, the means of going into the question : but I will take the opportunity of

---

[1] Is it possible that Hurrell Froude could have meant what he said (*Letters*, ii. 221) when he compared Newman's letter to Arnold "to a blow in the stomach"? Newman quotes it thus : " it is curious Froude compared my letter to Arnold to *a blow in the stomach.*"

&c.," and so he passes on to remarks about miracles in general.

In the first place, this is unfair; for he ought to have acknowledged—not without something approaching to shame —that the question of his "muddling" critic, "What has become of the oil for the last 240 years?" had really turned out to be a most pertinent one; and indeed it appears to have led Newman himself to discover that "*some* persons" —whether in the Church of Rome or not, he does not tell us—believe the oil to be now, and always, non-miraculous. In the next place, it betokens a culpable indolence; for it was surely in his power to write a letter of two lines to "The Superioress, The Convent of St. Walburga, Eichstadt, Germany," or else to the Bishop of the Diocese, if he preferred it; and by return of post he might have procured all the evidence (much of it unsound, but all of it interesting) which was sent to him in 1873, by a friend, the Rev. Corbinian Wandinger, apparently without any request on Newman's part, and which is to be found in the last edition of the *Apologia* (391-4). This evidence shows that St. Walburga's remains have sweated regularly "*from* 12 *October, the anniversary of depositing, to* 25 *February, the day of the death of St. Walburga,*" for centuries (except on an occasion of interdict, when *the sweating was suspended*); but that they will not sweat during the rest of the year, *except for special reasons*—as when the royal decree sanctioning the reopening of the Convent of St. Walburga was signed on 7 June 1835.[1] It shows also that at least two

---

[1] On this point, the evidence (302) is very interesting. The reader will soon perceive that the English is not Newman's.

"During all the year 1239" [the year of interdict] "not a single drop of liquor became visible on the coffin-plate of St. W. The contrary fact was stated on 7 June, 1835. *The case was opened on this day by chance,* passengers longing to see it. To their astonishment,

remarkable cures have been accomplished by it in this century; one of blindness ("persistent eyelid-cramp") attested by "the adjoined testimony of physicians" (which does not however appear as a separate or "adjoined" document but may possibly be embodied in the report);

they found the stone so *profusely dropping with oil that the golden vase fixed underneath was full to the brim*, whereas at this season *never before had been observed there any fluid*.

"*Some weeks later* arrived the long-wished-for royal decree which sanctioned the re-opening of the Convent of St. W., IT WAS SIGNED ON THAT VERY 7TH OF JUNE, 1835, by his Majesty King Louis I."

On this we may remark : (1) " the cave was opened *by chance*" ; it appears therefore to have been, *as a rule, kept shut*, during the non-sweating season ; (2) how therefore could it be ascertained that the relics *never* sweat from 25 February to 12 October, if, as a rule, *the cave is closed during that season ?* May there not have been other un-recorded exceptions besides the one mentioned above, which was only noticed "*by chance*" ?

(3) "The golden vase fixed underneath was *full to the brim*." We may reasonably suppose that this "golden vase," the receptacle of so precious a fluid, would hold a good deal more than one day's average supply : else there would be the obvious danger that the oil would be spilt and lost—which would be profane, besides being wasteful. Suppose it held three days' average supply (it probably, if it was to be on the safe side of profanity, held a good deal more—but we will say 'three'). Now the cave was *closed* at this season : therefore on 7 June, 1835, when it "was opened *by chance*," and was found "*full to the brim*," the obvious explanation is that the relics had been sweating, *at the average rate, for three days ;* consequently they had *begun sweating on* the *fourth* or *fifth* of *June*, 1835 ! What becomes then of the *coincidence* of the sweating with the signing of the decree on *the seventh* of June, 1835 ? The relics, it must appear, had been *too sanguine*, and had *antedated the happy event by at least three days !*

The Rev. Corbinian Wandinger (*Apol.* 391) tells us that there had " arisen a contest not long ago between two papers, a Catholic and a free-thinking one, about this very question, from which he ' collected materials.'" It is unfortunate that few, if any, of the " materials" collected from the latter source, appear in the report forwarded to Newman ; so that, in judging this question, we are not able to observe the golden rule of " hearing the other side."

the other, at St. Leonard's, Sussex, in 1858, which the Protestant doctor (394) refused to attest as miraculous, saying : " I believe the healing to be effected by the oil of St. Walburga ; but how, I don't know."

Why did not Newman get this information for himself? Was it that he was afraid of looking into the matter, as a possible bankrupt dislikes looking at his accounts for fear the balance should be on the wrong side? He may have thought it antecedently not improbable that miracles vouchsafed to former times of faith might be denied to modern incredulity ; so that he may have anticipated that a search in the eighteenth and nineteenth centuries might prove barren of miraculous fruit. More probably, however, his inertness was the logical result of his convictions. Strange though it may appear, he was right above in im-plying that he "had *no point to prove*" : it *was* proved already to his satisfaction ; additional evidence would not make the proof, *for him*, more cogent. *The belief in St. Walburga's oil, with him, seems to have been of the nature of belief in a God with us:* once *suggested by evidence*, the belief was grasped by faith and held for ever. The scaffold-ing of facts might be thrown down ; but *the faith remained.*

It is true that he has spoken of "a point" that "must be settled, of course, before the virtue of the oil can *be ascribed* to the sanctity of St. Walburga." But he ap-parently retains faith in the miracle himself ; for he goes on to say that (*Apol.* 303), "in a given case . . . the possibility of assigning a human cause for an event does not *ipso facto* prove that it is not miraculous" ; and that (*ib.*) "a Catholic," in a case of this kind, will not "admit that there has been no divine interference at all," "till some *experimen-tum crucis* can be found, such as to be decisive against" the supernatural cause. What *experimentum crucis* could be devised, he does not even suggest, nor does he indicate any belief that it could be devised. Probably, therefore, in admitting that "the virtue of the oil cannot be at present "ascribed" to St. Walburga, he means "ascribed in controversy, or, as against unbelievers": but, as regards himself, his own faith was altogether unshaken, both by the "some" who held that the oil had been natural always, and by the "others" who held that, though it had been miraculous once, it was natural now.

The important inference, then, from this "chain of evidence" constructed by Newman, is that he *had no notion of what " a chain of evidence" was, and had a supreme contempt for the facts necessary to construct such a "chain."* He showed his contempt for them at first, by not looking for them, and by deriding the critic who expected him to look for them; he shows his contempt for them afterwards by inserting in small print, in an obscure appendix, the testimony of his friend, the Rev. Corbinian Wandinger, sent to him in 1873, and by making no use of it in his text in order to prove the miraculousness of the alleged miracle. In p. 391 of this Appendix he calls the new evidence "Note on page 302": but there is no reference to it on page 302, not so much as a footnote, to call attention to it. Every one who knows how readers treat appendices, even when their attention *is* called to them, will readily believe that most of those who read Newman's own defence of St. Walburga will take no more notice of the Rev. Corbinian Wandinger's evidence on p. 391 than Newman himself takes of it on page 302 : and every one who knows how Newman despised such evidence, will believe no less readily that he was quite content that his readers should ignore it as completely as he ignored it himself. Why waste time about evidence and facts? Is not "Antecedent Probability" "the main point"?

CHAPTER VII

§ 25. *Why are they not all of "an historical character"?*

SEVEN miracles (134) "which have an historical character and accordingly are more celebrated than the rest" are enumerated with the promise that (135) "these and *other such* shall be considered separately." The seven are accordingly considered in an inquiry devoted to particular miracles; but no "*other such*," *i.e.* no other miracles "of an historical character" are added. In their place, there are substituted two miracles of a personal and comparatively private character, viz., the Change of Water to Oil by Narcissus, and the Change of the Course of the Lycus by Gregory Thaumaturgus. Why are these two put in the place of the "*other such*"?

That the former of these two was not considered by Newman himself a miracle of a historical character is proved by the fact that he himself mentions it, *apart from the "historical" miracles,* in the preceding section (133). And the latter, being mentioned by no original authority except Gregory Nyssen (118) "who lived about 120 years after" Thaumaturgus, can hardly be called a "historical" miracle. Yet the value of proof based upon miracles of the historical kind is obvious; they are open as it were to all the world; the converging testimony of many independent witnesses and of many circumstances, sometimes even the valuable because unwilling or indirect evidence of enemies, can be brought to bear upon them. Hence Newman was quite right in laying special stress on these miracles, and might be fairly charged with neglect of duty if he actually passed over "*other such*" miracles, having them at hand and yet substituting inferior miracles in their place. We have no right to impute to him such a dereliction. The fair and charitable, as well as reasonable, explanation, is that, when he came to look for the "*other such*," *he could not find them*. He was therefore forced to substitute for them the two private and personal miracles above mentioned. That was not his fault. His fault, if any, was, that he did not take us into his confidence, and tell us frankly that he had changed his mind, and *why* he had changed his mind.

We may be surprised that he passed over the Miracle of the Liquefaction of the Blood of St. Januarius for which, as I have pointed out above (p. 129) he " could not withstand the evidence " ;[1] but the explanation probably is, that he did not accept this Miracle till he entered the Church of Rome, and that, after that event, he did not think it worth while to modify the Essay in the direction of making the evidence for Miracles more cogent. On so unimportant a matter— unimportant at least as compared with antecedent probability—he probably thought that he had already spent more pains than enough.

---

[1] Comp. *Letters of the Rev. J. B. Mozley, D.D.* pp. 278, 279, "I do not remember myself ever expecting to be a spectator of the miracle of St. Januarius. Certainly it was *not a scene to confirm belief in miracles in any one who was shaky.*"

The following sections discuss, not the evidence for the several Miracles—which would require a volume to do it justice—but some prominent points in Newman's treatment of the evidence.

§ 26. *The Thundering Legion* (241—54)

The story is that, when a Roman army under the Emperor Marcus Aurelius, face to face with the enemy, was on the point of perishing through drought, some Christian soldiers in one of the Legions prayed for water. Rain fell, accompanied by lightning that terrified and routed their enemies and caused the Romans to gain the day; the Legion was ever afterwards known by the name of the Thundering Legion; the Emperor wrote to the Senate ascribing the victory to the prayers of the Christians. This story is told by Eusebius, *not on his own responsibility, but quoting Apollinaris and Tertullian ;* and Newman's conclusion is (251) : " Under these circumstances I do not see what remains to be proved. Here is an army in extreme jeopardy, with Christians in it ; the enemy is destroyed, and they are delivered. And Apollinaris, Tertullian, *and Eusebius,* attest that these Christians in the army prayed, and that the deliverance was felt at the time to be an answer to their prayers ; what remains but to accept their statement ? "

Upon this, we may remark :—

1. Eusebius (*Hist.* v. 5) "*attests*" *no part of the incident,* nor does he accept the responsibility of any part of it. He twice inserts "it is reported that," and adheres to "reported speech" throughout the narrative. The Pagan historians and the Christian writers, he says, differ as to the explanation of the facts ; and though he adds that " our writers, as

being friends of truth, have handed down the facts simply, and sincerely," (ἁπλῷ καὶ ἀκακοήθει τρόπῳ) this phrase does not exclude the possibility of unconscious exaggeration ; and he concludes with the significant words, "*But about these matters let each of my readers decide as he pleases.*"

2. Newman (242) *omits the second "it is reported that"* –which introduces the description of "the thunderbolts," and translates it as though it were the statement of Eusebius himself ; he *omits the significant conclusion* just quoted ; and he then goes on (251) to *make Eusebius "attest" what he has expressly declined to attest.* This is all the less excusable because he has shown himself perfectly alive to the meaning of the words " it is reported " in an earlier part of the Essay (122) : " The biographer not only is frequent in the phrases, '*it is said,*' '*it is reported,*' but he assigns as a reason for not relating more of St. Gregory's miracles that he may be *taxing the belief of his readers more than is fitting.*"

3. (242) "Again, Tertullian speaks of 'the letters of Marcus Aurelius, an Emperor of great character, in which he testifies to the quenching of that German thirst by the shower gained by the prayers of soldiers who happened to be Christians.' "

Now Newman is not here quoting from Eusebius. He refers us to Tertullian's *Apology*, ch. v. (the words of which *differ* from the extract in Eusebius) ; he *is professing to translate Tertullian ;* and the stilted style of the English might lead the reader to suppose that he is translating with scrupulous accuracy. But Tertullian's words are : " *Si* literae Marci Aurelii, gravissimi imperatoris, *requirantur* quibus . . . . contestatur," *i.e.,* "*If* the letter of the wise and judicious emperor Marcus Aurelius *were searched for and found*, in which he testifies. . . ." These words prove that *Tertullian knew of no such letter ;* he had probably heard a rumour about it, and was certain of it—as people will persist in being certain of convenient facts. This fault Newman elsewhere aggravates by calling this imaginary letter (246) "a formal document."

Bishop Lightfoot, *Apostolic Fathers*, part ii., vol. i. p. 473, confirms the view I have taken above. "The very language," he says, "in which he (Tertullian) asserts his claim, shows that he had *no direct and personal knowledge* of any such letter . . . He assumes that, *if sought among the archives*, the letter would be *found*." To this he adds, "Just in the same way he (Tertullian) elsewhere refers his heathen readers to *the official report which Pilate sent to Tiberius after the trial of Christ. He did not doubt that both documents would be found in the archives.*"

An interesting instance of the results of the doctrine of Antecedent Probability! First some Christian (i) *thinks* "There *ought to be* such a letter from Aurelius"; then (ii) some Christians say "There *must be* such a letter"; then (iii) Tertullian says "*There will be found* such a letter if you look for it"; then (iv) the cautious Eusebius, in his *Chronicle*, says "*It is said that* an epistle is extant"; then (v) Jerome, editing that Chronicle, drops the "*it is said*" and asserts boldly "*There is extant* an epistle"; then (at some uncertain date), but very early, (vi) the missing letter is *forged!*—(Lightfoot, *ib.* 474.)

4. Newman quotes (242) Tertullian *Ad Scapulam*, ch. 4, as stating that "Marcus Aurelius in the German expedition obtained showers in that thirst by the prayers offered up to God by Christian soldiers." But he omits the next sentence in which Tertullian says that, *whenever* there was a drought, and Christians and heathens prayed for rain, it was always the prayers of the Christians that *really* obtained the rain, and *that this was constantly happening.* This passage

shows that the so-called miracle was merely one of many (in Tertullian's opinion) wrought every year throughout the Roman Empire. As an advocate, Newman was not bound to give this ; as an inquirer, he was bound.

5. No other Father mentions this as a Christian Miracle, nor refers to the supposed recognition of it by the Emperor. Newman tacitly admits this silence ; but, after his manner (see p. 115 above), he adds a reference in a foot-note. " W. Lowth however refers to a passage in St. Cyprian, *ad Demetrian.* Routh, t. i. p. 153, It really seems *unreasonable to demand that every Father should write about everything.*"

True ; but if Henry V. or Henry VII., while persecuting the Lollards, had written to the House of Commons stating that he had been miraculously delivered from drought by the prayers of Lollards in his army, we might surely have expected that a good deal would have been heard about that, on the side of Protestant controversialists, during the next century or two. It must also force itself upon us that if the "passage in St. Cyprian, *ad Demetrian.* Routh, t. i. p. 153," was worth referring to, it was worth quoting ; for it is not likely to affect the general reader—except so far as it may leave him under the impression that " *after all, there may be something to be said on the other side.*" My previous experience in verifying Newman's references, and especially "Vid. Lucian. Peregr. &c. ap. Middlet. Inqu., p. 23," above (p. 115) has not induced me to think that it would be worth while to verify this one.

6. (254) "On the whole then we may conclude that *the facts* of this memorable occurrence are *as the early Christian writers state them . . .*"

The early Christian writers are three : Tertullian, Apollinaris, and Eusebius.

(i) Tertullian, as we have seen, states (on the strength of

his imagination) that Marcus Aurelius did what he did *not do*, and refers us to a document that had *no existence*. So much for Tertullian's "facts."

(ii) Apollinaris says that the Legion, in consequence of this miraculous thunderstorm, was called the "Thundering Legion." It was certainly called so (as Newman himself admits) *more than a hundred years before*, probably because the soldiers had on their shields an image of *Thundering Jupiter*. So much for the "facts" of Apollinaris.

(iii) Eusebius, as we have seen, attests *no* "facts," and so we can say nothing about them.

Further details are unnecessary. It will be sufficient to quote Newman's conclusion, viz., that *the thunderstorm occurred ;* but (254) "whether through miracle or not we cannot say for certain, but more probably not through miracle in the philosophical sense of the word. *All we know, and all we need know is, that* ' He made darkness . . and destroyed them.'" Here he quotes, in full, four verses from *Psalm* xviii. 11– 14.

Now this would be all very well for the conclusion of a sermon ; but it is not well, it is very ill, for the conclusion of an "Inquiry" into a particular Miracle, which, if it can be proved to be true by "cogent and complete evidence," will afford a basis for "recommending" a great number of other Ecclesiastical miracles to "the devout attention of the reader." For the serious "inquirer" into one of the alleged Nine great Historical Miracles of post-apostolic Christendom, it is mere trifling to be told that "*all he need know is*" *the truth of Ps. xviii.* 11-14. But the fact is that Newman *is* trifling. All his proposed inquiries are farces : and this is but one among many proofs of their farcical nature.

§ 27. *Change of Water into Oil by St. Narcissus* (255-60)

The following is Newman's account of this alleged miracle (255) : " Narcissus, Bishop of Jerusalem, when oil failed for the lamps on the vigil of Easter, sent the persons who had the care of them to the neighbouring well for water. When they brought it, he prayed over it, and it was changed into oil." A foot-note at the word " oil " refers to " Euseb. *Hist.* vi. 9," and gives us the very natural (but false) impression that Eusebius *relates this as having actually occurred ;* an impression all the more natural because we may remember what Newman has said before (133) : " Narcissus. . . sent persons to draw water instead ; which, on his praying over it, was changed into oil. Eusebius, who *relates this miracle, says that* small quantities of the oil *were preserved,* even to his time." On the following page (256) we are told that Eusebius relates another marvel, but not necessarily miraculous, about Narcissus ; how three men, who had falsely accused him of some great crime, and had imprecated three several curses upon themselves, were punished by the infliction of these very curses.

Now it is true that, on a later page (258), Newman says, " Eusebius notices pointedly that *it* was the tradition of the Church of Jerusalem." But this leaves us under the impression that "*it*" refers to *the whole* of this narrative about Narcissus, to the *non-miraculous,* as well as the miraculous part of it. In fact, however, Eusebius's " pointed " remark refers merely to the *first* of the two stories, the *miraculous* one. And further, Eusebius makes this *marked distinction between the two stories,* that he records the whole of the *miraculous* one with a " they say that," as a mere *report,* and the whole of the *non-miraculous* one as a *fact.* Hence

Newman's statement above quoted, "Eusebius says that small quantities of the oil were preserved even to his time," is *false*. What Eusebius says is, "and (*they say*) *that* among very many of the brethren, for a very long period, from that time right down to ours, a small specimen of the former marvel was preserved." The faults then, in this inquiry, are these, that by *mistranslation* on p. 133, and by *suppression* on pp. 225-60, we are left under the impression that Eusebius believed *these two stories to be equally credible*, whereas Eusebius, if accurately translated, tells us very plainly that he did not mind being responsible for the non-miraculous one, but *would not be responsible for the miraculous one.*

I could say more about this miracle and about the possibility of its being a true but non-miraculous occurrence, if Newman himself pressed it upon us as a miracle to be believed. But he declines to do this, although it is not easy to see why. He himself quotes (258) Jortin, (but without reference !) as quoting Pliny and Hardouin (but again without references !) to show that there were fountains "qui explent olei vicem." But it is apparently not for these, but for some other reasons (to me, after careful study of his words, quite unintelligible) that he gives up the miracle. He says that (258) "there seems sufficient ground to justify us in accepting this narrative as in truth *an instance of our Lord's gracious presence with His Church*, though the evidence is not so definite or minute as to enable us to *realize* the miracle . . . (259) we have *no doubt* about it, yet we cannot bring ourselves to say positively that we *believe* it. . . . I do not see that we can be said actually to *believe* in a miracle like that now in question, of which so little is known in detail, and which is *so little personally interesting to us.*"

What does Newman mean by "not *realizing*" the miracle?

If he means "not conceiving it vividly," "not drawing a clear picture of it"—is that defect of importance? In his *Letters* (ii. 274), he says to Keble, "My constant feeling, when I write, is that I do not *realize* things, but am merely drawing out intellectual conclusions—which, I need not say, is very uncomfortable." Here "not *realize*" seems to mean "not *really and heartily believe*"; and "draw out intellectual conclusions" seems to mean "draw out unpractical conclusions from unpractical, *i.e.* merely *hypothetical*, or merely *admitted*, or merely *professed*, principles." Now "not *realizing*," in this sense, means "*not believing in your heart* what you acknowledge that you are bound, both morally and mentally, to believe." For "not *realizing*," of this sort, "uncomfortable" is indeed a very euphemistic epithet; it might more justly be called "morally disastrous." Yet this view is confirmed by Newman himself who, when revising the letter to Keble just quoted, by way of explaining the passage about "not *realizing* things," added (*ib.*), "*Vide* a passage in my account of my Sicilian illness." We turn to it, and we find a passage written in 1834, in which he records his feelings during the illness of 1833, and pronounces them "in the main true" (*Letters* i. 416): "I seemed to see more and more my utter hollowness. I began to think of all my *professed principles*, and felt they were *mere intellectual deductions from one or two admitted truths.* I compared myself with Keble, and felt that I was merely developing *his, not my convictions.*"

This is a very painful confession indeed; for it amounts to saying that, when he was writing about religious matters, he felt that he did not *really believe*, and that he had no *convictions of his own.* Probably this is an exaggeration, springing naturally from a mind too self-introspective and apt to suspect evil where evil is not.

However, to return to the Oil of St. Narcissus ; if, by " not *realizing* " it, Newman means, as he appears to mean, " that he did not *heartily believe it*," we can hardly be expected to do what he himself did not do.   And, even if this meaning be denied, he has at least told us that "we cannot bring ourselves to say *positively* that we believe it," and that we cannot be said " *actually* to believe " in it. From all these rather bewildering propositions we seem to be safe in deducing at least this conclusion that the alleged Miracle of the Oil of St. Narcissus is not proved by evidence so "cogent or complete " as to commend other doubtful miracles to our " devout attention." Some of my readers may be disposed to go yet further, and to say that while perfectly " realizing " the alleged Miracle, they both " positively " and "actually " disbelieve it.

§ 28. *The Change of the Course of the river Lycus, by St. Gregory* (261-270).[1]

This incident is thus described (120) : "A large and vio lent stream. . . from time to time broke through the mounds which were erected along its course in the flat country and flooded the whole plain.   The inhabitants who were heathen, having heard the fame of Gregory's miracles, made application to him for relief.   He journeyed on foot to the place and stationed himself at the very opening which the stream had made in the mound.   Then, invoking Christ, he took his staff and fixed it in the mud : and then returned home.

[1] So described in the Table of Contents (p. x.), in the page-headings (261-70), and in the Index (p. 398) ; but on pp. 261 and Index, p. 397, it is called " *Miracle wrought on* the Course of the Lycus."

The miracles of this Saint are also described by Newman on pp. 118-21

The staff budded, grew, and became a tree, and the stream never passed it henceforth."[1]

This incident—which is described as being of similar character to the drying up of a lake at the prayer of the same Saint (*ib.*)—was related by Gregory of Nyssa (118) "who lived about 120 years after Gregory Thaumaturgus, and who, being a native and inhabitant of the same country, wrote from the traditions extant in it." Newman himself tells us that the biographer, frequently (122) uses the words "it is said," "it is reported," and that he (*ib.*) "assigns, as a reason for not relating more of St. Gregory's miracles, that he may be taxing the belief of his readers more than is fitting." Certainly some apology seems needed for such a miracle as (121) that of killing a Jew who was pretending death, as well as for others not mentioned by Newman but to be found (*sub voce*) in Smith's *Dictionary of Christian Biography*, in which we are told how Gregory desolated a city with a plague, and converted himself and his companion into two trees in order to elude their pursuers in a time of persecution!

What induced Newman to include in his Nine Miracles one found in such doubtful company and supported by such distant and unconfirmed testimony? His main reason seems to have been the belief that this particular miracle satisfied the following (267) "celebrated criterion of a miracle. . . that it should be sensible ; public ; *verified by some monument or observance ; and that, set up at the very time when it was wrought.*"

---

[1] Gregory Nyssen (*Migne*, vol. iii., p. 932) gives the prayer made by Thaumaturgus on this occasion, and says that the staff became a tree "*immediately, after no long time,*" which, I suppose, is the Greek way of expressing "almost immediately." He places the miracle far above the stopping of the Jordan by Joshua, and the drying up of the Red Sea by Moses. These details are not mentioned by Newman.

Now of course the force of this test of a "monument" depends upon its being obviously *erected for the purpose of attesting the fact in question.* A natural rock in the shape of a loaf of bread, will not "attest" a miraculous supply of bread ; but a rock *so shaped by the hand of man* might be some "attestation." In fact the "monument" "verifies" a miracle only so far as it approaches to the nature of an *inscription ;* and it is only when we have before us a monument of this kind—say, for example, the brass lectern which, at Leighton Buzzard, was said to have been constructed in memory of the gigantic buzzard which gave its name to the place (*Beau désert*), or the she-wolf suckling Romulus and Remus, set up in the Roman forum—that it is worth while considering its date and how far the verification is real.

Again, an "observance" may be a weighty verification, if it points *distinctly to a particular incident, showing that this and nothing else could have been its cause,* or at all events that this satisfactorily accounts for the "observance." But, as there is a natural tendency to find picturesque causes for results, care is needed before accepting at once an "observance," *e.g.* the institution of the order of the Garter, as a proof of a certain fact, *e.g.* that a particular lady's garter was picked up by a particular king upon a particular occasion.

Now what is the "monument set up at the very time when the miracle was wrought?" It is a *tree !* Gregory's staff, which budded and became a tree !

One would not pursue the subject further—for it ought not to be matter for jest, and yet cannot easily be matter for argument—if it did not show the tortuosity to which a clever man is driven who has brought himself to take plea-sure in believing such portents as these. In the first place, how can the tree be said to have been "set up when the *miracle was wrought,*" since, as Newman admits, there was nothing, for some years to come, to show that there *had been* a miracle (268) : " the success of St. Gregory's restraint upon the stream *could not be known till after an interval, or rather only in a course of years.*"

It ought rather therefore to be called *a prediction* that there *would be* a miracle than a monument showing that there *had been* a miracle. In the next place, what is there to show that the staff was erected *as a monument* or prediction ? We know that then, as now (Wetstein, *ad Luc.* xvii. 6), the custom of keeping together the embankments of the Nile by planting trees was so common that it was legally punishable to cut down such a tree. Why may not this sensible Saint—a pupil of Origen's, versed in physics, who (the reader may be quite sure) *has not said a word about a single one of his own miracles in his own extant works*, but who was by no means incapable, in a limestone or volcanic district, of predicting the " drying up of lakes " and the removal of vast rocks and some other so-called thaumaturgic acts—have made his unbelieving and barbarian neighbours practise what he himself had seen when he was staying with Origen in Egypt? He may have told them to plant saplings, and may have set the example himself—not without prayer, doubtless. The thing answered. Gregory's tree, or perhaps the biggest of the trees, became known as " Gregory's staff : " the *name* (121) (said his biographer) of the tree, viz. " the staff," existed even to his days as " a memorial of Gregory's grace and power." Why not ? But where is the miracle in all this ? And how is it reasonable to call the tree a " monument " of the miracle ?

And again, what is the " observance " ? None is recorded. Not even an annual pilgrimage to the tree ; nothing but " the conversion of the people benefited," which (268) " is, in its results, of the nature of a standing observance." But what is the proof—except the legend of Nyssen writing 120 years afterwards—that they *were* converted by *this* miracle when—according to Newman and Nyssen—*there were so many other miracles* to convert them?

Newman's only reply is, in effect, that they *must* have been converted *somehow by this river-miracle*, because Nyssen says so; and that they *could not have been converted by the mere restraint of the Course of the Lycus*, because that could not have been known to be a miracle at all for years afterwards; and *therefore* there probably was *something else* to convert them (268): "some probability is thereby added to the idea that there was something impressive and convincing, and such *the miracle wrought upon the staff would have been in a very eminent way.*"

Thus among his Nine select Miracles, Newman deliberately brings forward one, on the ground that it can satisfy sceptics because it is "verified" by a "monument" and an "observance"; and then he alleges, as an "observance," the fact (not proved) that people were converted by this particular miracle (not proved); and, as a "monument," he alleges a natural object, the existence of which is quite consistent with the absence of a miracle, and which can only be called a "monument" of a miracle on the supposition that the "monument" itself is a portentous miracle, requiring another "monument" to "verify" it!

Surely a miracle of this sort can recommend other miracles to none but those who have an actual hatred for the orderly course of Nature, and who take a pleasure in seeing what Newman ventures to call (103) its *prestige* lowered.

§ 29. *Appearance of the Cross to Constantine* (271—286)

The fourth miracle is the appearance (A.D. 311) to Constantine and his army—shortly before his victory over Maxentius—of a luminous cross in the sky, accompanied by a luminous sentence in Latin (or Greek, for accounts differ) " By this, conquer."

I shall do little more than give, in Newman's words, that testimony, " which *alone*," he says (281) " is direct and *trustworthy*," and his comment on it.

(281) " *Eusebius declares on the word of Constantine, who confirmed it with an oath, that Constantine, on his march, saw, together with his whole army, a luminous Cross in the sky above the mid-day sun, with the inscription, ' In this conquer : ' and that, in the ensuing night, he had a dream in which our Lord appeared with the Cross, and directed him to frame a standard like it as a means of victory in his contest with Maxentius. Such is the statement ascribed by Eusebius to Constantine ; and it must be added that the historian had no leaning towards over-easiness of belief, as many passages of his history show.*" A foot-note, added to explain " *over-easiness of belief*," says that Eusebius " omits mention of the dove in the martyrdom of Polycarp, of the miracles of St. Gregory Thaumaturgus, &c. In such miracles as he does record, he is careful not to commit himself to an absolute assent to them, but commonly introduces qualifying phrases."

The conclusion to which Newman leads us, then, is obviously this, that whereas Eusebius omits, or cautiously qualifies, *other* miraculous narratives, but inserts, and does not qualify, the *present* one, *Eusebius believed this miracle to be a fact and a miraculous fact*.

Now this affords one among many other instances showing how the truism that "the *direct* effect of evidence must be to create a presumption in favour of a fact," leads Newman, in practice, to neglect the *indirect* effect of evidence. For, if we consider the position of Eusebius in relation to this miraculous narrative, we shall see that he was obliged to weigh his words very carefully, and consequently that we ought to weigh them carefully too. He was writing, not a history of the Church nor of the times, but a Life of Constantine. He could not possibly omit a narrative imparted to him by the Emperor himself, confirmed by an imperial oath, and (no doubt) familiar to the imperial family and household. He could not here use his favourite device of interpolating "it is said," "it is reported," "they say." Still less could he openly express his disbelief of the story, and his belief that the lapse of twenty-six years from the time of the alleged occurrence had weakened or confused the Emperor's memory and unduly strengthened his imagination. But what he could do was to write (*Life of Constantine,* i. 28), "that a most wonderful sign appeared, which, *had any other person given a relation of it, would not easily have been received as true ;* but, *since* the Emperor himself told it to us who write this history, *a long while afterwards, who would hereafter doubt* of giving credit to his narrative ?" [1]

---

[1] Newman does not seem to credit this statement of Eusebius ; he seems to feel (and reasonably enough) that if this public portent occurred, Eusebius *must have known of it, a quarter of a century before, at the time when he described the battle ;* and so he makes the curious suggestion that Eusebius may have omitted it *because it was not* "*a public event*"—being witnessed by *only,* say 30,000 *men,* constituting an imperial army—(282) : "It is remarkable too that *even* Eusebius does not mention it in his History, but in his Life of Constantine, as if, *instead of its being a public event, it were but a visitation or providence personal to the Emperor.*"

Yet Newman himself with perfect justice says that (273) "the

Was it easy for a court-historian (for a man who writes an Emperor's life for an Emperor's family, *is* a court-historian) to express much more clearly the meaning that we can read between these words?—

"Although I wrote a detailed history of the imperial victory over Maxentius and of the divine favour vouchsafed to Constantine, and a good many years have passed since that, yet I never heard a word about this miracle at the time when I was writing; nor, since then, did I ever hear a word about it from any one of the many thousands who (if it took place) saw it, or from any one of the many more thousands to whom (if it had taken place) they must have spoken about it. Of course apparitions of an indefinite kind are common enough, and I don't stick at trifles; I have myself (*Life of Const.* ii. 6) related an apparition of phantasmal soldiers which appeared in the cities of Asia, not long after the alleged vision of the Cross. But even there I inserted 'they say,' so as to be safe. *But a sentence, seen by* 30,000 *men, written in the sky*—that's quite a different thing! Well, probably the Emperor saw something like a Cross in the sky, and I dare say his courtiers saw it; I am *sure they* saw it if he told them *he* saw it. Then on the same night, he had a dream, and saw, in his dream, the words, IN THIS CONQUER. Then, in after years, he gradually came to mix the sight and the dream, the Cross and the sentence, up together. And then, because

approaching conversion of the Roman empire in the person of its head, was *as great an event as any in Christian history*," and that (*ib*) " if any event might be said to *call for* a miracle, it was this." Surely, the most public " event" in Christian History "called for" something more than a private or " personal " miracle. Newman generally shows great respect for Eusebius; but it is interesting to see how, on this and other occasions, he can persuade himself (where it is convenient to do so) that the historian must have been an absolute fool.

his officers had said they saw the *Cross*, he came to fancy, many years afterwards, that they had said they saw the *sentence ;* or perhaps—for I know what human nature is in the Imperial Court—some of them may have humoured him by saying they *did* see the sentence.

" What am I to do with this miracle ? I will be as fair as I can. *It would not exactly do for me to say I don't believe* this story, as it stands ; *but I may venture to say that none would have readily believed it if the Emperor had not attested it by his oath.*"

If this is not an improbable explanation of the passage of Eusebius, Newman committed a double error of judgment. In the first place he ought to have given the passage—containing as it does *the only " direct and trustworthy testimony "*—in the exact words of the historian, so that we might have formed a judgment of the *indirect,* as well as the direct, *effect of the evidence.* In the next place, he is wrong in leading us to the inference that the cautious historian believed the story. That inference, it is true, is not stated ; it is only implied in the words above quoted : "Such is the statement ascribed by Eusebius to Constantine . . . . and it must be added that *the historian had no leanings towards over-easiness of belief" :* but if the intention had been —which I am sure it was not--to deceive the reader, the words could not have been more skilfully put together. That Eusebius "ascribed" the words to Constantine there is no doubt ; just as the *Times* daily "ascribes" words to members of Parliament in its Parliamentary reports. But Newman quietly assumes that, because Eusebius *reported* what Constantine said, Eusebius therefore *believed* it ; and that is a very different thing.

One more noteworthy feature in Newman's discussion of this miracle is the manner in which he tries to explain how a whole army could see a luminous Greek or Latin sentence in the sky promising them victory; how, after seeing it, they could march through the towns and villages of Gaul and Italy; how, after obtaining the miraculously promised victory, they could enter Rome in triumph amid the acclamations of the senate and people : and yet the Emperor, his generals, officers, and soldiers, could form so unanimous a conspiracy of silence before the battle, and adhere to their conspiracy with such resolution after the battle, that the careful historian Eusebius, writing a detailed account of the battle together with the events that preceded and followed it, made no mention whatever of this portent in his history, and further, when writing twenty-six years afterwards, tells us in effect, that he never heard of it from any one but the Emperor, long after the alleged occurrence, and that, but for the imperial oath, no one would readily believe it.

This difficulty Newman meets by saying that (283) : "the troops of Constantine saw the vision and marched on [*surely the " marching on" would be the very thing to circulate the news*]; they left behind them a vague testimony which would fall misshaped and distorted on the very ears that heard it, which would soon be filled out with fictitious details because the true were not forthcoming." [*How, about so very definite a matter, could the testimony be "vague"? Three words could easily be remembered or written. No doubt, we might expect exaggerations. But why should we expect silence about the plain fact that* IN THIS CONQUER *had been seen by, say,* 30,000 *men written luminously in the sky?*]

Besides this, he has really nothing to allege except that an army (283) "is *cut off from the world*, it has no home, it acts as one man, it is of an *incommunicative* nature or at least does not admit of questioning."

An army on the march "cut off from the world"! An

army entering Rome, as liberators, "incommunicative"!
As if the Duke of Cambridge could have marched from
Manchester to London during the Crimean war with 30,000
men who had seen, simultaneously with himself, IN THIS
CONQUER written in the sky, and could have kept the
secret, he and the 30,000, so quiet—for some inscrutable
reason and by some inconceivable means—that Mr.
Kinglake writing the history of the war, should know
nothing about it, and should hear of it for the first time long
afterwards from the Duke himself, and should then
declare, twenty-six years after the alleged portent, that if any
other person but the Duke had related it, and *if the Duke
had not confirmed it with an oath,* " *it would not easily have
been received as true* "!

§ 30 *St. Helena's Discovery of the Holy Cross* (287—326)

The alleged miracle, or rather miracles, are these, 1st,
the discovery of the Cross by Helena the mother of
Constantine A.D. 326 ; 2nd, miraculous cures by which it was
distinguished from the crosses of the two thieves, simultaneously discovered; 3rd, the miraculous multiplication of the
wood, in the form of relics scattered through Christendom.

The most interesting feature in Newman's inquiry is his
method of dealing with the silence of Eusebius, who is said
to have written in 337 A.D. about eleven years after the
alleged Discovery.

All who describe the discovery of the Cross agree that it
was found in the course of an excavation ; and Eusebius, in
his *Life of Constantine* (iii. 21—40), thus relates the motives
that led the Emperor to undertake this work.   Impious men,
he says, had heaped earth upon the Holy Sepulchre ; more
than that, they had actually built a Temple of Venus upon

these accumulations, so that it might well seem hopeless to
recover the actual Cave which had received our Lord's body,
but which now seemed lost and perhaps shattered beneath
the foundations of a heathen temple.   However the Emperor,
stimulated by Divine encouragement, determined at all
events to destroy the Temple of Venus and to build an
Oratory on the sacred soil below.

The historian then gives a minute account of the excavation itself, revealing the Sepulchre "contrary to all
expectation," as though " the monument of our Saviour's
resurrection " itself experienced a resurrection in being
restored to the light of day ; of the Emperor's reception of
the marvellous and almost miraculous news ; and of his
determination to build a Church over the Sepulchre and
the site of the Crucifixion.   But he nowhere mentions any
discovery of the Holy Cross in the course of the excavation ;
nor does he mention Helena, the Emperor's mother, as
having anything to do with the matter.   Now the discovery
of the Cross, if true, is felt by all to be the central event of
the narrative.   Eusebius could not (it would seem) omit the
very core or kernel of his story— an event also reflecting such
lustre upon the Emperor whose life he was writing, and in
whose career the Cross had played so prominent a part.
There are very many other grounds for disbelieving in St.
Helena's Discovery story ; but, at the very outset, *the negative
testimony arising from the silence of Eusebius* is almost fatal
to it, unless that silence can be explained.

How then shall this deadly silence be neutralized ?   One
way, under ordinary circumstances, would be to say (252)
" It really seems unreasonable to demand that every Father
should write about everything "; but that would be too
audacious here.   Newman therefore resorts to the following
fallacy, not stated, but quietly assumed : " If an author

omits anything, however unimportant, we ought not to be
surprised at his omitting anything else, however essential."
On this he bases the following argument, in effect : " Eusebius
while describing Helena's visit to the East in some detail,
does not say that she visited Jerusalem ; but she could not
have left unvisited so sacred a place. Well then, since he
omits her visit to Jerusalem, and yet that must have been a
fact, we are justified in assuming that, although he omitted
her discovery of the Cross, yet that may have been a fact
too."

This plausibility bursts at once at the touch of the following truism : " The silence of an author concerning some
ordinary alleged fact not necessary to his context does not
throw suspicion on the allegation ; but silence about some
fact extraordinary or necessary (if true) to give completeness
to the context, does throw suspicion on the allegation."

Besides, to any one who attentively examines the narrative
of Eusebius, and who can understand the meaning of
implied mention, it will be obvious that the historian is not
really "silent" about Helena's visit to Jerusalem, but that
he omits *express* mention of it because, *whereas elsewhere she
did several notable things, she did nothing notable here.* The
reader shall judge for himself. After describing at great
length (*Life of Constantine*, iii. 25—40) the discovery of the
Holy Sepulchre by the excavators under the orders of
Constantine, the Emperor's joy, his orders for the construction of the Church of the Holy Sepulchre, and the details
of the building—and all this without one word about
Helena—he then in a single section tells us (*ib.* 41) that the
Emperor adorned with offerings the cave at Bethlehem and
the cave on Mount Olivet (whence our Lord was said to
have ascended), "and these places he adorned most magni-
ficently and [at the same time] eternized the memory of his

own mother who was ministering (διηκονεῖτο) so great a good to mankind : for (*ib.* 42), in regard that she had resolved to pay the debt of her pious affection to God. . . . she came in haste that she might visit the land which all should reverence, and, with a care and solicitude truly royal, might make a visit to the Eastern provinces, cities, and peoples. But after she had given a due veneration to that prophetic expression which runs thus, ' *Let us go to worship at the place where his feet have stood*' (Ps. cxxxii. 7, *Septuagint*), immediately she left the fruit of her own piety even to posterity ; (*ib.* 43) she forthwith dedicates two Churches " ; and then he describes in detail the buildings she erected at Bethlehem and at Olivet, the Emperor's offerings thereat, and Helena's subsequent death.

In the face of this evidence, if we were to accuse Eusebius of being " silent about Helena's visit to Jerusalem," might he not defend himself with a just brusqueness? " 'Silent about Helena's visit to Jerusalem ' ! What do you take me for, or what must I take you for? Helena visited Jerusalem, of course. Did I not as good as say so to any reader with a spark of sense? Did I not say she visited Olivet ? Did I not say she built a church there? I gave my Christian readers credit for knowing *where Olivet is*. How *could* she visit Olivet without visiting Jerusalem ? How *could* a person visit Primrose Hill and build a church on the top of it without visiting London ? Helena visited Jerusalem of course, as she visited also Nazareth and the other sacred places ' where Christ's feet had stood ', *but I omitted those because she did nothing in those*, while I inserted Bethlehem and Olivet because she did *something in these*."

This would seem a very reasonable defence. And the inevitable conclusion from the historian's silence *in this context, and in the special circumstances of the case*, is one of two : *either* (1) Eusebius, writing ten years after Helena's alleged discovery of the Cross, and having the amplest possible means for obtaining the most minute information, had nevertheless *not heard of the allegation ; or* (2) he had heard of it, and *disbelieved it.*

How natural for us to adopt here the same explanation of the historian's silence which Newman himself gave us above (281) : "the historian, *i.e.* Eusebius, had *no leaning towards over-easiness of belief" !*

But Newman will have none of this explanation *here.* Instead of arguing *here,* "He omitted it because he did not believe it," he argues, in effect : "He omitted ; but he must have known it ; and he need not necessarily have omitted it owing to disbelieving it ; for we find him omitting other things that he must have believed to be true." "It *must have been well known to Eusebius,*" says Newman, for ten years after he wrote, Cyril of Jerusalem publicly declared that fragments of the Holy Cross, miraculously multiplied, had filled the world. We agree : *it must have been well-known to Eusebius.* Why was he silent then ? Because *he rejected it as a discreditable imposture.*

What has Newman to say against this explanation ? Simply this (295) : "His silence about it did not *necessarily* proceed from disbelief ; because he is *silent about St. Helena's search after it,* nay, as I have said above, *even about her visiting Jerusalem,* an historical fact which cannot be gainsaid." In other words the historian's silence about one fact, which we deny, is to be explained by his silence about a second fact, *which we deny also,* and about a third fact which the historian implies, but had *no motive for expressly mentioning.* Test this reasoning by a more modern application, and how will it sound ? "So-and-so's silence about the discovery of the sea-serpent by Drake during his voyage round the world, did not *necessarily* proceed from disbelief; because—he is *silent about Drake's having fitted out an expedition to search for the sea-serpent*, nay, as I have said above, *even about Drake's having touched at Java*, an historical fact which cannot be gainsaid "!

---

§ 31. *Further Details of the alleged Discovery*

Those who care to pursue the subject further may be interested in the following details :—

1. The only original evidence (293) for the *discovery* of the Cross is that of Cyril of Jerusalem concerning the *multiplication* of the wood of the Cross, in his Catechetical Lectures, said to have been delivered by him as a Priest A.D. 347, where he says (*Catech.* iv. 10) "the whole world is filled with the wood of the Cross," and uses many similar phrases.[1]

[1] A close examination of these phrases might lead a charitable modern reader to think that they might originally bear a spiritual meaning. Cyril's very effective lectures must have been made all the more effective by his power of calling to witness the Sepulchre, the Stone, the Clefts in the Rock, all of which were before the eyes of his audience. In the same way, he would point to the Cross. "The Cross," he says, "brought mankind together, subjected the Persians, tamed the Scythians, heals diseases, drives out devils." It would be an easy transition to say, "The Cross has filled the world," "All partake of the Cross in a spirit of faith." The next transition is from "the Cross" to "the Holy Wood" or "the Wood of the Cross." Then we have only to suppose that these expressions were taken literally; and that the mistake was found to "tend to devotion," or to be "edifying"; and that it seemed a pity to discourage a "pious belief."

Such an explanation might not perhaps make Cyril's conduct seem better, but would make it more intelligible. And the same explanation, I think, might apply to some other Ecclesiastical miracles such as the sacred Bread becoming a cinder (134) in the hands of an unworthy com-

2. A possibly genuine letter of Cyril (294) (the gross flattery of Constantius renders it probable that, at all events, it was written early, when such flattery was worth perpetrating) says to the son of Constantine : " In the time of thy father. . . the salutary Wood of the Cross was found in Jerusalem, divine grace granting the discovery of the hidden holy places to one who laudably pursued (ζητοῦντι) religious objects."

But Newman's translation, which I give above, fails to point out (1) that the *masculine* ("one who was pursuing" or " (*him*), when pursuing") *excludes Helena*, no less decidedly than Eusebius does ; (2) that the words "*was found* in the time of," by no means indicate that Constantine had found the Cross ; on the contrary they are consistent with the supposition that the Cross had appeared after the first news of the discovery of the Sepulchre.

3. Newman quotes (292) Eusebius's commentary on Ps. lxxxvii 13, " Dost thou show wonders among the dead ? " It runs thus, " If any one will give his attention to the marvels which in our time have been performed at the Sepulchre and the Martyry of our Saviour, truly he will perceive how the prediction has been fulfilled in the event." He seems to think that this must allude to the " miracles of healing" by which, according to the later writers, the true Cross was distinguished from the Crosses of the Thieves, and adds, in a foot-note, " Zaccaria strangely denies the

---

municant. The Priest used the expression metaphorically; the Congregation took it literally ; and, between them, they made a miracle.

If Cyril was an impostor, it will be an early illustration of what Pope Gregory said (Dean Church's *Miscellaneous Essays*, p. 227) to a Greek correspondent of his, " We have not your wit, but neither have we your cheating tricks (*imposturas*)." Gregory also (*ib.*) asked John the Faster, Patriarch of Constantinople, whether his noted abstinence obliged him to "abstain from *the truth*."

allusion ;" but even if it did refer to acts of healing, such acts do not postulate the discovery of the Cross; surely the Holy Sepulchre would have sufficed to produce them! And miracles of faith-healing (of a kind) were so common that they might possibly have occurred at the discovery of the Sepulchre, without in the least obliging Eusebius to break his minute and gradually developed narrative by inserting them.

But those who have noted the expression of Eusebius above, viz. that the discovery of the Sepulchre was "*contrary to all hope*," *and a kind of resurrection of the scene of resurrection itself*, and those who refer to Constantine's letter expressing his joyful *amazement* at the discovery as being "a miracle which no rhetoric could set forth" (*Life of C.* iii. 29) will (as it seems to me) believe that the "marvels" of the Eusebian Commentary refer to the bringing to light of the lost Sepulchre, and to nothing else.[1]

4. (299) Ambrose (395 A.D.) and Chrysostom (about 394 A.D.) speak of *three* crosses, and say that the true one was known from the crosses of the thieves by the title which Pilate had fixed on it.

But Paulinus and Rufinus (about 400 A.D.), and Socrates, Theodoret, and Sozomen (about 440 A.D.) say that the true Cross was known by a miracle wrought, either on a corpse,

---

[1] In the letter of Constantine above quoted, occur the only words in Eusebius that seem capable of suggesting the Cross, viz. τὸ γνώρισμα τοῦ πάθους, "the *token* of the *passion*." But it must be remembered that the excavation was supposed to have brought to light, not only the Sepulchre, but also Golgotha ; and it seems quite possible that this phrase may have been used *briefly* to mean "the tokens, or signs of recognition, of the *suffering, death, and resurrection* of Christ." In a very few years, μαρτύριον became the regular word to denote the whole site and the Church above it ; but this letter was written immediately upon the receipt of the news of the discovery, and so γνώρισμα may here be used for μαρτύριον.

N

or on a sick person.   Paulinus adds "that the portion of the Cross kept at Jerusalem gave off fragments of itself without diminishing."   Most of these writers, including Socrates, "speak of the nails as found at the same time."   "Such," says Newman (300), "is the evidence arranged in order of time."

But why, while mentioning "Socrates," has Newman omitted the important evidence of that historian (i. 17), who tells us upon the authority of "almost all the inhabitants in Constantinople," that the Empress Helena erected a magnificent church on the sacred site which *she called* New Jerusalem,[1] and that she forwarded one half of the Cross to Constantine ! who *enclosed it in a statue of himself,* erected in the market-place of Constantinople ! and that the nails that had pierced Christ's hands and feet were *converted by the Emperor into* " *bridles and a helmet which he used in his military expeditions* " !

The fact is, that—as is indicated by the variations between "three crosses " and one cross, miracles and no miracle, this miracle and that miracle—*all these later writers knew nothing whatever about the Discovery of the Cross except from rumour or from one another.*   And this last paragraph from Socrates, if Newman had inserted it, would have tended to show the hollowness of all this later testimony.   But Newman's theory is that the " *direct* effect of evidence " must be to create a presumption in favour of the alleged fact, and cannot create a presumption the other way ; and his *practice* is, to apply the same rule to the *indirect* effect of evidence.

5. All this unsatisfactory variation in the evidence, Newman not only regards as of no account, but finds a

---

[1] A mere misunderstanding of a Eusebian metaphor ! Eusebius means that *Constantine* built a church, which rose up—*a New Jerusalem, so to speak*—over against the Old Jerusalem.

parallel to these exaggerations in the Samaritan Woman's exaggeration, " He told me all that ever I did ;" and he seeks to turn the tables against serious seekers after truth, and make a joke of Protestants who would probably have wished to (298) "cross-examine" the woman !

6. (301) "The very fact that a beam of wood should be found undecayed after so long a continuance in the earth would be, in some cases a miracle." [1]

It would.   But Newman does not see that, on this supposition, we must also suppose—if *three* crosses were found—that there were *three* miracles.   For if two crosses were found half rotted, and one miraculously sound, the discoverers would have known at once the true Cross, and would have needed no test to distinguish it from the others.

Therefore we are called upon to believe that the crosses of the two thieves were *miraculously preserved—in order to create a preliminary confusion, so that a miracle might be wrought afterwards for the purpose of distinguishing them from the true Cross.*   I said above "Newman does not see" this. That was a rash assumption and an injustice to his throughgoing consistency.   Very probably he *did* see it, and liked the miracle all the better.

Again, Newman, who adds (301) "there were too many bones surely in 'the place of a skull' to discriminate the fact," evidently supposes that Golgotha, "the place of a skull," was a common burial-place for malefactors.   Then why not for the crosses of other malefactors as well as for the crosses of the two thieves, and of our Lord?   And, if so, why were

---

[1] Newman says (287), "it was the custom of the Jews to bury the instruments of death with the corpses of the malefactors," and gives references, which I have not examined.   Nor do I know whether this custom extended to crucifixion, and whether the Romans acted on it.

only three crosses found? Ought there not to have been
nearer three hundred? And, on that supposition, ought
there not to have been three hundred miracles wrought on
the three hundred crosses? For why should a miracle be
wrought upon the cross of the impenitent thief, and none
upon the crosses of the poor fellows, much less guilty perhaps, who had suffered a week before, or a month, or a year
before? This is a great difficulty. Socrates gets us out
of it—but gets us into a greater one—by telling us that
the three crosses were found, *not on Golgotha* but *in the
Sepulchre* (ἐν τῷ μνήματι).

7. After giving in detail (287—8), but without any references, the later legendary account which describes Helena
as searching " among other objects," for " the Cross," and
" availing herself of the assistance of the most learned," &c.,
Newman adds (289) " Hitherto the *main outlines of the
history are confirmed by Eusebius*, though. . . . "; and again
(295) " From the evidence of St. Cyril *and the passages of
Eusebius*, we gain then as much as this : that the discovery
of the Holy Cross was a received fact twenty years after St.
Helena's search for the Holy Sepulchre ; that it was
notorious . . . ; hence that the professed discovery must
have taken place . . . ; and that it must have been well
known to Eusebius . . . ; further that his silence about it
did not necessarily proceed from disbelief."

This is extremely misleading. The first passage represents
Eusebius as " confirming " that about which he is absolutely
and conspicuously silent. And although the second passage
is not exactly false, it leads the careless reader to blend
together " Cyril " and " the passages of Eusebius," instead
of keeping in mind that *whatever Cyril attests, Eusebius not
only does not attest, but, by implication, denies.*

In ordinary writers such language would be scarcely honest.

8. "Such," Newman tells us (300), "is the *evidence* arranged in order of time in behalf of this most solemn and arresting occurrence."

We have seen what it is : (i) Eusebius gives *no positive evidence* for it, and powerful negative evidence against it ; (ii) Cyril gives evidence for the multiplication of the wood of the Cross, but *none as to its discovery*, except in a possibly genuine letter which says that "it was found in the time of Constantine," but it does not add "by whom ; " (iii) a host of writers follow, who record conflicting and, at least in one case, disgusting legends—nothing, so far as we can judge, that is derived from any trustworthy authority.

But what as to "the *silence* arranged in order of time "? This question is suggested to us by a foot-note appended by Newman to the word " occurrence " in the last quotation : "St. Jerome too says of St. Paula A.D. 386, ' Prostrataque ante Crucem, quasi pendentem Dominum cerneret, adorabat ' "—which makes us say in amazement, " Can this,— which might be said about any woman before any Cross in any Church—be intended to prove that the ' cross ' here mentioned was *the discovered Cross ?* " And then we reflect that Jerome lived in Bethlehem for twenty-four years (from 386 A.D. to 420) and *would know all about the real Cross if it was in Jerusalem.* Yet he must be supposed (from Newman's taking refuge in this quotation) to say, in the whole of his voluminous works, not a word about it. Nor does Athanasius (so far as Newman helps us) who was in Alexandria about the very time when, *teste* Cyril, " the whole earth," and therefore of course Alexandria, was being " filled with fragments of the Cross." Yet Athanasius, shortly after 355 A.D. spent six years in seclusion and writing, and was not averse to recording wonders, as is seen from his Life of St. Anthony. Nor are the Eastern Bishops

Gregory Nazianzen and Gregory of Nyssa called to give evidence.

About an ordinary miracle such silence would be perfectly intelligible.   But if in their childhood or youth the true Cross of Christ was found, and if in their youth or middle age, fragments of this Cross were being imported into every diocese in Christendom, it would be scarcely satisfactory to explain silence on so profoundly interesting and so practically important a matter by the ordinary expedient (252)— " It really seems unreasonable to demand that every Father should write about everything."   Yet Newman suggests no other explanation.

§ 32.   *The Death of Arius* (327-333)

The alleged facts are these, and there is no reason to doubt their substantial truth.   Constantine, on a Saturday, had ordered Alexander, Bishop of Constantinople, to receive the heretical Arius into the communion of the Church on the following day (Sunday).   The bishop refused, and retired from the anger of the Emperor.   At 3 P.M. on that same day the Bishop prayed, in the presence of Macarius, that, if Arius was destined to communicate to-morrow, he himself might be dismissed from life so as to escape contamination ; or else, if God purposed to spare the Church, then that Arius might be "taken away."   This prayer reported by Macarius to Athanasius, has been recorded by the latter in his treatise on the death of Arius.   That same evening, Arius, in the square of Constantine, was suddenly seized with bowel-complaint and died.

Putting the moral question absolutely aside, we have to ask what proof is here of a miracle.   We have no proof that poison may not have been employed by some of the baser

partisans of the Athanasian party, without the sanction of
their leaders. We have no knowledge of the state of Arius's
health at the time, nor of the extent to which it may have
been impaired by the excitement of a long controversy
(though it seemed likely at the time to end in his favour) ;
by the knowledge that a large part of Constantinople
was praying for, or at least desiring his destruction ; or
by other purely physical causes. We have no knowledge, and no power of knowing, how many other
Christian Bishops have prayed that their adversaries might
be "taken away," and prayed in vain. Supposing such
prayers to have been uttered, say, 10,000 times, is it
miraculous, is it even improbable, that, *say ten or eleven
times in ten thousand*, a man so prayed against, should *die
at the very time when he was wished to die ?* Besides, no
one asserts in this instance, that the death occurred simultaneously with the prayer. If that had been the case, we
might have been more interested in the story, as a possible
instance of "brain-wave" influence of a malignant kind ;
but the most that is asserted is, that it took place one or two
hours afterwards. Nor can the advocates lay stress even
upon the shortness of the interval as being only "one or
two hours " : for the Bishop of Constantinople, who had been
for some time prepared for the crisis, had already (327)
"shut himself up in the church and continued *in supplica-
tion for several days and nights*." How many times therefore
may he not have uttered already this prayer that Arius
might be "taken away"? Probably for "*several days and
nights*" *before it actually took place.*

"But," it may be urged, "the case of Arius ought not to
be confused with that of any casual man prayed against.
He represented Heresy incarnate. Nor is the 'shortness of
the interval' to the point, but the fact that he died before

communicating. The *nearer*, in fact, *to his triumph*, the more apparent the miracle." The former of these pleas may make a miracle in this case appear to some minds more *antecedently probable ;* but we are not now considering antecedent probability, but evidence of the miraculous ; and undoubtedly an extraordinary amount of coincidence might impress us as verging on evidence of the miraculous. But let us grant the force of the latter objection ; "*the nearer to the triumph,* the more apparent the miracle." Probe this objection, and what does it amount to? Simply to this, that the objector prefers *one kind of coincidence to another :* he thinks it, so to speak, more effective, more dramatic, that Heresy incarnate should die, *not* at the moment when he was being prayed against, but *at the moment when he was kneeling at the altar, on the point of receiving the sacred elements.* We agree. It would have been more effective ; much more effective. But *an interval of a whole day* makes the miracle—from the point of view of *that* coincidence— *very ineffective.* If that was intended, it ought, so to speak, to have been managed better.

In all this, we are supposing (perhaps uncharitably) that Macarius has not in the least exaggerated the prayer of Alexander—although of course there would be an immense temptation, *after Arius's actual death*, to read into the prayer of Alexander a very much more precise request than perhaps was actually uttered—and that Athanasius has not exaggerated what Macarius reported to him. We give the advocates of the so-called Miracle the full benefit of the facts, and we say that the evidence of the facts (for the purpose of proving a miracle) is neither cogent nor complete enough to " recommend other miracles to our attention "— still less to our " *devout* attention."

§ 33. *The Fiery Eruption on Julian's Attempt to Rebuild the Temple* (334-347)

There is better evidence for this, than for any of the preceding miracles. The facts are, as stated by Newman, that the Emperor Julian, early in the year 363 A.D. gave orders for the rebuilding of the Temple of Jerusalem, and that the work was given up before Julian's death in June 363 A.D. It is alleged that some special deterring incident, whether thunderbolts, fiery eruption, or what else, caused the work to be given up, and that this was of a miraculous nature.

The first witness is Gregory Nazianzen, who wrote at Nazianzus, late in 363 or early in 364, two invectives against Julian, in which he describes the "notorious wonder in the mouths of all." Whenever wonders "in the mouths of all" are described by those who have not seen them, we know what to expect. Accordingly we are not surprised to hear that (335) "the spades and pickaxes" used for the excavations, "were of silver, and the rubbish was removed in mantles of silk and purple"; that the miraculous fire which stopped the work (336) met some who fled from it, at the door of a neighbouring church to which they were resorting for safety "and forced them back with the loss either of life or of their extremities"; and that afterwards (*ib.*) "in the sky appeared a luminous cross surrounded by a circle."

Some, besides Newman, have thought that Julian himself (338) bore witness to his own failure in a very long letter (of uncertain date and only fragmentarily preserved) written about the duties of a priest :[1] but there are two objections to this belief.

In the first place there is an objection as to time. On

[1] *Dictionary of Christian Biography*, iii. 491.

March 5, A.D. 363 Julian began his Persian campaign, which, one would suppose, would not have left him leisure during the preceding month to write a very long letter upon sacerdotal subjects. If, as Newman says (335), "*in the year 363, Julian. . . determined* to rebuild the Temple," it would seem that the *actual operations* would hardly begin till February; and, allowing only a month for the workmen to excavate and get down to the foundations near which (as we shall presently see) the flames are said to have burst out, the eruption would not take place till *the beginning of March at earliest* (about which time Julian would be quitting Antioch for Persia), and may very well have been a month or two later. Then we have to bear in mind that, according to Newman (336), "the workmen returned to their work," but the fire burst out "*again and again*, as often as they renewed the attempt." And this implies more waste of time. Thus, there seems no time for the news to come to Julian in Antioch, and for Julian to compose a letter (of which a fragment amounts to *twenty-two pages* in his works) upon the Duties of a Priest, with a disputable allusion to the failure of operations in Jerusalem, which he must be supposed to have heard a day or two before. This objection tends to prove that the letter must have been written at an earlier date, before the attempt to rebuild the Temple, and that the supposed allusion is not an allusion to that attempt.

In the next place there is an objection based on the wording of the letter, which contains these words (338): "'Those who reproach us on this head, I mean the Prophets of the Jews, what will they say about their own Temple, *which has been thrice overthrown and is not even now rising* (ἐγειρομένου δὲ οὐδὲ νῦν)"? There is no difficulty in supposing that the words "*thrice* overthrown" refer to the *three*

Temples, of Solomon, Ezra, and Herod respectively. It is, of course, true that Ezra's Temple was not "overthrown" by the Idumean Herod except so far as was necessary to repair and rebuild it; but such rhetorical hyperbole is a very natural exaggeration of Pagan contempt, amounting to no more than this, "These boastful Jews, who scoff at our Gods as not able to protect their images and temples, should remember that their God was equally unable to protect his temple, and that, not once merely, but *thrice*. Their God had *three* temples in succession on the same site; and where are they now?" In this there is no difficulty whatever; but there is a portentous difficulty in supposing that, in the words "thrice overthrown," Julian is including *his own abortive attempt, which had got no further than excavating and beginning the foundations, and of the failure of which he must be supposed to have received intimation, say, four or five days previously!*

This letter was therefore almost certainly written at an earlier date than 363 A.D. and the words following the sentence just quoted rather confirm that view (338) : "This I have said with no wish to reproach them [*i.e.* the Jews], inasmuch as I myself, at so late a day, had in purpose to rebuild it." This may very well refer, in an earlier letter, to a project that had floated before Julian's mind at various times but had never yet been seriously considered; but it cannot surely be with any probability supposed to mean that the Ruler of the Roman Empire *having four or five days ago* received from his Legate intelligence that the workmen at Jerusalem had been checked in their work by a fiery eruption or eruptions, *writes already of his imperial purpose as a thing of the past!* And not merely writes about it, but writes *allusively, as though there were nothing novel in it, nothing that any one could not fully understand!*

These two objections, based severally on the date and on the wording, of Julian's letter are fatal to its attestation of the fiery eruption. The real solid testimony is that of Ammianus Marcellinus (xxiii. 1), an impartial historian, who served under Julian in the Persian campaign and who, twenty years afterwards, recorded the interruption of the building of the Temple by terrible balls of fire (globi flammarum) which repeatedly leapt forth (crebris assultibus erumpentes) near the foundations and made the place inaccessible for the workmen; "and in this way, since the fire persistently repelled them, the undertaking dropped (hocque modo, elemento destinatius repellente, cessavit inceptum)."

Now if Ammianus had written nearer the time of the alleged incident, or had added a statement of the evidence upon which he based his story, the details might have been worth considering. As it is, the circumstances, while favouring belief in his veracity, do not justify us in accepting anything more than the fact that the rebuilding of the Temple was *generally believed* to have been stopped by some supernatural fiery manifestation. The historian was probably in Persia, or on his way to Persia, at the time of the occurrence ; he probably heard it, on his return from the campaign, when it was "in every one's mouth," as Gregory Nazianzen said, and he would almost inevitably hear it in an exaggerated shape. When the death of Julian crushed the hopes of the Jews and the Pagans, it became the interest of every one (including Julian's own legate, who would naturally avail himself gladly of a pretext for dropping the imperial project now that the Emperor was dead) to affirm the miraculous interruption. It was the interest of none (except those whose voices were *not handed down to posterity because they were not on the winning side*) to reduce the miracle to its real level.

Ammianus himself inserts it—not probably in chronological
order, which he by no means always observed (*Dictionary of
Christian Biography*, iii. 504)—as the most prominent of a
series of evil omens which preceded Julian's death. He
expressly says of another evil omen, mentioned in the same
section, that word was brought to the Emperor about it. *He
does not say this about the omen at Jerusalem.* We have therefore no ground for thinking that the historian (who was with
the Emperor at the time of the occurrence) heard of it till
after the Persian campaign. But he seems to have set it
down in later years, as if it showed that the God of Jerusalem,
as well as the Gods of Rome, predicted evil to the Emperor.
This being the case, the popular rumour fell in with his own
views of the truth ; he believed it to represent the truth, and
related it accordingly.

It is certainly strange that Cyril of Jerusalem—who was
on the spot during the alleged occurrence and who was said
by Rufinus in the next century to have predicted the failure
—and that Jerome who, lived at Bethlehem twenty years
afterwards, are absolutely silent about the story. " Why,"
asks Newman (340), "should Ammianus be untrue because
Jerome is silent ? " Because, replies Gibbon by anticipation,
" the same story which was celebrated at a distance might be
despised on the spot." This probably represents the
fact.

The rebuilding of the Temple was probably stopped by a
violent thunderstorm or thunderstorms [1] ; and the panic

[1] The curious statement that crosses were imprinted on the bodies
and clothes of persons present, is illustrated, in' the original edition of
Newman's Essay (clxxxii.) by some parallel instances quoted by War-
burton from Casaubon and from Boyle. Such crosses, or cross-like
impressions, are said to have followed not only a thunderstorm, but also
an eruption of Vesuvius : " these crosses were seen on linen garments,
as shirt-sleeves, women's aprons, that had lain open to the air, and upon

caused by these, not improbably heightened by religious feeling, and closely followed by the death of the Emperor, led to the final abandonment of the undertaking. Christian writers of the fourth and fifth centuries vied with Gregory Nazianzen in exaggerating the natural phenomena into a suspension of the laws of nature : (336) all the tools of the workmen were melted down ; there was an earthquake ; the new excavation was filled up ; the old buildings in the neighbourhood were thrown down ; numbers of Jews were buried in the ruins ; the fire met those who fled to a church "at the door, and forced them back with the loss either of life or of their extremities" [*Gregory Nazianzen, fourth century*] ; "the fiery mass," says another, " ranged up and down the street for hours " [*Rufinus, fifth century*] ; "there is no reason for doubting any part of this narrative " [*John Henry Newman, nineteenth century*] /

§ 34. *Recovery of the Blind Man at Milan* (348—368)

(348). " The broad facts connected with this memorable interposition of Divine Power are these : St. Ambrose, with a large portion of the population of Milan, was resisting the Empress Justina in her attempt to seize on one of the churches of the city for Arian worship.   In the course of the contest he had occasion to seek for the relics of Martyrs, to be used in the dedication of a new church, and he found two

the exposed parts of sheets ;" " fifteen were found upon the smock-sleeve of a woman," "eight in a boy's hand," "their colour and magnitude were very unequal, and their figures discrepant."

Chrysostom (ed. Montfaucon, vol. v. 271, &c.) mentions " crosses imprinted upon garments " as a sign that had occurred in his generation, close to the mention of the Temple of Apollo that was overthrown by a thunderbolt, and separated from "the wonders in Palestine" which he mentions subsequently.

skeletons, with a quantity of *fresh* blood, *the miraculous token* of martyrdom. Miracles followed, both cures and exorcisms; and at length, as he was moving the relics to a neighbouring church, a blind man touched the cloth which covered them and regained his sight. The Empress in *consequence* relinquished the contest ; and the subject of the miracle dedicated himself to religious service in the Church of the Martyrs, where he seems to have remained till his death."

Such and no more, is the information given us by Newman : not a single quotation from an original authority; not even a reference to an authority ; not a word to tell us whether the man was born blind, whether the cure was complete or partial, nor to tell us where, if we cared to take the trouble, we could get this and other evidence for ourselves.[1] Almost all Newman's " Inquiries into the Evidence for Particular alleged Miracles " partake of the nature of impostures, but this perhaps deserves to be acquitted of that charge ; for, by its insolent and audacious contempt for evidence, it shows, on its very face, that it does not profess to be an Inquiry.

In reality there is nothing at all that can claim to be called miraculous in the two details which alone suggest a miracle viz. (1) the discovery of blood, (2) the healing of the blind man.

(1). As to the blood, Newman calls it above, "*fresh*"; and hence he entitles it " the *miraculous* token of martyrdom." But here he seems to have mistranslated Ambrose whose words are (*Letters*, i. 22, § 2.), " ossa integra, sanguinis plurimum." Even if Ambrose had said so, or says so in some other passage, and even if there is some exaggeration in the " plurimum," we ought to be prepared

---

[1] A few facts about this miracle are mentioned, with references, in an earlier part of the Essay ; but no reference is given to them here.

for that, in one writing, as he was, under great excitement,
on the very day of the discovery. Under this influence, for
example, he tells us that the bodies of the martyrs were (*ib.*)
"*of a wonderful size* like the stature of ancient times." Still,
though in this passage Ambrose says nothing about fresh
blood, he certainly does say that there was "a good deal of
blood"—possibly using the phrase with some reference to
the circumstances, so that it might mean, "much more than
might have been expected." But the existence of blood is
quite consistent with the course of nature, if the body is kept
from the air. That the blood of a beheaded man might
remain uncongealed for many years we know from the
case of Charles I. When his remains were examined,
165 years after his death, "the head was found heavy
and wet with a liquid that gave to writing-paper and linen
a greenish-red tinge"[1] : and if, as appears possible, the
blood of the beheaded martyrs was preserved from the air
in an urn, there is no reason why it should not have been
found uncongealed. Thus we remove from Ambrose the
charge of imposture which has been brought against him
in connection with this miracle.

(2). As to the healing, although Ambrose himself (*Letters*,
i. 22), with an inconsistency pardonable enough in a harangue
to the people delivered at the very time of the miracle,
exaggerated (*ib.* § 18) the cure even to the level of the
healing of "the man born blind" (John ix. 1.), yet we know
(*ib.* § 17) from his own evidence that the man, Severus by
by name, was not born blind, but had to give up business
because he lost (apparently gradually) the use of his eyes
(*deposuerat officium postquam inciderat impedimentum*). This
being the case, we are reminded of the case of Matilda

---

[1] Sir H. Halford's *Essays and Orations ;* I am indebted for this fact,
and for the reference, to my friend Dr. John Shaw.

Makara mentioned above (p. 147) whose cure, in 1856, is fully described in the *Apologia*, p. 393. That was a case of "the instantaneous removal of *the most pertinacious eyelid-cramp* which (*sic*) Matilda Makara during many months had hindered" (comp. *impedimentum*, above) "in the use of her eyes and kept in blindness, and the simultaneous recurrence of the full eye-sight, *phlogistic appearances still remaining in the eyes*."

This German-English is somewhat obscure; but it is at all events so far intelligible that we can understand that Matilda Makara, though very much better, and indeed all but well, was not quite well: "*phlogistic appearances* still remained in the eyes." And this suggests the same question as to our Milanese Severus. Did he still retain "phlogistic appearances"? Was the case quite satisfactory? There are indications that it was *not* quite satisfactory. That, at least, seems to be a reasonable inference from the assertions of the Arians which, but for Ambrose himself, would not have been handed down to us (*ib.* § 17): "Negant esse eum illuminatum, sed ille non negat se sanatum . . . . *Isti beneficium negant* qui factum negare non possunt." These words appear to show that, although the man really was very much better, and though a genuine act of faith-healing had been performed, yet the Arians at all events denied that his sight was *fully restored:* they could not deny that *it had been done*, but they said that, when done, it was *no benefit to him*.[1] It was perhaps well for the credit of the miracle, under these circumstances, that the danger of a relapse was not incurred by letting Severus go about his business as

---

[1] This seemed to me so startling an admission from Ambrose that the question suggested itself, "Could *beneficium* here mean 'a good deed,' a 'deed done by the Holy Spirit and not by the Devil'?" I do not think however that the word could have that meaning.

before, exposed to the questions and criticisms of sceptical or Arian physicians. He probably had enough eyesight to move about in a church, and accordingly in a church he remained. Many years afterwards, says Paulinus, Ambrose's secretary, *nunc usque religiose servit.*

Some other fabulous incidents attached to this story, vanish when looked at. Ambrose had the resting place of these Martyrs revealed to him " in a dream," says Augustine, who was present in Milan at the time. But Ambrose himself, writing to his own sister on the day of the discovery, says that it was a kind of " prophetic glow " which suddenly made him declare he would consecrate the Church if he could find the relics of Martyrs. Then, as to the discovery itself, as soon as it was made, Ambrose himself tells us (*ib.* § 12) " old men now repeat that they have heard in old days the names of these Martyrs and *that they have read (their) inscription (audisse se aliquando horum martyrum nomina, titulumque legisse)."* What more natural than that Ambrose should have heard one of these old men repeating a tradition of this kind, viz., that he had "read the inscription of Protasius and Gervasius in the basilica of Nabor and Felix"? Perhaps Ambrose heard it and forgot it. Perhaps he half forgot it. In the crisis of the conflict with Justina, a half-remembrance comes back to him in the form of a " prophetic glow " *veluti cuiusdam ardor praesagii*) : " I will have those relics," he says to himself, "and I shall find them "—or, with a slight difference, "You shall have those relics," a Voice says to him, "and you shall find them "— " somewhere before the shrine of Felix and Nabor." Groups of workmen, perhaps half a dozen groups, straightway set to work to " clear away the rubbish " (*jussi eruderari terram*). One of these groups finds *signa convenientia*, " signs appropriate to an interment." The rest stop. The Martyrs are found. Everybody is in hysterics. The very finding is a miracle !

On the whole, I think we ought to agree with Augustine (ed. Montfaucon, vol. i. 15, *a*) who tells us that, when he asserted that *the days of miracles were past* in his times, he was well aware of the healing of Severus, being present in Milan at the time. There are many other acts of this sort, he says, more than he can enumerate. He evidently does not think much of it. Neither need we. On the whole, if Matilda Makara's still remaining "phlogistic inflammations" were not severe enough to prevent her from going about her work, while Severus was so far from being in condition to do so that the flippant Arians could say, even with some particle of truth, that his cure "*was no good* to him "— it would almost seem as if Matilda Makara ought to supplant Severus in the "Particular Inquiry," at least so far as strength of evidence is concerned. Both narratives appear to point to acts of faith-healing, and both are very interesting ; but the older story is very much exaggerated ; and neither of them indicates anything like a suspension of the laws of Nature, or a miracle of any sort, even of a popular sort.

As for Newman's discussion of it, we have not much ground (from his point of view) for blaming him for devoting *fifteen pages* (352—368) to the proof that there is nothing unscriptural, or shocking in "the *fresh* blood," and that the Miracle affords no encouragement either to idolatry or to rebellion against the civil power ; while he gives us *no help whatever towards a serious inquiry into the evidence.* We cannot here very well accuse him of suppressions when he tells us really nothing at all. The only serious faults are two statements opposed to truth, one wholly, the other partially, both contained in the following sentence (351) :

"'They denied the miracle . . . but they did *not hazard any counter-statement* or distinct explanation of the facts of the case . . . *They did nothing but deny*—except indeed we let their actions speak for them. One thing then they did ; they gave over the contest. *The Miracle was successful.*"

(i) "They did not hazard any counter-statement." They did. *Beneficium negant,* "they deny the benefit." They did not deny a cure after a sort ; they *denied that it was of any real good.*

(ii) "The Miracle was successful." This is partially opposed to the truth. In Fleury's *Ecclesiastical History* (i. 106) Justina's desisting from the contest is conjecturally explained as arising in part from "her apprehensions of the Emperor Maximus," who "wrote a letter" deprecating persecution of the Trinitarians. Considering that Newman's Essay was originally an Introduction to Fleury, and indeed originally *referred the reader to that History for the facts of this very miracle*, it would be very unfair—if it were not, more probably, nothing worse than gross carelessness—to attribute Ambrose's success simply to the Miracle, and to ignore altogether the alternative explanation suggested by the very History for which he was writing an Introduction, and to which he originally referred his readers for the facts.

§ 35.   *The Power of Speech continued to the African Confessors deprived of their Tongues* (369—387, and 391—2)

Having discussed Newman's treatment of this alleged miracle above (pp. 13-30) I need do nothing here except call attention to the chapter-heading, in which the reader will see no mention of the word "miracle"; the same conspicuous absence will be noticed in the page-heading, which is " Power of Speech in the Confessors deprived of their Tongues"; and in the Index (p. xi.) "Speech without tongues in the instance of the African Confessors." But in the original Essay the chapter-heading was, " *The Miracle* upon the African Confessors in the Arian persecution mutilated by Hunneric"; and the page-heading, " *Miracle* on the Confessors mutilated by Hunneric." The inference is obvious. Newman gives up the miracle : and we give it up too.

CHAPTER VIII

A GRAMMAR OF ECCLESIASTICAL ASSENT

THE reader has now seen placed before him Newman's theory and practice of assent to Ecclesiastical miracles; and a short summary of these will constitute in outline a kind of "Grammar of Ecclesiastical Assent," the result of adopting which would be to commit the adopter in practice to belief in almost any Ecclesiastical miracle that is not patently immoral. How can we construct such a Grammar?

(i.) We are to begin by laying down the Antecedent Probability of post-apostolic miracles, as follows. Reminding our readers that they admit—what, for the sake of argument, they are supposed in this treatise to admit—that God did once suspend the laws of Nature in certain ways for a special purpose, we shall call on them to admit, as a "first principle" (see p. 101 above), that it is likely that God will afterwards repeatedly suspend the laws of Nature in ways quite different, and often, apparently, for no purpose at all.

(ii.) We are then to assume that, wherever God is manifesting His will—and where else is He so likely to manifest it as in the Church?—He will work miracles; which will therefore be as proper to Ecclesiastical History and the lives of Saints as deeds of daring and skill will be to profane History and the lives of soldiers and adventurers (see above, p. 127).

(iii.) For the "first principle" in (i.) and for the assumption in (ii.), there is no basis of fact at all. But that is the beauty of them; for they consequently cannot be disproved by facts, if we are resolved to believe in them without facts. Taking therefore our stand on this impregnable position of Antecedent Probability, we are to asseverate that this is "the main point," and, if this is established, our task is (190) "nearly accomplished."

(iv.) Now, in order to meet the objection that some of the Ecclesiastical Miracles are grotesque and unworthy of an All-wise Author, *e.g.* (29,) "the petrifaction of a fowl dressed by a person under a vow of abstinence; the exorcism of a demoniac camel; stones shedding tears at the barbarity of persecutions &c.", we are to urge (149—53, 157, 162—3 &c.) that in Nature, as in the Church, there are certain unexpected and grotesque phenomena: and, if God makes monkeys and snakes and the like, why, we shall ask, should He not manifest His supernatural character and His personal attributes by exorcising (through His Saints) demoniac camels, and petrifying fowls dressed in improper circumstances? Continuing our remarks, upon the "kill-or-cure principle," we are to point out that in a few cases, as in the instance of Elisha, the Scripture Miracles manifest the same characteristics.

(v.) The next point is to prepare ourselves for dispensing with "legal proofs" as to miracles. For this purpose we are to declare that Probability (not Faith) is the guide of life; that we believe in a God Himself merely (*Apol.* 199) upon a probability, though a transcendent probability, and that we ought to be prepared to believe in Christianity, and in

Miracles, upon various degrees of probability. "We shall miss Christ," so we shall assert, "if we will not go by evidence in which there are (so to say) three chances for revelation and only two against"[1]—that, at least, is what we shall say in our first attempt at a Scheme of Faith; in a second or amended scheme, we shall declare that, say, "a dozen to two" is the right proportion [*being, in reality, absolutely ignorant as to the real proportion, because Christian Faith has nothing to do with probabilities, chances, and pro- portions of this kind*].

(vi.) In the next place, before coming to the dangerous ground of evidence, we are to distinguish evidence as to *fact*, from evidence as to *miraculousness;* and we are to indicate, vaguely perhaps at first, a line of reserved defence on which we can fall back in the event of our miracle being proved to be explicable by natural causes. We are to urge that God may work (172) "through natural principles even when miracles *seem intended* as evidence of His immediate presence"; that He (*ib.*) "is likely to intermingle the ordinary and the extraordinary when His object is "merely" " to confirm or encourage the faithful or to rouse the atten- tion of unbelievers "; and that (*ib.*) "*it will be impossible to draw the line between the two.*"

(vii.) And now, since we can avoid it no longer, coming at last to the quite subordinate consideration of *evidence as to facts*, we shall make a great many admissions as to the exaggerations, embellishments, and even impostures that may be expected in the province of Ecclesiastical Miracle : but all these, we shall say, so far from militating against the truth, on the contrary, *rather confirm the truth, of Eccle- siastical miracles* (171) "*on the whole.*" For what does

[1] From *Tract* 85, quoted by Mr. R. H. Hutton (who adds the subsequent alteration) *Cardinal Newman*, p. 57.

hypocrisy prove except the existence of virtue ?   And in the same way, impostures and pretences of miracles—what do they prove except the existence of *the real miracles* which the former strive to imitate ?   For (*ib.*) : "such counterfeits become, *not a disproof, but a proof,* of the existence of their prototypes."

(viii.) In order to dissipate as far as possible the un favourable impression created by the vast number of confessedly false Ecclesiastical Miracles we shall divide all Ecclesiastical Miracles into three classes, (*a*) the certainly false, (*b*) the certainly true, (*c*) the possibly true but also possibly false.   Then we shall (229) preface the candid admission that (*a*) "so many " are not true, with the moderate statement that (*b*) " others " have been proved to be true ; and we shall add that (*c*) "a *great* number of them, so far as the evidence goes, are neither certainly true nor certainly false."

Then we shall demand—and surely it is fair—that our readers, while prejudiced *against* class *c* (" *a great* many ") by the *falsehood* of class *a* (" *so* many "), shall also be prejudiced *for* class *c* by the *truth* of class *b* (" others ").

But, although we do not mind saying—in order to prevent our reader from expecting really solid evidence of a miracle —that (229) " he must not expect that *more than a few* miracles can be presented with evidence of so cogent and complete a character as to *demand* his acceptance," *we shall certainly not tell him that the proportion of the certainly false to the certainly true, is, say at a moderate computation,* 100 *to* 1, *but, more probably,* 1000 *to* 1.

We shall also be very careful, in this context, *not to say a word about the necessity of "going upon probabilities" ;* for this would lead us to regard any alleged Ecclesiastical miracle as being, antecedently, in all probability false, the statistical probability against it being 100 to 1, *or perhaps even* 1000 *to* 1.

(ix.) Next, in order to prepare our reader to believe upon very scanty and confused evidence, and to disregard tokens of exaggeration, and not to be too ready to suspect imposture, we shall dose him with truisms such as these (180) : "the *direct* effect of evidence is to create a presumption, according to its strength, in favour of the fact ; it does not appear how it can create a presumption the other way"; and then, in practice, we shall act as if the word " direct " were omitted, and so we shall contrive to forget, and lead our reader to forget, that "the *indirect* effect of evidence *may* create a presumption *the other way*."

(x.) We shall ignore in practice—although we have repeatedly admitted in theory—the very great temptations which have induced ecclesiastical writers to invent or exaggerate miraculous narratives. Hence, our disposition will be to accept any miracle, as a matter "of course," in the life of any Saint, unless there is definite positive evidence *to prove that the Saint did not work the miracle in question.* We shall demand "*legal proof*"—and every one knows how difficult it is to obtain legal proof of a negative—either by proving an *alibi* for the Saint, or by showing that some one was on the spot and saw the Saint doing something else at the time ; or else, we shall demand a proof that the act was immoral, or that the Saint was no Saint, but a heretic. If none of these proofs be forthcoming, we shall be ready to receive any miracle, however astounding—and indeed, the more astounding and supernaturally portentous the better, because it is so much the more " characteristic " so to speak, of (our conception of) the personal attributes of God, and so much the better calculated to destroy the (103) "*prestige*" of the Laws of Nature—upon almost any evidence however slight.

For, we shall say (179), "How does *insufficiency* in the evidence create a positive prejudice against an alleged fact ? How can things depend on our knowledge of them ? "

(xi.) Hence, we shall take an entirely different view from that taken by ordinary historians of the "argument from silence." It will not occur to *us* that, if a man knows all about *a miracle*, he will be *much more likely to tell us all about it than about the ordinary affairs of life.* Why should he ? Since we regard a miracle as a quite common-place affair, we shall be hardly more surprised at a biographer for omitting a few miracles in the life of a Saint than at a traveller for omitting to tell us the names of all the railway stations that he passes on his journey. It will seem to us a shocking thing, and the mark of an irreligious and ill-taught mind, to reject any miracle that tends to edification ; "it is difficult," we shall say (179), "to see how its (*i.e.* the evidence's) mere *insufficiency* or *defectiveness* is a justification of *so decided a step.*"

(xii.) Hence, when Eusebius gives us a minute description of the Discovery of the Holy Sepulchre by Constantine's agents, and gives us the very letter of Constantine written upon the occasion, and gives us the most petty details of the construction of the Church of the Holy Sepulchre, but *omits to say that at the same time there was discovered the very Cross upon which the Saviour died*—which Cross was said by Cyril, some ten years afterwards, not only to have been then discovered but to have now filled the world with its miraculously multiplied fragments—we shall reply that Eusebius *must* have known it, *because* Cyril, ten years afterwards, knew all about it.

Then, if our reader asks us why Eusebius omitted it, we shall reply that Eusebius *omitted other things*, which certainly happened, *e.g.* the fact that Constantine's mother visited

Jerusalem ; and, generally, we shall act upon this useful principle that, *if an author omits any one fact however super-fluous, we ought not to be surprised at his omitting any other fact however essential.*

Lastly, if our reader, dissatisfied with this explanation, asks whether Eusebius may not have omitted this story for the same reason for which (as we have confessed) he omitted other marvellous stories, viz. *because he had* (281) "*no lean-ing towards overeasiness of belief,*" we shall be hard put to it. But our best reply will be, that the Antecedent Proba-bility of the Discovery and Multiplication of the Holy Cross is so great, and the probability of fraud in so sacred a matter is so small, and the consequences of admitting fraud are so shocking, and the argument from silence is so unsafe, that no properly taught or religiously disposed mind ought to re-ject this Miracle.

(xiii.) In the same way we shall meet another very awk-ward objection based on "the argument from silence," viz. that, although a great number of Saints have had miracles attributed to them, and some of these Saints have been authors, and voluminous authors too, yet in the whole of Ecclesiastical History—so it has been alleged and we have not been able to contradict it—*not a single saintly author has ever made mention of a single miracle of his own.*

For example, St. Ambrose of Milan,—so says his biographer Paulinus (§ 28)[1]—cured a child named Pansophius of an unclean spirit, and, a few days afterwards, when the child died, the Saint, imitating exactly the proceedings of Elisha with the child of the Shunammite widow, raised the boy to life again. Now to this same Pansophius, in after years, St. Ambrose addressed a book of instruction ; but neither here nor elsewhere does St. Ambrose give us the least hint of

[1] *Dictionary of Christian Biography*, i. 97.

this miracle. "*He has not mentioned the fact in his writings,* but by what feeling the omission was prompted it is not for me," says Paulinus, "to judge. Again, we have seen that St. Gregory Thaumaturgus dried up a lake, changed the course of a stream, converted his staff into a tree, miraculously moved a rock, and so on; and yet, if we examine his books, "*no light is thrown upon his thaumaturgic renown by his extant writings,* which are conspicuous for their philosophic tone, humility, self-distrust, and practical sense."[1] In the same way, says Gibbon (219), " Bernard of Clairvaux, who records so many miracles of his friend St. Malachi, *never takes any notice of his own,* which, in their turn, however, are carefully related by his companions and disciples."

This objection demands from us a very careful answer. We shall meet it by recalling the distinction between Scriptural and Ecclesiastical Miracles. The former were given to attest the truth; the latter were often given for (116) "no discoverable or direct object :" the former were deliberate and confident; the latter (220) "commonly *tentative*," *i.e.,* often tried and only sometimes successful, "scarcely more than experiments." Then we shall say (221), " Under these circumstances, how could the individual men who wrought them appeal to them themselves ? *It was not till afterwards, when their friends and disciples could calmly look back upon their life and review the various actions and providences which occurred in the course of it, that they would be able to put together the scattered tokens of Divine favour, none or few of which might in themselves be a certain evidence of a miraculous power.*" It will be urged against us that St. Paul—although he did not equal or even approach St. Martin of Tours or St. Gregory Thaumaturgus, or a host of others, in the multitude of striking and manifest suspen-

[1] *Dictionary of Christian Biography,* ii. 730.

sions of the laws of nature; although he seems to have performed little more than acts of faith-healing; and although he clearly discourages the laying of much stress upon miracles—nevertheless *does* distinctly mention, and clearly assume, in his letters, that he performed such ' signs '; and we shall be asked to explain why the Apostle in his few extant pages, makes mention of these comparatively insignificant acts of his, and yet, in the subsequent eighteen centuries not one of the post-apostolic thaumaturgic and voluminous writers lets drop a syllable of similar confession of his own miraculous power.

In answer to this we shall briefly reply that, as regards the apostolic miracles (221), " these were intended to be instruments for conversion ; " but afterwards, when miracles became superfluous, the power of working them (221) " could not but seem to imply some *personal privilege,* when operating in an individual, who would in consequence be *as little inclined to proclaim it aloud as to make a boast of his graces.*" " As well," we shall add with a touch of indignation (221), " might we expect men in their lifetime to be called Saints, as workers of miracles " !

N.B. Here it will be best to close the discussion of this point, for fear our inquirer should ask us whether St. Ambrosius acted " tentatively " when he raised Pansophius from death " imitating exactly the proceedings of Elisha " ; and whether St. Gregory Thaumaturgus acted " tentatively " when he was challenged by a heathen priest to make a stone move, and made it move accordingly ; and whether the same Saint " acted tentatively " when he " changed the course of the Lycus " in response to the appeal of his heathen neighbours, and so on ; and it might also be difficult to answer the question whether St. Martin, who stopped a heathen procession by the sign of the Cross, and made a falling tree reel round (in answer to a heathen challenge), and warned off a fire, &c., acted "tentatively," and why he should not have been called both (221) "a saint and a worker of miracles in his life-time."

(xiv.) Having thus scotched that deadly and serpentine adversary, the "argument from silence," and having also shown that the insufficiency and the confusedness of evidence are very subordinate considerations, we shall have prepared ourselves to act as if *evidence itself were a very petty matter, not worth taking much trouble about.*   Consequently, having our minds full of Antecedent Probability, and knowing perfectly well what our witnesses *ought* to say, we shall be able—in all honesty (of a sort), and *all the more effectively*, because we are honest (after a fashion)—to *make our witnesses say what they ought to say, e.g.* by omitting little phrases here and there, such as " it is said," " it is reported ; " by heightening a convenient, and softening or suppressing an inconvenient, expression ; and by occasionally building up a whole super-structure of solid conclusion upon two or three references which we shall place in a footnote, and which, when examined, will be found to refer to (practically) nothing.

Thus, for example, since, all through this subject, our really great difficulty is the fact that the certainly false Ecclesiastical Miracles are to those which we can, with any decent show of evidence, call the certainly true, in the pro-portion of, say, 100 to 1, or, more probably, 1,000 to 1, we shall keep this steadily in the background.   Of course we should be charged with want of candour if we did not make the admission *somewhere ;* but we will reserve it for the very last section of our Essay and then put it neatly thus (238-9) : " it *as little derogates* from the supernatural gift residing in the Church that miracles should have been fabricated or exaggerated, as. . . and, *as the elect are fewer than the reprobate, and hard to find among the chaff, so false miracles at once exceed and conceal and prejudice those which are genuine."*

Again, as an instance of building much inference on little foundation, we shall boldly declare (173) that, after all, if Ecclesiastical pretences of miracles have abounded, so also have they "abounded" even *in the primitive Church*, *"from the first hour."* And as foundation for this, we will give four references in a foot-note, showing that, *outside the Church*, Simon Magus, and some vagrant Jews, attempted miracles; and that a half mad heathen ventriloquist called St. Paul "a Servant of the Most High God;" and that there was once a Christian who turned Cynic Philosopher, and who was ridiculed (probably with some allusion to Christians) by the satirist Lucian *towards the end of the second century.*

(xv.) We ought to be now prepared to believe any edifying miracle upon any basis of evidence. For consider the strength of our position.

We can say of any edifying portent that *there is nothing of any importance against it, and much to be said for it.* The "argument from silence" has been shown to be futile. The argument from direct negation is practically impossible. For how often has a witness said, "*I was by the side of such and such a Saint at such and such a time,* and I know he did *not* work such and such a miracle"? How indeed *could* a witness protest *beforehand* against a miracle of which he knew nothing and suspected nothing—unless indeed, we suppose that he was *miraculously inspired* so as to foreknow (what he could not know by nature) that, a century or two hence, a miraculous story would spring up? Or, if he *did* say it, and if, in some few cases, a sober witness *did* deny the truth of some legend that had sprung up in his own lifetime, how often would a miracle-loving posterity preserve the testimony?

Thus, we have, practically, *nothing against us, and a good deal for us.* The confusion of testimony, the lateness of testimony, the insufficiency of testimony, are not to induce us to reject a miracle. These deficiencies, therefore, though not for us, *cannot be against us.* On the other side, testimony *of any sort* (unless the witnesses are heretics, or absolute knaves) is in favour of a miracle, to *some* extent : Antecedent Probability is in favour of a miracle, to *a vast* extent. We must decide by probability. Therefore we decide that the miracle is true. Q. E. D.

N.B.—We have forgotten all about Statistical Probability, which is 100 to 1, or 1,000 to 1, against us. Never mind ; we must continue to forget it, or we must turn it off by saying, "Anything can be proved by Statistics."

But it is not enough to believe. We must make people believe that we believe. And in order to make people believe that we mean what we say, it is necessary often to say a little more than we mean.[1] So we must conclude, for the sake of the truth, with just a spice of insolent aggressiveness, of which the following is a specimen (390) : We are "quite prepared to find those views themselves condemned by many readers as subtle and sophistical. This is ever the language men use concerning the arguments of others, when they dissent from their *first principles*—which take them by surprise, and which they have not mastered."

This will furnish an appropriate conclusion to our *Scheme.* If an untoward discovery of facts should result in our having to surrender one of our miracles and to end our *Scheme,* after all, with less confident words, by confessing, about a certain miracle, that (393) *"Catholics are prevented from*

[1] See note on p. 45 above.

P

appealing to it for controversial purposes," we will at all events save the reader's time, and the interests of Ecclesiastical truth, by relegating these last ill-omened words to an Appendix where they will never be read—never at least by the sort of people whom alone we can hope to convince.

CHAPTER IX

§ 36. *The Art of Lubrication*

ECCLESIASTICAL Logic is of little use without Ecclesiastical Rhetoric : so very much depends upon the way of putting things. This latter Art includes several important departments, any one of which might almost claim for itself the title of a Minor Art.

There is, for example, the " Art of Oscillation." This is of two kinds. Sometimes, when you have made up your mind to a certain conclusion, you fix upon two extreme propositions between which your conclusion may appear to lie as the happy mean. The one extreme is an apparently liberal concession to your reader ; the other is a really exorbitant demand upon your reader. Between these two extremes you " oscillate," so conciliating him by your reasonable candour that you make him half afraid to resist your unreasonable extortion. Thus, by a continual process of logical tacking between admissions and assertions, you steadily, though slowly, progress towards your end, and at last you so bewilder and confuse him that finally with a sense of relief he drops into your conclusion as a kind of

P 2

compromise, and is half disposed to thank you for not asking more.

Another device is, to "oscillate," through the whole of a period, between two meanings of a phrase, and to end by using it in the sense in which your reader will admit it to be true. If you do this neatly, you leave him under a vague impression that *in the other sense*—the sense in which he does *not* admit its truth—the phrase is *somehow also true ;* and, without testing that vague impression, the average reader (who is a very lazy, careless creature) passes on to the next sentence.   Meantime, you have instilled your venom.

Then there is the Art of " Assimilation," or " Drawing Parallels."   The skill, in this, consists in cheerfully assuming that cases *are* "parallel," when they are *not* really parallel, except in some small particular that is not to the point.   No precepts can communicate this Art.   Sometimes you may succeed by a breezy, open, audacity.   Suppose you want to prove that there *was* such a person as Aladdin and his Lamp, or St. George and the Dragon (see below p. 227) ; you can draw a " parallel " between them and some famous historical but ancient characters.   But you must do it suddenly and without flinching : " Take a parallel," you must say, " not Aladdin and his Lamp, nor St. George and the Dragon, but Moses, or Lycurgus," and this barefaced boldness will often answer very well, especially in ephemeral controversy.   You will really get people—*some* people—to fancy that there *is* a parallelism between Aladdin and Moses, or between St. George and the Dragon and Lycurgus.   At other times, it will be safer, and almost as effective, to slip your " parallel " into a parenthesis, with a " just as," or " as if," or some other innocently subordinate conjunction.   However, when all is said, the Ecclesiastical

Assimilator, or Parallelizer, *nascitur, non fit.* Some specimens, which shall be given below (pp. 227—240), will be
better than general rules.

Thirdly, comes the " Art of Lubrication," or, so to speak,
"greasing" the descent from the Premises to the Conclusion.   But I am not sure whether this Art does not, strictly
speaking, include the other two.   For both your "Oscillation" and your "Assimilation," if they are to be effective,
are to be "greasing," or smoothing, processes.   However
passionately you may desire, and indeed may have determined on, your conclusion, you must never forget the precept
of Hamlet, to preserve "a smoothness" in the very "tempest
of your passion."   Yet it may be worth while to mention
one or two special lubricating devices, such as, dropping
some qualification of the premises ; repeating the old premise in new words, two or three times, and each time with
a slightly different meaning ; beginning with "which *may be*"
and then dropping into "which *is*"; admitting candidly—
candour is sometimes very effective—that a difference exists,
then stating that it is not a radical difference, then that it is
merely "a difference of degree," then that it is, practically,
no difference at all.   The one thing needful is, that
the descent should be so continuously smooth that no
hitch or break may cause your reader to pause and ask
"What am I coming to next ? "—until you have brought
him to the conclusion to which you would have him come.

In order to "lubricate" well, four qualifications are
necessary, and some of these apparently, but not really,
incompatible with each other.   First, a nice discrimination
and delicate handling of words, enabling you to form,
easily and naturally, a great number of finely-graduated
propositions, shading away, as it were, from the assertion "*x* is white," to the assertion "*x* is black";

this must be carried to such a perfection as to become an instinctive art, which you can practise, as
it were, with your eyes shut, without thinking about it.
Secondly, an inward and absolute contempt for logic and
words and for the understanding generally, for your own
understanding as well as other people's : this will enable you
to lure yourself onward, and other people too, from proposition to proposition, with pretty plausibilities, and all the
while without any sense of dishonesty or loss of self-respect,
because you will say to yourself, " After all, if this or that
is not quite true, does it so very much matter?   Who knows
what is 'quite true'?   *We are going in the right direction :
that is the main point.*   If I want to coax a child to come to
me, I hold out my watch ; when he takes hold of the watch
I substitute a penny ; when he begins to suck the penny I
substitute a chocolate.   What is the harm of this?   And
what are men—in comparison with the 'quite true,' the
absolute truth—but babies?   And what am I but a baby
too ?   And what are words but toys and sweetmeats for
grown-up babies who call themselves men ? "

The third qualification is an intense and passionate longing
for a certain conclusion on which, as upon a goal, you may
fix your eyes so intently that you can see nothing else and
are quite blind to the exact force of the expressions which
drop from your lips.   To this some may object, " Surely
your third qualification is inconsistent with your first.   How
can you be 'blind to' that which you use with 'nice discrimination'? "   But I anticipated that objection by saying
that the accomplishment of word-shading was to be carried
to such perfection as to become an instinctive art which you
can practise " with your eyes shut."   Or we may put it thus,
" You are to pick your meanings nicely with one half of
your mind and be blind to them with the other half."   If

any one replies, "This state of mind is too subtle for me," my reply would be, " I never said it was not ; I hope it is. It *is* too subtle; much too subtle for any but a very complex, tortuous nature."

Fourth, and last, comes the most important qualification of all, the power of self-deception. With the aid of this, having deceived yourself, you the more perfectly and artistically deceive others.   No artist, and therefore no lubricator, can be so truly artistic as when he entirely conceals his art not only from others but even from himself, by being—for the time at least—unconscious of it.   For the purposes of Ecclesiastical Rhetoric, a contempt for logic is perhaps essential : of the other qualifications, an artistic power of word-shading is good ; a mind bent on a foregone conclusion, is perhaps better ; but a perfect power of self-deception is unquestionably the best of the three.

§ 37. *A specimen of self-deceptive Lubrication*

The following specimen of self-deceptive rhetoric will need but a few words to make it intelligible.   In October, 1840, Newman had written to Keble, avowing the Romanizing tendencies of his teaching and asking whether he should resign the Vicarage of St. Mary's, Oxford.   He felt that he could not trust his own feelings, or ascertain the impressions and convictions whioh were the basis of his difficulty, but he hoped that perhaps Keble might supersede the necessity of going by them (*Apol.* 132) ; what he wanted from Keble was leave[1] to remain at St. Mary's.   Keble, who did not at all realize the real position from the hints and

---

[1] *Letters*, ii. 318, " What I wanted to get from him was leave to do so," *i.e.* to remain.

interrogations in which Newman conveyed it, gave him provisional "leave" to remain (*Apol.* 135) : "It would be said "—writes the spiritual adviser—" ' You see he can go on no longer with the Church of England, except in Lay Communion '; or people might say you repented of the cause " [*i.e.* the Tractarian Movement] "altogether. Till you see, [your way to mitigate, if not remove, this evil], I certainly should advise you to stay." To this Newman replies as follows (*Apol.* 135-6) :—

"Since you think I may go on, it seems to follow that, under the circumstances, I ought to do so. . . . Say, that I move sympathies for Rome : in the same sense does Hooker, Taylor, Bull, &c. Their arguments *may be* against Rome, but the sympathies they raise *must be* towards Rome, so far as Rome maintains truths which our Church does not teach or enforce. Thus, it is a *question of degree* between our divines and me. I *may*, *if so be*, go further ; I *may* raise sympathies more ; but I *am* but urging minds in the same direction as they *do*. I am doing *just the very thing which all our doctors have ever been doing.*"

In order to understand the skill and self-deceptive subtlety with which Newman here bridges over the wide gulf between himself and the English divines whom he mentions, we must bear in mind (1) that in the previous year he had expressed to two friends (1839) the possibility of his being forced to join the Church of Rome ; (2) that he was in a condition of mind that would have horrified the Anglican divines by the gloomy and almost despairing views he took of the National Church ; he had, for example, in 1839 (*Letters*, ii. 288), mooted the question, whether the Church of England might not have "grace, " even though she were "*schismatical*," and might not be allowed at least to "put herself into *a state of penance*"; (3) that, in this year (1840) he describes himself (*Apol.* 122) as being "sore about the great Anglican divines, *as if they had taken him in*"; (4) that he had begun (*ib.*) "to wish for union between the Anglican Church and Rome, if, and when, it was possible"; (5) and yet that, *at this very time*, he felt that *opposition to the Church of Rome* was a *necessary part* of Anglican theology; that he who could not protest against the Church of Rome was *no true divine* in the English Church; and that no one "*in office* in the English Church, whether Bishop or *Incumbent*, could be otherwise than in *hostility to the Church of Rome.*"[1]   No opinion is here expressed that Newman's theological opinions, *in themselves*, necessitated his resignation; but, *from his own point of view*, the conclusion seems as clear as daylight, "I cannot any longer avow myself to be *in hostility to the Church of Rome;* an Incumbent who is not *in hostility to the Church of Rome* is *no true divine* in the Church of England; therefore I can no longer call myself a *true divine in the Church of England*." And again, "The Anglican divines have taken me in, I am *sore* about them; therefore I can no longer preach from the pulpit of St. Mary's, Oxford, in the spirit of an Anglican divine; I cannot honestly do what they did; and so I ought to go."

What can be clearer? But now see the consummate art with which Newman beclouds and obfuscates what seems to us so clear, and mystifies and confuses his reader all the more because he has mystified and confused

---

[1] *Apol.* p. 156, "I have felt *all along* that Bishop Bull's theology was the only theology on which the English Church could stand.   I have felt that opposition to the Church of Rome was part of that theology; and that he who could not *protest against the Church of Rome* was no *true divine in the English Church*.   I have never said, nor attempted to say, that any one *in office* in the English Church, whether Bishop or Incumbent, could be *otherwise than in hostility to the Church of Rome*."

himself, so that at last he and his reader drift quietly and easily into the haven of the desired conclusion, viz. that he and the Anglican divines are *doing precisely the same thing*.

Every step is worth noting for the delicacy of its smooth suggestiveness of something false.

1. In the first place, introducing the great Anglican divines, he does not say, "their arguments *were*, as a fact, against Rome," but, "their arguments *may be* against Rome"; and then, instead of saying, "but the sympathies they raised, *although they were not actually towards Rome, ought logically to have been so*"; he continues, "the sympathies they raise *must be* towards Rome."

2. Then he introduces that most fallacious of truisms "the question of degree," preceded by a "Thus"; where the "thus" suggests that *what preceded must be satisfactory*, since the conclusion that follows cannot be denied : "*Thus*, it is a *question of degree* between our divines and me."

3. "I *may, if so be*, go further ; I *may* raise sympathies more."

This is an understatement disguised under a "may." In his previous letter to Keble, Newman had himself confessed, "I fear I must allow that, whether I will or no, I *am* disposing them," *i.e.* his hearers in St. Mary's, "towards Rome." In November of that same year (*Letters*, ii. 319) he quotes the Virgilian "tendimus in Latium" to express his tendencies, not as going *all* the way to Rome, but as going *toward* Rome ; and the quotation was a familiar one in the mouths of some of his pupils who were ready to substitute "to" for "toward." Only three months before this letter, one of Newman's followers (*ib.* 291), "a most simple-minded conscientious fellow, but as little possessed of tact and common sense as he is great in other departments," had actually preached, in Newman's place and from Newman's pulpit, what Newman himself confessed to be "*totidem verbis* the Roman doctrine of the Mass; and, not content with that, added, in energetic terms, that every one was an unbeliever, carnal, and so forth, who did not hold it." Now, would " the Anglican divines " have had to make *anything like* this confession about "disposing their hearers," or have talked about "tending to Latium," or have had to admit that followers of theirs had preached "*totidem verbis*, the Roman doctrine of the Mass"?

Take away the rhetoric, and the passage ought to have run, "*I do, I must frankly admit, go a great deal further. I am convinced, from practical experience, that I raise sympathies a great deal more*—if indeed I was right in saying that the Anglican divines, as a fact, raised sympathies *at all* toward the Church of Rome."

4. " I *am but* urging minds in the same direction as they do."

Having used "I *may*" above, where he ought to have used "I *do*"; he now compensates for this by using "I *am*" for "I *may be*," or for "I might suggest that I may be." Also the cleverly inserted " but," meaning "only" and being combined with "same," gives the reader the impression of "*only the same* thing."   And now, with "*only the same* thing" in his mind, the reader, or rather the writer, drops gently into the conclusion, which would have astounded him if he had not been so smoothly and imperceptibly led towards it, viz., that every Anglican Divine worthy of the name, in every period of the Church of England, has not only done what Newman was doing then, but has "ever been doing" it :—

5. "*I am doing just the very thing which all our doctors have ever been doing.*"

§ 38. *The Art of Oscillation*

" Oscillation " means bringing your reader to a pre-
determined conclusion oscillatively, that is, in a zig-zag
fashion, by oscillating between two extreme boundaries, just
as you might send a billiard ball onwards by successive re-
bounds from the cushion on this side and on that, or as you
might tack with a vessel, or might bring a jibbing horse up
to some object that scares him by letting him go first to
one side, then to the other, pulling him round now this way
and now that, till you get him at last face to face with the
thing.

It does not need much knowledge of human nature to
teach us that this is a very effective art.   The mind jibs,
so to speak, at coercion, and is always more interested in
whatever it approaches unexpectedly and obliquely.   But it
is essential that the limits of oscillation should be carefully
defined, not of course in your reader's mind but in yours.
He may be allowed to think himself indefinably free ; but
you, besides seeing your conclusion straight before you,
must also keep in view the barriers, on this side and on that,
fixed and firm, beyond which you must not give him his
head : otherwise he will give you the slip.

The two limits or barriers are, on the one side, superfluous and excessive candour and, on the other, excessive
and extravagant demand.   At one moment you make such
liberal concessions as to cause your reader to exclaim,
" How very reasonable ! "   At another you make so large
an exaction (generally, a good deal more than you expect
to get) that he is disposed to say, " Surely this is rather unreasonable "; though at the same time he feels that you
have been so very reasonable before that perhaps he is wrong

in thinking you unreasonable now. In the end you may propose a compromise in which you gain a good deal more than you are entitled to.   But there is also another advantage in this device.   By dangling before your own eyes now one, now another of two long series of alternative propositions you so confuse yourself and weary your own mind with the very thought of arguing or balancing arguments any longer, that, having your conclusion ready, you are glad to drop into it as a relief.   And the same applies, of course, still more to your reader, who is likely to be a great deal more confused than you are.

The following, though an imperfect specimen, will serve very well as an introduction to the art :

1. " If we *will* doubt " [*i.e. If we are obstinately resolved to doubt*], " if we will not allow evidence to be sufficient which *merely* results in *a balance* on the side of revelation ; if we will determine that no evidence is enough to prove revealed doctrine but what is *overpowering ;* if we will not go by evidence in which there are (so to say) *three* chances for revelation and only *two* against, we cannot be Christians ; we shall miss Christ either in His inspired Scriptures, or in His doctrines, or in His ordinances." [1]

Here, all you have made up your mind about is the *conclusion, viz.* that your reader is bound to believe.   You begin—it is almost always best to begin thus—with a very reasonable statement, implied, though not expressed, in the words, " If we *will* doubt "—which makes your reader say, " *will* doubt ! *resolve* to doubt !   Of course I have no right to do that ; it is quite reasonable to demand that I should keep my mind open."   Then, oscillating to the extreme of extortionate demand, you order him to believe upon "merely' " a balance."   Then—having staggered him with a command

<hr />

[1] *Cardinal Newman*, by Mr. R. H. Hutton, p. 57.

to believe (with a practical and life-influencing belief) in the
most momentous truths upon 'a balance' that may mean a
probability of 1,000 to 999 ; and having suggested by the
emphatic "*will*," here, as before, that he must be *extremely
obstinate and perverse* if he *resolves not to believe* upon a probability of, say, 1,000 to 999—you oscillate once more
towards the side of mild reasonableness : "your reader,"
you say in effect, "must not be unreasonable, must not
ask '*overpowering* evidence.'"   And now, lastly, having
pacified him and stroked him down and slightly confused
both yourself and your reader—for neither he nor you
know what the 'balance' or the numerical 'chances' are to
be—you oscillate back again to the "balance" view of the
matter, but with an appearance of compromise : you will
not expect him to believe on a balance of 1,000 to 999, but
you threaten him with the heaviest penalty of which a
Christian can conceive unless he will believe *on "a balance"
of 3 to 2.*

Perfect in one respect—the confusion on the part of the
reasoner, who has not the least glimpse of what the 'balance'
or 'chances' are, or ought to be, and who confuses his
reader the better because he is confused himself—this
oscillative specimen is imperfect in another.   It is too
short.   It ends too abruptly and asks what appears
to be too much.   Newman felt this himself, and, in a
subsequent version of this passage, he substituted 12 to 2
for 3 to 2.   But to make it perfect, the oscillation should
have been continued through three or four more clauses,
showing that between 12 to 2 and 3 to 2 there is "only a
difference of degree," and so, by smooth transitions, landing
the reader in the conclusion that the two ratios are "the
very same," and that any one who is reasonable enough to
believe at all and not to require "overpowering evidence,"

will be ready not only to believe upon a "balance" of
12 to 2, but also upon "a balance" of 3 to 2, or perhaps
upon any " balance " whatever.

2. For further illustrations, the reader is referred to the
next chapter.   Only one or two more will be given here.   In
the following passage, Newman desires to prove that "fear"
must always exist in the Christian life.   He himself felt a
religious "fear" that bordered on abjectness, and in his
Doctrine of Development he regards "love," not as being the
basis of Christian belief, but merely as a kind of " *Preservative
Addition* " to Fear.[1]   Now, it is true that in the Old Testament, the "fear" of God is a common motive ; but in the
New Testament—although the Hellenistic Vocabulary sometimes used "fear" where "awe" or "reverence" would have
been more appropriate—" love " is so prominent, and "fear "
so much in the background that Newman's task is somewhat difficult.   He achieves it, however, by beginning, as
usual, with a candid admission ; then by using "fear" for
"awe" or "reverence," speaking of it as an "evangelical
grace " and yet as seeming (which it ought *not* to seem)
"contradictory" to love ; then by saying that "love" *is
necessary, from the first*, in order to make Christian "fear"
differ from servile dread, and yet implying that love is
almost non-existent at first side by side with the " prominent
ecclesiastical *grace* of "fear " ; then by implying afterwards—in
the words "Love *is added*"—that love *did not exist at all at
first* in the religious life ; and finally by introducing a quotation from St. Paul which refers neither to "fear," nor to
"awe," nor to "reverence," but simply to "*sorrow*," and
which—if St. Paul's context is examined—will be found to

---

[1] *Cardinal Newman*, by Mr. R. H. Hutton, p. 183.   In the edition
of 1878, instead of "preservative," the word "conservative" is used.

have nothing whatever to do with the matter in hand. Here is the passage :—

"Thus we know that no temper of mind is acceptable in the Divine Presence without love [1]; it is love which makes Christian fear differ from servile dread [*more correctly, "it is Christian love which takes away servile dread, and substitutes awe"; or "which transmutes servile dread to awe"*]; . . . . yet in the beginning of the religious [2] life fear is the prominent evangelical grace [*"fear" CANNOT be a "grace," unless Christian "love" has first partly or wholly transmuted it from servile dread to awe*] and love is but latent in fear [*hardly true, if love has partly, or wholly, transmuted, servile dread*], and has in course of time to be developed out of what seems its contradictory [*say rather, that, in course of time, love wholly purifies away the dross of servile dread, and leaves the pure metal of reverence; love is not "developed out of" fear, any more than admiration is "developed out of" envy, or friendship out of hatred*]. Then, when it is developed, it takes that prominent place which fear held before, yet protecting, not superseding it. Love is added [*this is not true, unless it means "MORE LOVE is added"; the "religious life," rightly so called, could not begin without love, if by "religion" is meant "the religion of Christ"*], not fear removed [*"fear," in the sense of "servile dread," IS entirely removed*] and the mind is but perfected in grace by what seems a revolution. [*There is no "revolution" at all, nothing but a steady progress, after the real "religious life" is once begun, a progress in which "love" transmutes "servile dread"*]. 'They that sow in tears, reap in joy'; yet afterwards still they are 'sorrowful' though 'always rejoicing'" [*true; but not to the point. There is nothing "contradictory" between "sorrowing," e.g., under persecution or physical suffering, and*

<hr>

[1] In the 1st ed. "but love."   [2] In the 1st ed. "Christian."

simultaneous "rejoicing" in the Divine grace and help ; but there is a contradiction between the "love" of God and the "fear," i.e. the "servile dread" of God.]

3. In 1852, Newman wished to convince the Romanist Prelates in Ireland that literature ought to have free scope in their proposed course of University education. A University, he wished to say, *ought to have, for its object, " to fit men of the world for the world."*

Now, considering that " the world" *i.e.* the "world of men," is, in Newman's eyes, a very shocking scene indeed : created indeed by God, but (*Apol.* 241) conveying "no reflexion of its Creator ; " and that (*ib.*) "the sight of the world is," to Newman, " nothing else than the prophet's scroll, full of lamentations and mourning and woe," the task presented obvious difficulty. Want of space prevents the quotation of the passage in full :[1] but the method by which he overcomes the difficulty may be briefly indicated.

He " oscillates" between the two possible meanings of "prepare men *for the world.*" This phrase may mean " prepare men to live *in the world, i.e., in this world " ;* or it may mean "prepare men to contend *against* the world," as one may be said " to prepare *for* an enemy." In the former sense, of course, one might speak of gymnastics and bodily exercises, as a " preparation *for* the world," with little, if any, reference to the preparation *against this* world and *for* the world *to come.* In the latter sense, some would say that a University education *ought*—by purifying the emotions, strengthening the judgment, ennobling the character—to do a great deal more than "prepare men *for this world" ;* it *ought* to prepare men for the world to come, and ought not to be mentioned on the same footing as mere physical training.

[1] *Discourses on the Idea of a University,* ix. 8, quoted by Mr. R. H. Hutton, *Cardinal Newman,* pp. 218, 219.

Q

With consummate boldness, Newman begins by taking the former—the ignoble and worldly view of University education—putting the higher view into a parenthesis and, so, getting rid of it :—

"Why do we educate except to *prepare for the world?* Why do we cultivate the intellect of the many beyond the first elements of knowledge, *except for this world?* [*Note "this world," a rise upon "the world."*] Will it be much matter in the world to come whether our bodily health, or whether our intellectual strength, was more or less —except, of course, as this world is, in all its circumstances, a trial for the next [*Thus, in a parenthesis, and with an "of course," and "in all its circumstances," (as being a truth too general and abstract to take up the time of practical men), this very important view of the question is put on one side*]. If, then, a University is a direct [*"direct," another rise !*] preparation for this world, let it be what it professes [*again, a rise implying that there is something of hypocrisy if a University aims at being more than a preparation for "this world"*]. It is not a convent; it is not a seminary; it is a place to fit men of the world for the world." [*A climax ! admirably introduced by the method of "the Plausible Antithesis," which first insists that a thing is "not black," and then implies that it is consequently "white"— suppressing the possibility that it may be "grey." In the present instance, a University may be "not a seminary," and yet not "a place to fit men of the world for the world," ; it may be something between the two. Note also "men of the world"—a huge assumption ! Note, lastly, "fit," substituted for "prepare ;" there being this difference between the two, that you* CAN *speak of "*PREPARING *for the world, as an enemy," but* NOT *of "*FITTING *for the world, as an enemy."*]

Now having uttered this "aculeate saying,"—"to fit *men*

of the world for the world"—to which, if allowed to pass un-
noticed, he could afterwards appeal, in defence of unex-
purgated Aristophanes and generally unrestricted freedom—
he hastens on to appease (and devotes forty lines to
appeasing) any not unnatural alarm in his Romanist
audience, by taking the *other* view of the phrase "*prepare
for* the world," as meaning "*prepare against* the world," or
"prepare *to meet the temptations* of the world " :—

"We cannot possibly keep them from plunging into the
world. . . but we can *prepare them against* what is inevitable, and it is not the way to learn to *swim in troubled waters*
never to have gone into them." Then a plea is put in for
Homer, Ariosto, Cervantes, Shakespeare, and "the masters
of human thought," that "they would have in some sense
educated him " [(*i.e.*, the student] " *because of their incidental
corruptions*" ; and the Irish Prelates are finally warned that,
if they turn the world out of their University, the young
man will find his University in the world. Thus the period
ends with a conclusion well adapted to commend itself to
his hearers, viz., that the great authors of Europe are to
educate the youth of the Roman Church "*because of their
incidental corruptions*" ; and that a training in literature must
be given because young men must be *prepared against* what
is inevitable. And yet there remain on record—in case
there may be need to appeal to them—those memorable
words, "A University is a place to *fit men of the world for
the world.*"

§ 39. *The Art of Assimilation, or, Drawing Parallels*

In the *Apologia* (1st ed. Append. p. 37) occurs the following extract from one of "the Lives of the Saints :" "On
what evidence do we put faith in the existence of St. George,

the patron of England ? Upon such assuredly as an acute critic or skilful pleader might easily scatter to the winds ; the belief of prejudiced or credulous witnesses, the unwritten record of empty pageants and bauble decorations. On the side of scepticism might be exhibited a powerful array of suspicious legends and exploded acts. Yet, after all, *what Catholic is there but would count it a profaneness to question the existence of St. George ?* " This is called by Kingsley, " nonsense," and is said to " sap the very foundation of historic truth."

" Well and good," replies Newman (*ib.*), " take a parallel ; not St. George but Lycurgus." He then shows, on the testimony of Grote, that authors differ as to the birth, travels, death, and mode of proceeding, political as well as legislative, of the reputed legislator. Next, he triumphantly quotes the following passage from Thirlwall, " Experience proves that scarcely any amount of variation as to the time or circumstances of a fact, in the authors who record it, can be a sufficient ground for doubting its reality." And thereupon, very effectively, (for the purposes of ephemeral controversy) he swinges Kingsley for virtually accusing Thirlwall of " talking nonsense which saps the very foundation of historic truth."

Here, no doubt, a part of the skill consists in the audacity, the brisk cheerfulness, with which the words "take a parallel" are used in order to induce the reader to assume that there *is* a parallelism between the mythical St. George of dragon associations and the supposed legislator of the Spartans. The boldness of the "parallel" stuns the reader, for a moment, like a blow in the face, and makes him forget what Thirlwall means by "facts." Thirlwall is not speaking about the so-called "*facts*" *of ecclesiastical tradition*—where there have been operating all sorts of disturbing influences such as sectarian feeling, love of marvel, desire to find relics and martyrs and miracles in this or that church and to extol them at the expense of some other church—but of "facts" in Grecian History, in which, when we quit the region of myth, evidence is for the most part fairly trustworthy. The Swiss, who have given up the legend of William Tell, would perhaps say that Thirlwall went too far in the general proposition above quoted; but still, applied to Grecian history generally, and in particular to the mere existence of some notable man who did something—we are not very clear what or when—in the way of legislation for Sparta, the proposition may perhaps pass muster. At all events it is not "nonsense," as it would be if Thirlwall meant to say that the variations of different authors as to the labours of Hercules, or as to the wonderful deeds of Bacchus, are not sufficient ground for doubting their reality. Practically, in dealing with Lycurgus, not as a mere name but as a legislator, Thirlwall reduces him to very little, saying, some thirty pages after the passage above quoted, "In the institutions hitherto described we have found nothing that can with any probability be attributed to Lycurgus"; and assuredly Thirlwall would not have said to Grote, "After all, what student of Grecian history is there but would *count it a profaneness to question the existence of Lycurgus?*"

But let the reader turn to the "parallel," viz. St. George (*Dict. of Christian Biography*, ii. 645). He will there find (if we pass over two inscriptions of doubtful date, evidence apparently not known to the writer of the above preface, and therefore not to the point) that the earliest evidence to the existence of the Martyr is derived from a decree of a council 494 A.D. (*i.e.* 191 years after the alleged martyrdom in 303 A.D.), which, while acknowledging the Martyr's existence and title to respect, condemns the current

Acts of St. George. Turning to these *Acts,* we find ourselves
in a region of legend no doubt of which is not "profanity"
but self-respecting common sense—tortures, miracles, a
magician, Athanasius by name (no doubt a wicked Arian
device, to induce posterity to confuse the magician with the
great champion of orthodoxy,) and a metaphorical triumph
over the devil which, a century or two later became a literal
triumph over a dragon: and then, says the *Dictionary,* after
a century or two more, the horse was added: and any
number of legends followed.

It is therefore no exaggeration to say that the only source
of information on which the author above-mentioned was
relying for his knowledge of the *acts* of St. George was this
Arian forgery, condemned and exploded by an orthodox
Council. Now, surely there is no *moral* step of any importance in passing from this proposition. "I know nothing
whatever about the *acts* of so and so," to the proposition,
"I do not even feel sure that so-and-so *existed.*" Why then
should it be called "profaneness" to question the existence
of this supposed Saint who is known mainly as the hero of
an Arian forgery? Surely the real "profaneness" consists
in mentioning the belief or disbelief in such "existences,"
in the same breath with the words "sacred" or "profane."

2. Another "parallel"—but almost too audacious to be
effective—is that in which he compares together belief in
Ecclesiastical Miracles on the whole with belief in English
History on the whole, and asseverates that the former belief is
as reasonable as the latter. Besides the "parallel" itself,
the reader should notice, in the passage I am going to quote,
the use of the pronoun "they." At the beginning, it means
"the *miracles* of Ecclesiastical History": but later on, it
means, not "the *miracles,*" but "*the histories containing
these miracles*"—a very different thing. The reader must

also bear in mind that, by Newman's own admission, the
false miracles in Ecclesiastical History are as much more
numerous than the true ones, as the fragments of (239)
"chaff" are more numerous than the grains of wheat
which they "conceal." This being kept in mind, he will
not need much comment to do justice to the following
" parallel " :—

(*Apol.* 1st Ed. p. 55).   "Such then is the answer I make
to those who would urge against us the multitude of miracles
recorded in our Saints' Lives and devotional works, for
many of which " [*i.e. which (miracles)*] "there is little evidence, and for some " [*i.e. miracles*], "next to none. We
think them [*i.e. the multitude of miracles, say* 120,000, *of
which by far* (239) *the greater part are* (229) "*certainly not
true* "] true, in the same sense in which Protestants think
the history of England is true. When they say that, they
do not mean to say that there are no mistakes, but no mistakes of consequence, none which alter the general course
of history. [*But* 100,000 "*certainly not true*" *miracles,*—
"*concealing*" 100, *or even* 1000, *true ones, and* 19,000 *possibly
true ones—are surely* "*mistakes of consequence,*" *and* DO "*alter
the general course of history* "] . . . They do not stake their
credit on the truth of Froissart, or Sully, they do not pledge
themselves for the accuracy of Doddington. or Walpole, they
do not embrace as an Evangelist Hume, Sharon Turner, or
Macaulay."

By this time Newman has almost worked us up to his
conclusion : but here we must pause to call attention to
this really magnificent instance of his skill in contriving
to say, at, or near, the end of his period. *something that shall
carry his reader along with him,* something that shall force
us to say "How very true !" Here, for example, we can
hardly help saying, "I never looked at the matter in this

light. But really there is a great deal in it. 'Pledge myself'
for the accuracy of that scandal-monger Walpole ! ' Embrace '
Hume, or Macaulay, as 'Evangelists' ! Not I ! And yet
I cannot deny that I *do* accept English History *as a whole*.
And so perhaps I *ought to* accept Ecclesiastical History *as a
whole ?* " But, at this point, if we looked back, we might
find that we had been asked, not to accept Ecclesiastical
History as a whole, but Ecclesiastical *Miracles* as a whole
(of which 100,000 out of, say, 120,000 are false). Therefore,
to keep us from looking back, Newman now pins our attention
on *History*—not on special facts in History—by urging
that "we do not think it necessary to commence a religious
war " against our English historical abridgments, catechisms,
books of archæology, etc. (ignoring the fact that we *do* make
a religious war against inaccuracies and myths in English
history, wherever we find them) ; and *now* he is quite ready
for a conclusion in which he will drop the word " *Miracles* "
—after brief preliminary mention of it—and substitute
" *histories* " :—

" And so as regards the miracles of the Catholic Church ;
if indeed miracles never can occur, then indeed, impute the
narratives to fraud [*there is no question about whether they
can occur, the question is whether they* DO *occur ; but even
if Ecclesiastical miracles do occur, we are bound, by his own
admission, to say that the vast majority of them are false, and
that a great number of them are due to fraud*]; but, till you
prove they are not likely [*thus he throws on Protestants the
task of proving the Antecedent Improbability of miracles,
whereas it is his business to prove that they are antecedently
probable ; and he omits the consideration that the Statistical
Probability against any alleged Ecclesiastical Miracle is,
1000 to 1, or, on the most favourable supposition for him, say,
100 to 1*], we shall consider the HISTORIES WHICH HAVE

COME DOWN TO US true on the whole, though in particular cases they may be exaggerated or unfounded."

Thus he has left, sticking fast in the mind of his reader, that barbed assertion which he discharged at us in his first sentence or two, viz. that "the multitude of *miracles*" is to be considered "true" on the whole ; but he ends with the more moderate demand that "the *histories*" are "true on the whole." To this, of course, we shall reply that we are ready to be perfectly impartial. The history, for example, of St. Ambrose shall be treated in the same way as any biography in English History. We will listen to St. Ambrose himself, to his contemporary Augustine, to his secretary Paulinus, to those who have analysed the evidence, such as Fleury, Milman, Newman, the Dictionary of Christian Biography, and others—just as we would listen to Holinshed, Bacon, Hume, Sharon Turner, Macaulay, Green, Bright, and Gardiner, writing about any English king. We will also take into consideration those motives—peculiar to Ecclesiastical as distinct from Secular History—the strength of which Newman has himself admitted, and which have resulted in the vast mass of certainly false Ecclesiastical miracles. Finally, when we find Paulinus ascribing to St. Ambrose (see above, p. 204) the miraculous raising of Pansophius from death, in a manner imitating, and with a success equalling, the well-known miracle imputed to Elijah,—while Ambrose makes no mention of it, even in a treatise addressed to Pansophius himself, and Augustine also makes no mention of it, but speaks of the age of miracles as past—we shall, in this case, eliminate the miraculous element not merely because it is "unlikely" but because it is certainly not proved to be true, and, further, as we should say, it is satisfactorily proved to be false. And so of the rest.

3. Here is another "parallel" noteworthy for its subtlety and compactness, and for the clever play on the word " natural " :—

(*Apol.* 1st ed. Append. p. 50) "If miracles *can* take place, then the *fact* of the miracle *will be a natural explanation* of the report ; just as the fact of a man's dying *accounts satisfactorily* for the news that he is dead."

Here " accounts satisfactorily " is used as being parallel to " will be a natural explanation." And thus the sentence cleverly implies the following proposition, " As *actual death satisfactorily explains* a report about a man's death, so *an actual miracle* will *satisfactorily explain* a report about a miracle " ; the utility of which proposition may be discerned from another of the same kind, " As the report of a man's death *is satisfactorily explained by* his *actual death*, so the report that there are in Central Africa monkeys a hundred feet high, will be *satisfactorily explained by* the *fact that there are actually such monkeys.*" The real question, of course, is, whether *other* explanations of the report will not be *more* " *natural*," and " account" *more* " *satisfactorily*," for the report.

The words " If miracles *can* take place " are superfluous, except so far as they rhetorically suggest " probably take place," or " regularly and frequently take place, so as to constitute a kind of natural course of their own." If that was the meaning, it ought to have been stated. What is the use of such an " if-clause " as this :—" If there *can* be in the sun rational bipeds, each as large as the moon, then—"? We grant they *can* be. But *are* they ?

So stated as not to bewilder and mislead, the sentence should have omitted this (logically, but not rhetorically) superfluous " if-clause " ; and should have run thus : " The fact of a miracle will be *one* explanation of the report of a miracle; just as the fact of a man's death will be *one* explanation of the report of his death."

This would have been quite true; but it would not have helped Newman much. Every one knows that, on one occasion, "the fact" of Lord Brougham's death was *one* explanation, but not the true explanation, of "the report of his death"; and "the fact" is always *one* explanation, but not always the true explanation, of other similar "reports," say, on the Stock Exchange. We are ready to make the same admission as to any Ecclesiastical miracle : "The fact of the miracle will be, or would be, *one* explanation of *the* report about it." That is true; so true as to be a truism—so very true as to be wholly useless to the philothaumaturgic soul.

4. The following "parallel" deserves special attention, and shall be our last. It is drawn between "the religious honour" paid to relics and the "civil honour" paid to some object of historical antiquity.

In order to appreciate it, we ought to bear in mind the Romanist theory, which justifies, not only "religious honour," but even "devotion," to such relics; a "devotion" that has really and truly penetrated the heart of many a believer and—there is no reason to doubt—has resulted in many marvellous instances of faith-healing. The origin of this "devotion" is well expressed in Newman's *Development of Christian Doctrine* (p. 401) : "I call attention to . . . . the *devotions* which both Greeks and Latins show towards bones, blood, the heart, the hair, bits of clothes, scapulars, cords, medals, beads, and the like, and the *miraculous powers* which they often ascribe to them. Now, the principle from which these beliefs and usages proceed is, the doctrine that Matter is *susceptible of grace, or capable of a union with a Divine Presence and influence.*"

Now, obviously, on this principle, it is of the highest
importance that the relics, "the hair, bits of clothes," and so
on—to which we are to pay our "devotions," and from
which we may possibly receive cures of diseases—should be
genuine, and not liable to the suspicion that they may be
impostures. If they are not genuine, if they are impostures,
the "bits of clothes" can hardly—we must suppose—be
"susceptible of grace," or "capable of union with a Divine
Presence and influence." To pay "devotion" to a *possible*
imposture, to pay "devotion," *even upon a probability*, to a
fragment of the True Cross, or to the very robe of our
Saviour, is surely abhorrent to the mind of a Romanist, as
well as a Protestant believer. Newman elsewhere comments
with severity (*Apol.* 19) upon the address " O God, if there
be a God," and asks, " Who can really pray to a Being about
whose existence he is seriously in doubt ? " And this seems
to apply, in a measure, to a devout believer paying his
"devotion" to a portion of the True Cross which Newman
believes (*Apol.* 1st ed. Append. p. 57) to be at Rome, or to
the Crib of Bethlehem which he believes (*ib.*) to be at the
same place, or to the Holy Coat at Trèves. If in any of
these "devotions," the thought of "probability" steps in,
must it not be fatal ?

We may perhaps go so far as to make *a pilgrimage* to
Trèves "upon a probability " ; but, when we have got there
and are on our knees, how can we possibly pray with
effect, if we have to begin our "devotion" thus : " O
Holy Coat, *if Thou art a Holy Coat—for the Dictionary*
of Christian Antiquities says there are twenty-one Holy
Coats"? Or, for I do not suppose a prayer could be
actually addressed *to* a relic by any but the most ill-instructed
Romanist—how can we even pray to God that the touch of
the Holy Coat may heal our paralysis, or rheumatism,

"upon the probability" of its being genuine? "Almighty and most merciful God, *if this be indeed a genuine Holy Coat, heal my paralysis by the touch of it*"—to a Protestant, at all events, must sound very incongruous. Any act of faith-healing, from the Protestant point of view, is incompatible with the very thought of probability. And from the Romanist point of view, the "miraculous power" will surely *not be in* the Coat, nor will it *have* the "Divine Presence and influence," unless it is *really and truly* the Coat worn by our Saviour Himself; and how can the pious believer who is offering up the "devotion" *know* that this, alone of the twenty-one Coats, is not an imposture? Or, is the devotee to believe that, *as the wood of the Cross*, so too the Holy Coat, has been *miraculously multiplied?*

Now see with what wonderful tact and delicacy, in a treatise addressed to unbelieving Protestants, Newman draws his "parallel" between the Holy Coat and a *possible* jewel of King Alfred's; between "religious honour" (for, of course, "devotion" is carefully kept out of the way *here*) paid to the former, and "civil honour" paid to the latter; between country bumpkins in London coming to "see" curiosities in the Tower, and French peasants, "singing and piping"—no mention, you may be sure, of "miraculous powers," or of "grace," or of "a Divine Presence and influence," or of such people coming up "on the probability" of being healed, or of fathers and mothers coming up to pray, "on a probability," for ailing children too feeble to come up for themselves—on their way "to *see* the Holy Coat at Trèves."

Here is the passage, which forms a fit climax to this collection of "parallels" :—

(*Apolog.* 1st ed. p. 53) "There is in the museum at Oxford, a jewel or trinket said to be Alfred's; it is shown to all comers ; I never heard the keeper of the museum accused of hypocrisy or fraud for showing, with Alfred's name appended, what he might or might not himself believe to have belonged to that great king [*this ignores two very important differences, 1st, that we have not here the coat, say, worn by Alfred during the Baking of the Cakes; and 2nd, that the keeper of the coat is not supposed to know that* TWENTY OTHER COATS, CLAIMING TO BE THE SAME COAT, *are in existence*] ; nor did I ever see any party of strangers who were looking at it with awe, regarded by any self-complacent bystander with scornful compassion.   Yet the curiosity is not to a certainty Alfred's.   The world pays *civil honour* to it on the probability ; *we pay religious honour to relics, if so be, upon a probability*.   Is the Tower of London shut against sight-seers, because the coats of mail and pikes there *may have* half-legendary tales connected with them ?   Why then may not the country people come up in joyous companies, singing and piping, *to see* the Holy Coat at Trèves ? "   And then, without stopping for a word of comment, or allowing even the break of a paragraph, which might have given his reader time for thought, he hurries on to another clever " parallel " between God and Queen Victoria :—" to see the Holy Coat at Trèves.   There is our Queen again, who is so truly and justly popular," and so on, for a page and a quarter !

Now, notice first, the " if so be " in " we pay religious honour to relics, *if so be*."   " If so be," and " so be it," in Newman's letters, are often superfluous except for rhetorical purposes.   But there is no superfluity here.   There is a definite object, viz. to preserve the writer from the accusation that Romanists *regularly* " paid religious honours to relics upon a probability."   To such a charge, " if so be " gives him the power of rejoining, " I said nothing of the kind; I said that we did it, *if so be, i.e.* that we *might* do it, *on occasion.*"

Notice, next, the skill with which "devotion" is altogether ignored and yet such a substitute is put in its place that the writer can fairly say he *meant* "devotion." Thus, it may happen that some unwary antagonist—furious at the "parallel" between the "coats of mail" in the Tower which "*may* have half-legendary tales connected with them" and the Holy Coat, which *has* a tradition (largely believed by Protestants to be a lie) not only "connected with it," but also acted upon—may lose his temper, may forget how much might be implied in "religious honour," and may fasten on the word "see" in "to *see* the Holy Coat," as though Newman were suppressing (and he really *is, almost,* suppressing or, at least, unfairly subordinating) the "devotion," or what Protestants would sometimes popularly call "worship," paid to the relic. In that case Newman leaves himself free to turn round and reply, with splendid effect, "*I* did not ignore devotion," "*I* did not ignore what you Protestants call 'worship.' 'Why do *you* suppress the truth? Why do *you* garble my words? *I said* we paid *religious honour* to relics, if so be, on the probability." And this is what *actually happened* between Kingsley and Newman. Kingsley in his fiery, straightforward, but slightly clumsy way, had said, "To *see*, forsooth! to *worship*, Dr. Newman would have said, had he known (as I take for granted he does not) the facts of that imposture." Hereupon, Newman is down on him at once :—

"Here, if I understand him, he implies that the people came up, not only to see, but to worship, and that I have *slurred over* the fact that their coming was an act of religious homage, that is, what *he* would call 'worship.' Now, will it be believed that, so far from *concealing* this [*note the clever transition, from " slurred over," to " concealing." New-man* HAD REALLY *" slurred it over; "* he had NOT *(speaking technically")* *" concealed" it.* *This exemplifies a useful rule of Rhetoric, viz.* *" State a charge against you as it* IS *; refute it as it is* NOT *"*]. I had carefully [*yes, too " carefully," so " carefully" that a little carelessness in the reader would make him overlook it*] stated it in the sentence immediately preceding, and *he suppresses it ? " *[1]

Now this is a crowning and artistic triumph of Ecclesiastical Rhetoric. The passage has not been reprinted in the later editions of the *Apologia ;* but it deserves permanent recognition as a kind of high-water mark, showing what " parallels " may be drawn, and with what consummate skill any " parallel " may be defended, by an Ecclesiastical Rhetorician working upon the principles of an Ecclesiastical Logic, and always having in his mind an Ecclesiastical ideal of truth. This kind of reasoning has been too effective during the nineteenth century, in one way, to deserve to be entirely forgotten in the twentieth, where possibly it may be effective in another way.

[1] The italics, in " he " and " he suppresses " are here Newman's.

CHAPTER X

THE Lubricative, or Ecclesiastical, method of proof appears to have been in common use before Newman's time among Romanist controversialists, at least if we may credit the following passage from Donne's *Sermons* (p. 657, ed. 1640) in which the descent from "it may be," to "it probably is", and from a possibility to a probability, is treated as a well-known controversial trick :—

"They obtrude to us miraculous doctrine of Transubstantiation and the like upon a possibility only : 'It *may be* done,' they say, 'God *can* do it.'" [For this use of "can," compare Newman's phrase above, p. 232, "If miracles *can* take place, then the fact of the miracle will be a natural explanation of the report."] " . . . . For *Asylum haereticorum est omnipotentia Dei* is excellently said, and by more than one of the Fathers, 'The omnipotence of God is the Sanctuary of Heretics'; thither they fly to countenance any such error—'This God *can* do; why should you not believe it ?'

"Men proceed further than so, from this possibility to a probability, 'It will abide argument, it hath been disputed

R

in the Schools and therefore is probable ; why should you not believe it?' . . . . They will go further than this prob- ability to a verisimilitude, 'It is more than merely possible, more than fairly probable ; it is likely to be so, some of the ancient Fathers have thought so'; and then—'Why should you not believe it?'

" Further than this verisimilitude they go too. They go to a *Piè creditur*, 'It may be piously believed, and it is fit to believe it, because it may assist and exalt devotion to think so,' and then—'Why should you not believe it?'"[1]

This quotation appears to preclude us from crediting Newman with the invention of the Lubricative method of proof; but he carried it to a height of perfection hardly to be found in the range of English literature and possibly not even in the great special pleaders of antiquity.

§ 40. *An Exhortation to Pious Belief*

Take, for example, the passage in which Newman pre- pares the Protestant or general reader for a belief in Ecclesiastical miracles by dispelling the prejudice against them as impostures, by admitting that it is a question of probabilities, and by appealing to the fairness, the judgment, the dispassionate consideration, and calm reasonableness, of the sensible reader. It begins with a very wide and candid admission (as to miracles that are false), which disarms op- position : then it asks us to be reasonable, and not to expect too much in the way of evidence ; then it states that there is *something* to be said *for*, as well as *against*, a large class of miracles, while maintaining a careful silence as to *how much*

---

[1] I am indebted for this quotation (of which I have altered the spelling) to my friend the Rev. H. C. Beeching, the Rector of Yat- tenden.

can be said *for*, and *how much against*, on the basis of statistical probability; then it exhorts us to bethink ourselves of what is "our wisdom," *i.e.* apparently, the wise course for our own interests; then it bids us avoid the 'sin' of rejecting what *may possibly* be true; and finally it implies that we are to take into our hearts these miraculous possibilities "for our comfort and encouragement," thus committing us practically to a pious belief in a multitude of (possible) lies— a belief all the more subtly demoralizing and dangerous because we can never be delivered from it by the light of reason, since we are to *keep it generally to ourselves*, and not to expose it to the test of controversy by "urging it upon unwilling ears." Part of the passage has been quoted above, but it needs to be considered as a whole and to be given in full; for no summary does justice to it. Here it is (230—231) :—

"An inquirer, then, should not enter upon the subject of the miracles reported or alleged in ecclesiastical history, without being prepared for fiction and exaggeration in the narrative to an indefinite extent. This cannot be insisted on too often; nothing but the gift of inspiration could have hindered it." [*Can anything be more candid? But is this consistent with what he has said elsewhere (p. 231 above) that in "the multitude of miracles recorded in our Saints' lives" there are "no mistakes of consequence." Which of these two incompatibilities is true?*]

"Nay, he must not expect that more than a few can be exhibited with evidence of so cogent and complete a character as to demand his acceptance" [*"More than a few"? Then surely we may expect that, when Newman sets forth a "few" miracles in detail, the evidence will be "cogent and complete." But we have seen that his "few" are* NINE, *of which he himself practically surrenders* THREE; *and the evidence for the rest is neither cogent nor complete. But we will give him* 100 *true miracles*] ; while a great number of them " [*say,* 19,900], "as far as the evidence goes" [*that means to say,* "*setting aside Antecedent Probability upon which I can always fall back if my evidence collapses*], "are neither certainly true nor certainly false but have very various degrees of probability viewed one with another ; all of them " [*say* 19,900] "recommended to his devout attention by the circumstance that others [*but how many ? Are there more than* SIX ? *If there are, why were they not substituted for the surrendered miracles ?*] of the same family [1] have been proved " [?] "to be true, and all prejudiced by his knowledge that so many others " [*But how many* "*others*" ? *What proportion do they bear to the true? Apparently, it is* 100,000 *to* 6 ; *but, to meet every demand,* say, 100,000 *to* 100, *i.e.* 1000 *to* 1] on the contrary, are certainly not true."

Then follows a truism, which has nothing to do with what precedes ; but it is introduced very artistically with a 'then.' The truism is, that "we are *not to reject what has a fair chance of being true*" ; but it is hitched on to what precedes, with a "then," as if a miracle against the truth of which the antecedent chances are 1000 to 1 *could* have "a *fair chance* of being true " :—

"It will be his wisdom then " [*i.e. the wisest course for his interests—an exquisitely veiled form of the* "*argument from cowardice*," *which is now on the point of being introduced*] not to reject, or scorn [*Why insert* "*scorn*" ? *Why try to create the impression that a man cannot reject a miracle from honest conviction, and humble reverence for Truth and the God of Truth ?*] accounts of miracles where there is a fair chance of their

---

[1] I have shown above (p. 9) that "of the same family" means Ecclesiastical Miracles, which are said by Newman not to be "of the same family" as Scriptural miracles.

being true " [*Of course no one would reject anything that has a "fair chance of being true" ; but Newman is applying this phrase to the intermediate class of Ecclesiastical Miracles, against any one of which there is, as we have shown, an Antecedent Statistical Probability of, say, 1000 to 1 ; and as to the particular evidence for any one of them, we are bound to think that it must be very slight : for otherwise surely that particular miracle would have been substituted by Newman in the place of one of the surrendered miracles*], but to allow himself to be in suspense [*what does this mean—" to be in suspense"?   To suspend his judgment ?   No indeed.   " Private judgment " is an abomination.   It means to hold oneself in suspense between " Yes " and " No " as to an allegation of fact, because, though the want of evidence ought to make us dismiss it (see p.* 93 *above) with a practical " No," our personal prospects may be improved by saying " Yes."*]

The "argument from cowardice," having been thus introduced, is now to be pressed upon us, veiled in different forms ; and superstition will be presented as aspiration, or as reverence, or as humility.   And at this point, the Art of Oscillation will be called in.   Just as, when the tide is coming in, even at its fastest, a wave will now and then fall a little behind the line of the wave before, only to prepare the way for a third wave that shall sweep on far beyond both, so here, we shall be told to " ask for light " about these doubtful miracles and to " do no more " ; and yet a few lines afterwards there will come an exhortation to *receive them into our hearts "for our comfort and encouragement."*   However, to resume ; the reader is not only " to allow himself to be in suspense," but also :—

"to raise his mind to Him of whom they may possibly be telling [*but, far more probably—by a probability of, say, 1000 to* 1 " *may* NOT *be telling"*], to " stand in awe and sin not " [*certainly, we ought to "stand in awe" of the God of Truth, and not to harbour in our minds what we have good reason for thinking false : and Newman has done well to quote Ps. iv. 4, because it suggests Ps. iv. 2, " O ye sons of men, how long shall my glory be turned into dishonour ? How long will ye love vanity and seek after falsehood ?"*] and to ask for light and do no more [*surely, if God has already given us the " light " of an antecedent statistical probability against any alleged miracle, say, of* 1000 *to* 1, *or even* 100 *to* 1, *that ought to be enough " light " for the present, until very " cogent and complete evidence " is alleged for the miracle*]; not boldly to put forward what, if it be from God, yet has not been put forward by Him. [*This is a very rhetorical breathing-space, telling the reader with a great appearance of moderation what he is* NOT *to do (which of course he would never have dreamed of doing) ; it is a recoil preparing for a sudden and rapid advance.*]

Next comes the advance :—

What He does in secret [*just now, it was, " what* MAY POSSIBLY BE *telling of Him " ; now, instead of, " what He* POSSIBLY MAY HAVE *done," we have " what He* DOES], we must think over [*a good phrase—" think over " ; for it may mean (but it does* NOT *mean) " think over rationally and soberly, pondering the evidence for and against " ; or it may mean (and it* DOES *mean) " think over lovingly and hoping that the story may be true, with such a fervour that at last you will believe it is true"*] in secret ; what He "has openly showed in the sight of the heathen " we must publish abroad, " crying aloud and sparing not " [*a truism, superfluous, except that it heightens our sense of the moderation of the writer, who says in effect, " See how much I do* NOT *expect you to do." Thus the writer also confuses us, casting a veil over what was quite to the point and absolutely false, by obtruding on us, under*

cover of moderation, what is not at all to the point though indis-
putably true; and thus we half forget to dissent from the
earlier falsehood while we are forced to assent to the later
truism].

Now it is time to bring into action the reserve of Potentiality, the doctrine of "It *may* be true"; and, at the
same time—the truth being regarded, not as the subject of
honest patient search, but as a prize to be fought for and
wrangled about—a distinction will be drawn between facts
that may be used in "controversy" and facts *that may be dwelt*
on for our own "comfort" :—

"An alleged miracle is not untrue because it is unproved
[*but, though it is not "untrue," it is non-existent ; and should*
be non-existent alike for our hearts and for our minds, for our
private faith and for our public controversy]; nor is it excluded from our faith because it is not admitted into our
controversy [*as if one should say, "Nor is a thief excluded*
from our confidence because he is not admitted into our in-
timacy," the obvious retort being that he is excluded for another
reason, viz. because he is a thief ; and similarly an unproved
alleged miracle is to be excluded from our faith, not because
it is excluded from our controversy, but for another reason,
viz. because it is unproved].

We are now ready for the conclusion, viz. that we are to
keep these doubtful miracles *in our hearts*—*i.e.* with the
result of getting used to them and believing in them. And
this will be persuasively put before us in a quotation from
Scripture ; and so the whole passage will terminate with a
final repetition of the soothing statement—so often and so
effectively made above—that, after all, something will *not*
be expected from the reader :—

"Some (miracles) are for our conviction, and these we
are to 'confess with the mouth,' as well as 'believe with the

heart ˙[*here again is the rhetorical device, described above as "The Plausible Antithesis," where the first term, which is unnecessary but undisputed, prepares the way for the second, which is necessary but disputed ; and the disputed clause is now to follow*] ; others are for our comfort and encouragement, and these we are to 'keep and ponder them in our hearts'[*those "others" are those against the truth of which the chances have been shown to be, so far as concerns Statistical Probability, say,* 1000 *to* 1 *; and we were told, just now, that we were to "ask for light" about them and "to do no more." Again, what does " keep and ponder in our hearts" mean ? It is an advance on " be in suspense about" and "think over in secret;" it means, as is clear from the addition, " in our hearts"—not "ponder" in the sense of balancing or weighing evidence, but " brood over lovingly," till at last we persuade ourselves that they must have happened because they are so very edifying*], without urging them upon unwilling ears."

Rhythmically, this last clause, " without urging them upon unwilling ears," is a little disappointing, savouring somewhat of bathos. Rhetorically, it is magnificent. " How very moderate !" we say ; " nothing surely can be more reasonable." And besides, the " not urging upon unwilling ears " is not a mere repetition of the previous "not boldly to put forward." It suggests to us that, by way of habituating ourselves to believe these (possibly) false stories, whether fables, legends, or impostures, we may not only poise them lovingly in our own minds, but also, when we get a " willing " ear, endeavour to habituate others to them. It is not at all a bad plan for preparing oneself to believe in anything, to try to habituate others to the thought of believing in it.

§ 41. *The Proof of the Assumption of the Mother of our Lord*

The next passage describes the death of the Mother of our Lord. Beginning, after his manner, with what every one admits, namely that "she died," Newman finally conducts us by the smoothest and most soothing transitions to the conclusion that "it cannot be doubted that we are able to celebrate not only her death but her Assumption."

The great skill of this passage is shown in two broad ways, besides innumerable fine traits here and there on which it would be endless to dilate. First, he takes advantage of the fact that *we know absolutely nothing about the subject.* So far from apologizing for this lack of evidence—he converts the absence of basis into a basis for a most solid and elaborate superstructure. He suggests that the *silence itself is a proof that there must have been something mysterious about it.* Secondly, at the very beginning, he strikes at once the key-note of Antecedent Probability, teaching us to expect and, as it were, to claim, that the death *must* have happened in this way or in that, because this way or that would be *fittest;* and thus he leads us to expect and almost to demand, something stupendously supernatural, because (so it is quietly assumed) she died, only "as a matter of form," and " her death was a mere fact, not an effect."

The reader will further notice that almost all the *facts* in this passage are *negations, e.g.,* " her departure made *no* noise in the world," "they sought for her relics, but they found them *not,*" "her tomb could *not* be pointed out." Almost all that is *positive*—except where after stating that "the tomb could *not* be pointed out," he adds, "or if it was found it was open " : and "there was a growth of lilies from the earth

which she had touched "—belongs to "rumour," "tradition," and "revelations made to holy souls," that is to say,
"visions." Beyond these remarks, the passage will need no
comments ; it speaks for itself.

"She died, but *her death was a mere fact not an effect ;* and
when it was over, it ceased to be. She died that she might
live ; she died *as a matter of form or,* (*as I may call it*) *a
ceremony,* in order to fulfil what is called the debt of nature
. . . . not with a martyr's death, for her martyrdom had
been in living ; not as an atonement, for man could not
make it—and One had made it, and made it for all—but in
order to finish her course and receive her crown. And
therefore she died in private. It became Him who died for
the world to die in the world's sight ; it became the great
Sacrifice to be lifted up on high as a light that could not be
hid. But she, the lily of Eden, who had always dwelt out of
the sight of man, fittingly did she die in the garden's shade,
and amid the sweet flowers in which she had lived.

" Her departure *made no noise in the world.* The Church
went about her common duties—preaching, converting,
suffering ; there were persecutions, there was fleeing from
place to place, there were martyrs, there were triumphs ; at
length the *rumour* spread through Christendom that Mary
was no longer upon earth. Pilgrims went to and fro ; they
sought for her relics, but they found them *not.* Did she
die at Ephesus ? Or did she die at Jerusalem ? Accounts
varied, but her tomb could *not* be pointed out, *or, if it was
found it was open ; and instead of her pure and fragrant body,
there was a growth of lilies from the earth which she had
touched.*

"So, inquirers went home marvelling and waiting for
further light. And then the *tradition* came wafted westward
on the aromatic breeze, how that, when the time of her

dissolution was at hand, and her soul was to pass in triumph before the judgment-seat of her Son, the Apostles were suddenly gathered together in one place even in the Holy City, to bear part in the joyful ceremonial; how that they buried her with fitting rites; how that, the third day, when they came to the tomb, they found it empty, and angelic choirs with their glad voices were heard singing day and night the glories of their risen Queen. But however we feel toward the details of this history (nor is there *anything* in it which will be unwelcome and *difficult to piety*), *so much cannot be doubted*, from the consent of the whole Catholic world, and the revelations made to holy souls, that, as is befitting, she is, soul and body, with her Son and God in heaven and that we are enabled to celebrate, not only her death, *but her Assumption.*"[1]

In the whole of Newman's works it would perhaps be difficult to find a passage more delicately and artistically constructed for the purpose of persuasion. I am not speaking of the style, which, with its "aromatic breezes," and "how that's," and the like, is a trifle florid for English prose—though even here it is noteworthy for the skill with which it avoids blank verse, except in the one place where (perhaps deliberately) it almost soars into actual poetry. But I am speaking of it practically, as really efficacious rhetoric, not showy, but perfectly adapted for its purpose.

If the *purpose* is steadfastly borne in mind; if it is once recognized that we really do not care a straw for historic truth; that the object is to construct something out of nothing, to infer substantial conclusions from imaginary premises—exemplifying in practice the subtle and penetrating power of such maxims as (231) "evidence" is not

---

[1] *Discourses addressed to Mixed Congregations*, quoted by Mr. R. H. Hutton, *Cardinal Newman*, pp. 202, 203.

"the test of truth"; and (179) "insufficiency in the evidence ought not to create a positive prejudice against an alleged fact"; and things may be true although the Fathers are silent about them, for (252) "it really seems unreasonable to demand that every Father should write about everything"; and (180) "the direct effect of evidence is to create a presumption, according to its strength, in favour of the fact attested: it does not appear how it can create a presumption the other way"; and (190) "in drawing out the argument in behalf of ecclesiastical miracles, the main point to which attention must be paid is the proof of their antecedent probability: if that is established, the task is nearly accomplished"; and (186) "if the Church be possessed of supernatural powers, it is not unnatural to refer to these the facts reported, and to feel the same dispositions to heighten their marvellousness as otherwise is felt to explain it away" :—in other words, if the search after the truth of facts, and the most sacred facts, is to be regarded not as an honest search at all, but as a war against the "*prestige*" of the laws of Nature, a campaign against evidence and common sense, a campaign in which the laws of orthodoxy militant allow as "fair," and excuse as "not unnatural," a degree of prejudice, blindness, and almost wilful exaggeration which a scientific man, in the interests of science would consider not only as professionally mean and discreditable but as tainted with moral turpitude—if, I say, this sort of work is to be done at all, I do not see how it could be done with a more consummate deftness, and with a grace more calculated to conceal its underlying foulness and falsehood than in the passage above quoted—the legitimate outcome and crowning achievement of Newman's method of applying probabilities to our aspirations after God, and faith to the facts of History.

APPENDIX

THE contempt for facts, which pervades the whole of the *Essay on Miracles*, is manifested with peculiar clearness by certain changes in the edition of 1870 (reprinted, without mention of change, in 1890) as compared with the edition of 1843. Probably few of my readers possess the latter. I shall therefore make no apology for describing these changes at some length.

I will begin with the inquiry into the alleged miraculous cure of blindness (348-368), to which I called attention above, as not containing a single reference to any original authority for the miracle. Such an omission would be discreditable in any case, but it is made more discreditable by the following explanation. The original essay of 1842-3 was written as an introduction to a translation of Fleury's *Ecclesiastical History*. Now this particular miracle was described in pages 104, 105 of that *History*. Consequently the reader was *originally* referred in the Introduction to the *History* itself for the detailed facts of the miracle, as may be seen from the following paragraph which (in 1843) introduced the narrative :—" *The history of this miracle occurs in the present volume* (pages 104, 105), and attention has been drawn to it in a work which appeared several years since (*Church of the Fathers*, ch. iii.). Yet it is so memorable an act of Divine Power that *one or two additional remarks* upon it cannot be out of place." And then after this introductory paragraph follow the "*one or two additional remarks*," beginning with the words, " The broad facts connected with it are these."

Now when the Introduction was reprinted as a separate Essay—if Newman attached any serious meaning to his " Inquiry " into the Particular Miracle—(one of Nine Miracles, be it remembered, which he desired to set before his readers because they had (134) "a historical character and are accordingly more celebrated than the rest," and which apparently he desired, or ought to have desired, to place before his readers (229), "exhibited with evidence of so cogent and complete a character as to demand his acceptance")—what was his obvious duty? Surely to include in the *Essay* the two pages of Fleury's *History* which give a detailed account of it. Otherwise, how could the reader form any judgment about it? For what would he have as a basis for his judgment—the history being absent—except the "*one or two additional remarks*," which no scholar surely, with a conscience, would venture to palm off as an " Inquiry "? But Newman did what no scholar —least of all a theological scholar—ought to have done. He was actually content to cut off the " history " of the miracle ; to reduce his " Inquiry " to "*one or two additional remarks*" about the Miracle ; and yet to call it an " Inquiry," as before.

" But," it may be asked, "does not Newman after all leave us the 'broad facts'? Surely he does not omit any matter of importance." Let the reader turn back to p. 191, and he will there find omission after omission of most important facts which tell against the miraculous hypothesis—omissions of evidence showing, 1st, that the man was not born blind, so that the blindness may have been curable by an emotional shock; 2nd, that the Arians admitted the cure but apparently *declared it to be only a partial one*, and that the cure *was* probably only partial; 3rd, that the dream which was alleged to have miraculously revealed to Ambrose the locality of the relics had no existence; 4th, that no miraculous revelation was needed, for old men still living had read the inscription on the tombs of the buried martyrs; 5th, that the "success" confidently attributed by Newman to the miracle is, at least conjecturally, *attributed by Newman's own authority (Fleury) in part to the political intervention of Maximius.* These omissions indeed will not seem surprising when the reader is informed that—while the disquisition on the morality and antecedent probability and evidence of the miracle occupies *nineteen* pages—the evidence itself, the "broad facts" themselves, are compressed into little more than *half a page!*

All this is very bad; and if Newman had done no worse than this, it would have been bad enough. It would have been an insult to truth, and to the faculties by which we may reasonably hope to attain truth, and to all students who are seeking truth by the reasonable use of their faculties. But at all events, so far, it would have been an open insult. The reader would have been told plainly : "The history of the miracle I have not thought it worth while to give you; but *you have my 'one or two additional remarks.'* Won't that do as well? *I know, and you know, we don't really want to 'inquire.' We want to believe. Now for that purpose, surely my 'one or*

two additional remarks' will suffice." This at least would
have been plain speaking ; there would have been no deceit.
And, in the edition of 1843, there is no deceit. The only
fault I have to find with that edition is, that it still maintains
the mockery of inserting, as the heading of each left-hand
page, " *Evidence* for particular alleged Miracles."

But in the edition of 1870, reprinted in 1890, the reader
is no longer thus openly insulted. Instead of that, he is
now *deceived*. The opening paragraph is altogether omitted ;
the reader is *not* referred to the pages of the history for the
facts ; he is *not* referred to the " Church of the Fathers,
ch. iii." ; he is left, without warning, without references, and
without facts, (for the " broad facts," mentioned above, are a
mere imposture, unworthy of the name) to enter solemnly
into the consideration of the " *one or two additional remarks*,"
as though *they* constituted a full and particular " *Inquiry* "
into one of those Nine great historical Miracles of Christian
Ecclesiastical History, which are to be exhibited " with
evidence of so cogent and complete a character as to
demand his acceptance."

A further comparison of the earliest and latest editions
of the *Essays* will go even beyond this. It will show
that the Inquiry into certain defined " historical " miracles
was *not originally intended to be a part of the book*, and ought
not to have that weight which is attached to it by the misleading alterations in the subsequent edition. In 1843 he
does not mention his purpose of inquiring into any miracles
of a special sort, but speaks of *taking up* " *two or three* "—
almost as though he were choosing them at random. In
1870 he exhibits himself as making a promise in an early
portion of the book, to discuss *certain definite miracles* later
on. In *both* editions, there follows the *same* " Inquiry into
particular Miracles," which does not deserve the name of

Inquiry; in both, the so-called "Inquiry" is largely casual and wholly careless and unscholarlike; and, so far, the two editions are on the same footing. But the last edition is in this respect inferior to the first, because the last conceals what the first admits with some degree of frankness, viz., that the Inquiry is a mere sop thrown to those who are startled by such truisms as that "Truth does not depend on evidence," and "As if moral and religious questions required legal proofs, and evidence were the test of truth !"

Here are the differences between the two editions :—

1843.	1890.
p. xxxvii.	p. 134.
"*Before quitting* this review of ecclesiastical miracles in the ancient Church, it will be right to *mention* certain isolated ones which have an historical character and are accordingly more celebrated than the rest. Such is the miracle of the Thundering Legion. ....African confessors who had lost their tongues in the Vandal persecution."	" Lastly, *in* this review of the miracles belonging to the early Church, it will be right to *include* certain isolated ones which have an historical character and are accordingly more celebrated than the rest. Such is the miracle of the Thundering Legion......... African confessors who had lost their tongues in the Vandal persecution. These, *and other such, shall be considered separately before I conclude.*"

We see then, so far, that the author originally avowed no intention of instituting any special inquiry into the seven "historical" miracles which he simply thinks it "right to *mention*" before quitting the subject. But the later edition so alters the text as to indicate that these great miracles are not only to be "mentioned," but also to be "*included*"—an ambiguous expression, which however appears to mean something more than "mentioning," and rather suggests "*reviewing*"; and this apparent meaning seems made

S

certain *by the addition of a distinct promise " to consider them separately."*

Now let us turn to the last words of the chapter introducing these particular miracles :—

1843.	1890.
"And now, after these preliminary considerations, let us proceed to inquire into the evidence and character of *two or three* of the miracles ascribed to that period of the Church in which the history which follows is included."	"And now, after these preliminary considerations, let us proceed to inquire into the evidence and character of *several* of the miracles in particular, which we meet with in the first centuries of Christianity."

These words " two or three " indicate the casual nature of the proposed Inquiry, and they are illustrated by another phrase, which (no doubt by a slip) has been allowed to remain in the latest edition, and which, until I examined the original edition, caused me a great deal of perplexity. He introduces his Inquiry into the Nine Miracles by saying (228) " it may be allowable . . . . to throw off the abstract and unreal character which attends a course of reasoning, by setting down the evidence for and against certain miracles *as we meet with them."* Going on the principle that Newman's words always mean something, and are never superfluous, I was puzzled to know what could be the meaning of these words " *as we meet with them*," till I perceived that the author *really did mean at first* to take up his miracles more or less at random " *as he met with them*," and that it was only afterwards that he to some extent recognized the duty of selecting those for which the evidence was most " complete and cogent."

My accusation then against Newman is this, that he has cancelled words and phrases that exhibited the casual and unscientific nature of his " Inquiry," and has substituted for them other words and phrases which make the " Inquiry" appear more deliberate and scientific ; while at the same time, instead of adding anything of weight or value to the " Inquiry," he has, at least in one instance—the alleged miraculous cure of blindness—actually removed from it the references which gave it the little worth that it possessed. Practically his conduct amounts to this. He strung together a number of loose, slatternly, and ill-arranged bits of evidence (I say nothing now about bias, distortion, suppression ; I am confining myself to the tokens of careless indifference) bearing on " two or three " Ecclesiastical Miracles. He inserted these in an Introduction to an Ecclesiastical History, where his readers might at least have verified some of his facts. He then published this slovenly work as an independent essay upon Ecclesiastical Miracles, making it *less* valuable than it was before, but introducing in the text changes which caused it to appear *more* valuable than before.

Such conduct is worthy of a bookseller's hack, not of one who aspires to be called a theologian. But we know well that Newman was absolutely indifferent to pecuniary temptations, and could not thus have degraded his pen for a bribe of any material kind. The reasons that actuated him were two : partly contempt for his readers, partly contempt for facts. He knew that the sort of people whom he hoped to bring over to his way of thinking would not take the trouble to verify his assertions, or investigate his facts ; and he knew also, in his own heart, that if all his facts were disproved to-morrow, he should continue to believe, and indeed take a greater pleasure than ever in believing, that the Miracles were both miraculous and true.

Richard Clay and Sons, Limited,
LONDON AND BUNGAY.

A Catalogue

of

Theological Works

published by

Macmillan & Co.

Bedford Street, Strand, London

CONTENTS

www.ingramcontent.com/pod-product-compliance
Lightning Source LLC
Chambersburg PA
CBHW060613030726
47498CB00005B/1661